W9-BZU-332

A Dog Named
CHRISTMAS

CHRISTMAS
with Tucker

A Dog Named
CHRISTMAS

AND

CHRISTMAS

with Tucker

GREG KINCAID

CONVERGENT BOOKS

NEW YORK

Sale of this book without a front cover may be unauthorized.
If this book is coverless, it may have been reported to the publisher as
"unsold or destroyed" and neither the author nor the publisher
may have received payment for it.

This is a work of fiction. Names, characters, places, and incidents either
are the product of the author's imagination or are used fictitiously.
Any resemblance to actual persons, living or dead, events, or locales is
entirely coincidental.

A Dog Named Christmas copyright © 2008 by Greg Kincaid
Christmas with Tucker copyright © 2010 by Greg Kincaid
Excerpt from *Noelle* copyright © 2017 by Greg Kincaid

All rights reserved.

Published in the United States by Convergent Books, an imprint of the
Crown Publishing Group, a division of Penguin Random House LLC,
New York.
crownpublishing.com

CONVERGENT BOOKS is a registered trademark and its C colophon is
a trademark of Penguin Random House LLC.

A Dog Named Christmas was originally published in hardcover in the
United States by Doubleday, an imprint of The Doubleday Publishing
Group, a division of Penguin Random House LLC, New York, in 2008.
Christmas with Tucker was originally published in hardcover in the United
States by Doubleday Religion, an imprint of the Crown Publishing Group,
a division of Penguin Random House LLC, New York, in 2010.

Library of Congress Cataloging-in-Publication Data is available
upon request.

ISBN 978-1-5247-6290-2

Printed in the United States of America

Cover design: Jessie Bright, based on a design by Rex Bonomelli
Cover photographs: (farm) George Contorakes/Masterfile; (black dog)
Eric Isselee/Shutterstock

10 9 8 7 6 5 4 3 2 1

First Mass Market Edition

CONTENTS

A Dog Named
CHRISTMAS

This book was always for my wife.
She has taught me so much,
not the least of which
is the value of a good dog.

···❖·❖·❖·❖·❖···

J ake seemed content with the Conner family, but even so, his departure was predictable. Mr. and Mrs. Conner lived on the edge of a growing city where subdivisions turned into ten-acre lots and where all too often people discarded beer cans, fast-food debris, and unwanted pets. Jake walked on, scruffy and half starved, with no tags. Mr. Conner found him resting on the back porch as an early February wind piled snow high on the driveway of their modest ranch home. They fed him, cleaned and vaccinated him, and then just waited. They put up "Lost Dog" flyers, but no one called.

A walk-on like Jake has a different status than a pet you purchase. A walk-on can just as easily walk off, the Conners told each other.

The weeks passed and Jake stayed. Mr. and Mrs. Conner did not understand why anyone would dump him. Though the vet had confirmed he was a little bit older, he was one of the more engaging dogs they had known. With an alert personality, he was eager to please, house-trained, well behaved, and could sit, stay, and roll over on command. He was a good companion, keeping close without intruding, and was also curious and a quick learner.

Jake lingered through the summer, gaining weight and

confidence in his surroundings, but by early fall, when his strength had fully returned, he seemed restless, like a pioneer yearning for his own territory, and would wander off at night and stay out for days and once for an entire week. He began roaming farther and farther away. The Conners tried fences and ties and even locking him up at night, but there were few bonds strong enough to keep him put for long. When the first frost collected on the still green grass and the moon was full, Jake left the Conner family to fulfill his own calling.

Speculation naturally followed. At the top of Mr. Conner's list was the assumption that Jake went home, back to wherever he came from. Mrs. Conner suggested that a wily female lured him away. The Conners' grown children wondered if Jake found a family with children to play with him, as their own children had when they visited their grandparents on weekends.

After the first few days, the Conners were concerned, but not alarmed. He was an important part of the family, but the Conners suspected that Jake operated by his own rules. As the days turned to weeks, and the weeks to months, his disappearance somehow seemed natural and the Conners just accepted his absence. A walk-on can walk off, they reminded themselves.

When they thought of him, they said things like, "He has Jake business to attend to. He'll come back if and when he is ready."

By the time winter came, Jake was like a faded old picture in a box of family memories. Occasionally at dinner, they would laugh and tell Jake stories, like the time a neighbor

chased him down the middle of their driveway, trying to recover a twenty-pound black trash sack that dangled proudly
from his jaws, or the time he chased a rabbit onto the frozen
pond and spun around like an Olympic skater. The rabbit
stopped and watched, seemingly laughing at Jake. Jake apparently thought it was fun too, for he backed up and did it
again, with the same result.

Mrs. Conner would grow quiet as she felt his absence in
her heart and then Mr. Conner would say, "Pass the potatoes . . . I'm sure he's fine."

When he left, Jake journeyed west away from the city and
the Conners' home. It felt good to be a full-time roamer. He
answered to no one. He had a freedom that few are brave
enough to own. He slept beneath the stars, under bridges,
in caves, in open fields tucked behind a log, or on the back
porch of some generous soul who could tolerate a hobo on the
road. He ate food that some might describe as unfit for a dog.
He did what he needed to do to stay nourished. To do so, he
honed the instincts lost to more modern times. He learned to
listen, his sense of smell became more acute, and he noticed
slight movements that would have gone undetected during his
domestic life.

He hunted like an animal. He waited. He journeyed. He
did not know how long it would take or how far he would go.
It would be right when he got there. He had given himself
over to instinct.

Like geese, salmon, and monarch butterflies, Jake was
being pulled to a very particular place.

It was often dangerous. As he moved through less friendly

neighborhoods, the residents had a way of making it clear that his kind was not wanted. They barely paid him a glance and were likely to pretend that he did not exist. They thought that showing him a little kindness would encourage him to stay and then they would never be rid of him.

If they were not ignoring him, they sent their hints in more obvious ways. One man threw a rock in his direction as he passed by. A carload of boys saw him walking on the side of the road one evening and they swerved in his direction as if it were funny to see him jump out of the way. Though Jake was unharmed, the message was clear. He needed to move on, keep heading west.

The animal kingdom was not generous toward him either. Dogs barked at him, skunks sprayed him, ticks bit him, and thorny bushes scraped at his sides. Still he kept going, aware that his journey was not yet complete.

These discomforts were minor inconveniences to Jake. He was content and at peace with himself. In the morning when he woke and stretched, his tired muscles felt good, never better. Hardship was the patina of his good life. There is no better state of mind for man or animal than being what you are and doing what you are meant to do. This harmony of existence and purpose is so rare that we forget it exists. Not Jake. Particularly, not today.

After the sun ascended to its midday vantage, Jake rested on a wooded knoll and watched as a young man in bright red tennis shoes wandered along a stream bank, aimlessly skipping rocks across the barely frozen surface of Kill Creek, bluntly named by the local Indians to suggest the abundance of wildlife that lived and died so near its banks.

As he watched the young man, the first thing he felt was a vague feeling of comfort and familiarity. Still, he cautiously waited, sensing that something was not quite right. After the man passed, he ambled down to the creek and drank deeply from the cool water that was yesterday's rainfall. There were smells that danced along the banks, like wildflowers, sweet hay, ancient oak, wet moss on limestone, and a strange, unfamiliar musky scent he could not place. He tried to separate the scent when he heard the slightest of sounds and spun around to see something, really only a blur, move away from him and into the deeper forest of hickory, walnut, red bud, and oak that flanked the creek.

He moved toward the woods and the scent grew stronger. Within a few moments, he found the tracks and made the connection. They were cat tracks. Enormous cat tracks. This was an engagement he did not want. He would not wait for the man to return. In the distance he could hear car engines, train whistles, dog barks, church bells, and the playful screams of children out for recess.

Jake stopped again and looked for the man in the bright red shoes and then moved toward the town sounds, hoping to find the thing for which he vaguely searched. Whatever it was that pulled him was growing stronger, persistent, and very near.

I spend more time now looking back than looking ahead, sifting through the years and pausing over the important events of my life. Maybe it's rare, but aside from the occasional sadness that accompanies us all, there is no litany of disappointments for me. Instead, there is a storehouse of good memories and special times. We all have some defining moments in our lives. Mine was a holiday that seemed perfect.

Of my five children, three boys and one daughter are grown and employed, but none is far away from this old farm we've called home for four generations. They come back for the holidays and sometimes for dinners, unsolicited advice, to borrow tools, or to just sit quietly on the porch with their feet propped up on the rail, listening to farm sounds, which lift our spirits even in the worst of times. They grew up here on land my great-great-grandfather purchased from the Blackfoot Indians. Just south of our house, a large stand of irises has spread over an acre of forest ground and hidden the remnants of his settler's cabin. Our memories on this farm are good.

Mary Ann, my wife, teaches English and debate at the Crossing Trails High School, from which each of the four generations of the McCray family have graduated. The more recent generations were spoiled by a school bus. The older two rode horses nearly eight miles each way and were not shy about recounting the details of their burdensome journey.

Then, there is Todd, my youngest child. By that Christmas he was old enough in years to be on his own, to have a real job like his siblings, but the immaturity that naturally accompanied his disability kept him home with his mother and me.

Todd looked like any other healthy twenty-year-old, but he had his own way of thinking about things. You'd know from watching or even talking with him briefly that something was unusual. Over the years, we tolerated some stares and whispers, but learned to think nothing of it. We loved and accepted everything about our youngest child, born to us later in life, a good ten years after we thought we were finished with diapers. Mary Ann, my wife of nearly forty years, frets over Todd and connects his problems with her late-life pregnancy.

I've learned that for every deficit one might see in Todd, there is an ability you don't see.

Todd always had his hands in his pockets and never seemed certain which direction he was going when he went out the door. His clothes seldom added up to an outfit, and his hair, the color of sun-bleached rope, was punctuated with cowlicks and curls. Sometimes he would sit near a herd of sheep for an entire day, just watching. Other days, he would find a river and follow it upstream, searching for the place where the water began. He never found this place, but that did not deter him from trying.

Todd also loved to paint. If I stood him in front of a building, he would paint it. However, there was one problem. His mother was convinced that our son would forget he was on a ladder and fall straight off and hurt himself. He was under strict orders to climb no higher than the third rung, which left many painting projects half finished.

To add to this peculiar feature, our neighbors seemed to enjoy giving Todd their leftover paint. However kind this may have been, it did not result in a harmonious color scheme. Our farm was painted with colors rejected by others, often for good reasons. Once again, we grew accustomed to the staring, and no one laughed harder at it than we did. We always thought of it as primer over which we would someday paint, but, like most eyesores, in time we stopped noticing. We took great pride in telling passers-by that we were the Midwest testing site for the Todd Paint Company.

Unless it was something he felt passionate about, Todd usually wasn't much of a talker, but he whistled from memory, and off-key, every tune that he ever heard from his friend and constant companion, the radio. I continually pleaded with him to take off the earphones so I could talk to him. He gladly complied, but rarely would he take them off unless he was asked first.

The one thing that defined Todd's life more than any other was his relationship with animals. He held them, raised them, loved them, and laughed with them. I am outdoors caring for animals all day. When finished, I want to leave the work behind, so I try to keep animals out of my house, but if one could be carted, crated, boxed, or stalled, Todd tried to bring it into the barn or garage and, more times than not, sneak it up to his room. This worked well enough for squirrels, rabbits, and baby birds, but not so well for skunks, snakes, and toads. To make matters worse, Todd's room was always a mess, which served as an excellent camouflage for a variety of uninvited guests.

As he got older, Todd finally accepted that he would have to set wild animals free. Not to do so was cruel. The only exception was for creatures that were injured or otherwise unable to care for themselves. As a result, every hurt, maimed, and lost animal within five counties somehow made its way directly to our back porch.

There was no money for veterinarians, so Todd became a bit of an animal medicine man. He was not at all shy about using the phone to ask for help. In fact, I often had to work hard to keep him off it.

He was very patient and determined in his rescue missions. And it was rare for anyone to turn Todd down because they were too busy. It wasn't that they felt sorry for him. He was one of those people who could capture you with his enthusiasm, and before you knew it his urgent need became your urgent need.

He would set out calling Jim Morton, our vet, who

in turn would give Todd the number of the U.S. Department of Agriculture or the National Park Service, depending on whether Todd's latest patient walked, climbed, flew, or slithered. One could amble into the room and find Todd talking to a professor of ornithology at the local university about a broken bird wing. Before long, it seemed like the entire American university system had abandoned world hunger and quantum physics. After all, there was the problem of Todd's bird that needed immediate attention.

Todd had a way of setting things in motion, and when he did, we dropped everything. I must admit, however, that I did not see this one coming.

One early December afternoon, Todd came running into the barn carrying his radio and frantically trying to scribble down a phone number. He handed me the wrinkled note.

"It's for a Christmas dog," he said.

"Slow down, Todd. What are you talking about?"

"The animal shelter wants you to adopt a dog for the Christmas holiday."

"Todd, they always want you to adopt a dog. That's what they do. Besides, we don't need another animal around here, and most definitely not a dog." We had been a dogless farm for many years, and I was not ready to change that arrangement. I had my own reasons for not wanting a dog—long-standing ones. It ended poorly with the last several dogs I let into my life and I was dead set against trying it again. I'd spent twenty years saying no to Todd's brothers and his sister and I saw no reason to change my mind now.

"It's just for Christmas," he said in what came as close to an argumentative tone as Todd could muster. "After that, you can take the dog back if you want. They have lots of dogs that don't have homes."

I pushed the scrap of paper into the front pocket of my jeans and hoped he would forget about it. But Todd continued with his innocent persistence that wore on you, yet was endearing. "Can I call them?" he pleaded as I tried to walk away.

"Todd, there is no use in calling. We've had this discussion before. We are not having a dog on this farm. We already have plenty of animals to care for. We don't need more. We've got work to do now." He was still looking disappointed. I wanted to give him time to adjust to a situation that he might have a hard time accepting. "Let's get some chores done and maybe we can talk about it later."

"It'll be too late by then. It will be closed and all the dogs will be gone." His voice quivered. He kicked at the earth with his large feet and hung his head. I knew he was only moments away from tears. Saying no to Todd was *never* easy.

I took the red handkerchief that I kept in my front overalls pocket and wiped the sweat from my brow. Just like the rest of us, it was sometimes difficult for Todd to accept that he could not always have what he wanted.

It would take time to walk him through this one. I playfully grabbed him in a headlock and rubbed my knuckles across the crown of his head until he started to laugh, then I released my hold and held him by the lapels of his jacket and said, "Come on, Todd, let's go finish the chores and then we'll talk about it more tonight. Those dogs aren't going anywhere, and if they did, that would be a good thing for them."

We had a ritual of chores that started with the chickens, passed a hog or two, and ended up at a corral where I kept cows and their calves. We, of course, fed and watered the stock, but beyond that, without ever thinking about it, we made sure each animal was healthy. You can't take a chicken's temperature and cattle don't sneeze when they're sick. You have to sense something is wrong, usually by the way they move or don't move.

Todd slipped between the rails of the corral and walked freely among the cows, touching and assessing each animal that he passed. Cattle and sheep are less domesticated than horses and don't generally like to be handled or touched, which made Todd's ability unusual. I watched him as he made his rounds and called out updates.

"The twins look good."

"Yeah, they do," I answered back.

"Old Two Stubs looks thin. Do you think we should worm her again?"

"Probably," I concurred, readying a mixture of corn and sorghum to pour into a long cylindrically shaped aluminum trough. The calves bawled as the larger cows jostled for a front-row seat. There are no manners in the feedlot. The biggest always win.

Todd stopped in his tracks as if he remembered something important. Surrounded by hungry, jostling animals but without the least bit of fear, he worked his way out of the corral. He closed the distance between us and then stood six inches from my face and just stared at me. I had no idea what was on his mind.

"What?" I finally asked.

"The cows are fine, Dad."

"So?"

"Could I call—now?"

"Todd Arthur McCray, enough about the dogs. Okay?"

He frowned and walked toward the house. Todd was such a good kid, but I needed more time to think about this one. If I decided against it, Todd was going to find it difficult to accept, but I knew I should not let disappointing Todd get in the way of making the right decision.

Truth was that I missed having a dog, but there were a lot of reasons to move slowly on this one. Certainly, it would make Todd and his mother happy. In fact, I knew darn well that if I let Todd or his mother so much as look at a dog, it would own the farm by sunset and I'd be lucky even to have a place at the dinner table. I could picture the chaos that would ensue.

"Where's your father, Todd? I don't believe I've seen him for two or three years now."

"What do you mean, Mom? Dad is still here. He's been

out on the back porch for the last couple of winters. You know, where you put him after we got the dog."

"Oh, yes, I remember now."

"Todd, get the dog and come to dinner, we're having prime rib. You know how Fido just loves prime rib. If there is any left over, put it out on the back porch for your dad and do tell him hello for me the next time you see him."

When it was time for dinner, or what my grandfather called supper, I walked past the porch on the south side of our home and into the mudroom at the back of the house. I sat on a bench and took off my muddy boots and overalls. I could hear Todd and Mary Ann talking at the kitchen table. He had started dog campaigning with his mother. As I expected, it took very little convincing. To her credit, she waited at least ten or fifteen seconds before she sold me down the river.

"Yes, Todd, I can see why you want the dog, and no, I don't understand why he would not want you to have one. Like you said, it's just for a week and then you can take the dog back if it doesn't work out for you. I heard the whole thing on the radio and it seems like such a nice thing to do for those poor dogs."

"I would take good care of him, Mom."

"Of course you would, Todd. Your dad knows that too. We'll just have to work on him, won't we?"

"Is there some reason I shouldn't have the dog?" I heard him ask.

"None. None at all," she said.

The discussion I wanted to have with Todd had just

occurred in my absence. Our home is not a democracy. It is a benevolent dictatorship. Queen Mary Ann had spoken.

From the mudroom bench I stood up and walked into the kitchen, took off my leather gloves, set them on the kitchen counter, and jumped into the conversation. "I know there are lots of reasons to give this dog program a try, but I still am not sure that it's a good idea."

Todd was not too worried about my concerns. "The radio said it was a good idea."

"Yes, I'm sure the radio thinks it's a good idea, but still I want to check into it myself. Can you two wait for me to do that?" I asked.

"Yes," Todd said with no conviction.

I smiled at him and said, "Hard time waiting, huh?"

"Can't wait."

"Big rush?"

He knew I was teasing him and he smiled back and said, "Can't wait."

"They're closed tonight. Do you think we should call the emergency number to check on this program or could you and your mother hold off until morning to discuss this further?"

He paused and it was clear that he was seriously considering calling the emergency number. "Todd!" I said.

He pondered his options and finally said, "I guess I can wait."

That night, after Todd went to bed, the dog issue was

discussed further. "Mary Ann, I am willing to consider the Christmas dog program, but I need more details."

I took a deep breath and continued on to a more sensitive subject. "The way you handled this whole thing with Todd irritated me."

"I have absolutely no idea what you are talking about," she said with the innocence of a spring lamb. This was a diversionary strategy the debate coach saved for those rare occasions when she knew I was right.

"Todd and I needed to talk about the program together. Reach an understanding about this. You know, have a discussion."

"Did I stop you from having that discussion?" she asked, knowing full well that she was avoiding the real issue.

"By the time I entered the room, you and Todd were pouring puppy chow in a steel bowl and you know it." I did not enjoy confronting my wife, but I was quite sure that what she had done was not fair.

"George, what are you talking about? I never did any such thing. I was just acknowledging Todd's feelings. You just need to admit that you cannot say no to Todd and please do not blame me for your inability to be tough with him."

I recognized a sly switching of gears in her attack. "What are you talking about?" I asked with an accusing tone in my voice.

"I am tired and I am going to bed. Perhaps tomorrow

we can have a more civil discussion on this subject. I do not feel like being yelled at and unfairly accused." My wife pushed her nose to the ceiling in mock indignation and left the room. I had seen this act before and there was no way I was going to fall for it this time.

I followed her into the living room. "You know I'm right, don't you?"

Cornered, she had to concede the point. "Well, perhaps I did give in a little too quickly."

"Five seconds?" I asked.

"I tried to make it to ten." Mary Ann then switched tactics again and said what was really on her mind. "Oh, George, why can't you just let Todd have the dog?"

"You know why, Mary Ann."

"I don't mean to be insensitive, but your bad dog history was a long time ago. Believe me, you would be better off to forget about it and try again."

"I'll think about it," I grumbled, and went into another room, sat in a chair, and rested my face in my hands and tried to think about something I didn't like to think about—my history of dog experiences.

When I was twelve years old my father was killed in a tractor accident and his parents—my grandparents— moved back into our house. Not knowing what else to do for me, my grandfather came home one day with an Irish setter. I grew up with the world's best dog, Tucker. No other kids lived near our farm, so Tucker became my best friend. We hunted, explored, and understood each other. No rabbit, quail, rattlesnake, or prairie chicken was safe from me and Tucker.

He somehow got me through what would have otherwise been a very lonely adolescence.

After I graduated from high school, the United States Army gave me a one-year, all-expenses-paid Vietnam vacation. Tucker, now an old man of a dog, patiently waited for me on the back porch for months, just like I was going to come home from football practice any minute. My grandmother wrote to me on April 7, 1969, to tell me that Tucker died on the back porch waiting for me to come home. His collar and tags still hang from an ancient nail in our barn. I missed him, but given where I was, I just moved ahead and tried to stay alive.

In June 1969, our patrol made its way into a village. The last and only living thing left was a half-starved dog of indeterminate breed. It was against regulations, but I kept that dog with me for the next four months. I hoped he would replace the empty space that came from being so far away from home and losing Tucker. We made him our platoon mascot and, after considering several worthy nominations, settled on the name "Good Charlie." He became my new best friend and the only sane and kind creature in a part of the world filled with brutality. He saved my life, but it cost him his own when he bounded ahead of me and stepped on a land mine.

It took me a very long time to get over grieving for Tucker and maybe even longer for Good Charlie. Not just because I missed the dogs, but also because they became important landmarks in my journey through the ugly war memories that are hard to shed. I still don't talk about either dog. Not even to Mary Ann. Some people may think I'm a dog grouch, but it isn't that simple.

I wanted to leave memories of guns and dogs back in Southeast Asia. My grandfather insisted that it was not safe to be on a farm without a rifle, so I kept his, a World War I .30-06 with five bullets, buried deep in my closet. Though I knew how to load and fire the old gun, I hoped it would never be needed. My dog memories were buried even deeper. People wonder why I don't have dogs on the farm. I let them wonder. Another dog was likely to bring back a flood of dark feelings, of losses and pain and lives cut short.

Deep in thought, I did not hear Mary Ann enter the living room. She startled me slightly with a hand on my shoulder. "George?" she asked.

"Yes," I said, without looking up.

"I'm sorry. We can forget about it this year. I should not have put you in this position. It was insensitive of me." She paused and then added, "I'll tell Todd that this is a bad year and we'll consider it next year. Maybe you'll be ready by then."

I reached out and held her hand. "No, Mary Ann, you're right. It's been almost forty years. That's long enough. It's time for me to get over this."

"Are you sure?"

"Yes, but there are still a few concerns I want to discuss."

"Like what?" she asked, without pushing.

"At the end of the week, we take the dog back. It's a one-week experiment. A nice thing to do for the holidays. Nothing more."

"Yes, George, I understand. That's how the program works. If you want to take the dog back, you can."

"You'll support me on this?"

"Of course I will. What else?"

"I want Todd to handle this responsibly. He feeds him and takes him out for walks, not you or me. Also, I think this is the perfect opportunity to get him to clean his room. No clean room, no dog."

"I agree," she said.

"Settled?" I asked.

"Done," she said.

I was inclined to give it a try. I felt better having an understanding with my wife. We had learned long ago that all couples fight, or at least argue from time to time. Mary Ann likes to say that it's not conflict itself, but unresolved conflict, that causes problems in life and marriage.

She grew up the daughter of the local banker and I wondered if getting everything she wanted as a child made it harder for her to say no to Todd. While I was in Vietnam, Mary Ann received her teacher's degree from Kansas State University. Between homework assignments, she wrote to me every day, and she was ready to marry me when I returned, shot up and crippled as I was. I quipped, "You only want me for my disability pension."

"That makes us even, George."

"Why's that?"

"You only want me for my teacher's salary."

I never questioned Mary Ann's sense of loyalty. She promised to be the best wife and the best mother any woman could be. She never let me down. We just did not always see things exactly the same way when it came to Todd.

This was going to be one of those occasions.

The next morning, Todd was dressed and in the kitchen earlier than usual, trying to keep his excitement under control. After breakfast, Todd and I made our way through the corral and down to the barn. I took out the scrap of paper with the number on it and picked up the phone extension that I kept on the south barn wall. From the barn, I could call the shelter without any interference from Crossing Trail's debate coach.

A hundred reasons for not making that call raced through my mind, but I dialed the number anyway and tried my hardest to forget each and every one of them. At some level, I suspected that Todd and Mary Ann were right. However uncomfortable it might make me, it wouldn't hurt me to have a dog around the house for a week.

Todd's life was hard. It seemed that every day we had to choose between trying to make his life better or just accepting that there were things in his world that we weren't big enough to change. Like the Christmas dog, the choices were not always easy.

The fact that Todd came to us so late in our lives sometimes made raising him more difficult. Every doctor we visited came up with a different diagnosis. I believe most were trying very hard to avoid telling us that Todd was mildly retarded. It's an ugly-sounding word. Nobody likes to say it. So, we heard *autism, learning disabled*. We heard *prenatal stroke, developmental delay, epilepsy*, and probably more. Truth was he just did not function at a high level. An exact diagnosis really didn't matter that much to me. All the doctors agreed that Todd would never get better.

He may have struggled at T-ball, soccer, and spelling bees, but we loved him and accepted him just the way he was, so what difference did it make? He needed us and we needed him—perhaps, even more.

Todd enriched our lives in countless ways, teaching us kindness, acceptance, and patience in a thousand little daily lessons. We came to understand what a special gift he was to us. When Todd was born, we vowed never to allow "I'm tired" or "I'm too old" to get in the way of doing what needed to be done for him.

I reminded myself of this vow as I dialed the phone.

"Cherokee County Animal Shelter," said a voice from the other end of the line. "This is Hayley."

I suspected that it was Hayley Donaldson, a former student of Mary Ann's and classmate of my daughter's. Clearing my throat to bring my mind back to the task at hand, I responded, "Hayley, this is George McCray. My son Todd is interested in something he heard on the radio about a Christmas dog."

"Oh, yeah, you're Hannah's dad, right?"

"That's right."

"What can I tell you?"

"Todd's given me a few details, but I want to make sure he understands." I glanced over at my boy. His eyes were beaming. And although it warmed me to the core to see him this happy, I was already getting an uneasy feeling about adopting a dog.

"Over the holidays, many of us like to do kind things for other people," Hayley began. "At the shelter, we offer animal lovers an opportunity to extend that holiday spirit to an animal. You come by anytime from around December eighteenth on and pick out your dog. You keep him until at least the twenty-sixth. We're pretty flexible on the dates. We're more concerned that the Adopt a Dog for Christmas program works for your family and that you have a good time with our dogs. You feed him and give him lots of attention, then bring the dog back if you want. Otherwise, our dogs stay in a three-foot-by-six-foot steel cage for the holidays. At this time of year, with so much of our staff off, there just isn't time to do much more than give an occasional pat on the head."

I raised my voice slightly for Todd's benefit and then carefully asked, "There is no obligation to keep the dog, right?"

"Absolutely not."

"Are there enough volunteers?" I realized the question was absurd.

"No, Mr. McCray. There are never enough volunteers. It seems that we always have more dogs than good homes for them."

I could see how Adopt a Dog for Christmas might work for us, but many questions still ran through my head. Was this just a scheme for the shelter's employees to get a few days off? How could the dogs possibly know that it was Christmas? Wasn't this a holiday for humans? Would I feel guilty when I returned the dog? Would Todd understand and accept the transitory nature of the program?

Ultimately, it was one of the times in my life when I took a deep breath and trusted that it would work. I was never one who believed that the road to hell is paved with good intentions. In fact, I believed just the opposite to be true.

"We'll come and take a look," I said, suppressing a sigh of reluctance.

"That's great. If you decide to adopt a dog for the holidays, there is some paperwork, but we know your family, so it's really just a formality."

"Thanks, Hayley. We'll see you in a couple of weeks."

Todd was obviously pleased that I made the call. He smiled, nodded his head, and walked away from the barn to conduct the latest in his series of painstaking experiments to determine just how well paint adheres in December. I assumed that after seven years on this experiment, Todd Paints was on the verge of releasing the shocking results of this research to the public: Paint does not adhere particularly well, or spread with ease, when it's nearly freezing outside.

It was cold for early December that year and we had an abnormally large amount of snow. Winter weather triggers pleasant memories for me. My grandfather had a very important job in Cherokee County. He drove a maintainer, or what we might call a grader today. The title of County Road Maintainer, which was only slightly less prestigious than "Your Honor," was bestowed upon him. At first, the maintainer was pulled by two large draft horses, named Dick and Doc. They were lavishly housed in giant box stalls in our barn. Later, the county acquired a maintainer that was powered by a diesel engine that was extraordinarily reliable.

It was my grandfather's job to keep the gravel roads graded in the summer and clear of snow in the winter. When I was a boy, a big snowstorm would cause our family to spring into action with tremendous urgency.

My grandmother would make coffee and put it into an old thermos. I could tell by the smell of the pot brewing in the predawn hours that it was a snow day. She would make up a sack of sandwiches and cookies large enough to feed my grandfather for several meals straight.

In the middle of the night, Bo McCray would start up that old grader. It would loudly spew and spat, daring the snow to fall, and then shoot balls of sparks into the dark snow-stained sky like a mighty titan awakening from a deep, centuries-old slumber. I liked the sound of the mammoth machine coming to life. Eventually the engine would smooth out and I could hear him pull out of the driveway, heading the maintainer west toward town. I would listen until the sound was gone, picturing the snow pushed aside effortlessly.

This was one of those familiar childlike images where we see adults towering above us with inconceivable power and ability. Eventually the roar of the maintainer disappeared into the night, but it left me with good thoughts about my grandfather moving all of that snow out of the way as I snuggled deep down into sheets of flannel and blankets of wool.

The heat from the wood furnace did not make it to the edges of the house that were relegated to the children. A glass of water set on my bedside table was likely to have ice in it by the early morning hours, but it somehow mattered less because I knew that the roads were clear and each day held endless possibilities, including a very good chance of a school-closing decision made after the school consulted with my grandfather, who was often kind enough to ask my opinion.

Sometimes Grandfather McCray would work twenty-four, or even thirty-six, hours straight, plowing snow. When he grew tired, my father would climb onto the maintainer and take a shift, and when I got older, after my father died, I took my turn. I loved the feeling of clearing the snow, and the admiration of our neighbors was considerable.

The elderly, sick, or poor were likely to wake and find

their own private driveways also cleared of snow—a brief detour my grandfather was sure the county could afford.

Our lives depended on my grandfather maintaining the roads. Many homes did not have phones to call for help and what phone service did exist was unreliable and frequently lost in bad weather. Without the roads cleared, there was tremendous isolation.

Over the Christmas holidays, we were the most popular people in Cherokee County, Kansas. Around four o'clock on the Sunday afternoon before Christmas, my grandmother and my mother would make a large pot of oyster stew, cook a ham, and make an enormous bowl of mashed potatoes. Aunt Elizabeth brought her famous cinnamon rolls and cherry pie, which my cousins and I fought over as if they were lost pirate treasure.

Around seven o'clock on that same Sunday evening, our neighbors showed their gratitude by dropping by with Christmas cookies, gifts, or homemade ornaments to string on our tree. Because we expected the company, my mother, and now many years later Mary Ann, made our old farmhouse seem like the Midwest regional office for Claus Enterprises. Half of our basement was filled with gifted decorations and no one dared, now or then, to throw away one piece of worn-out holly. Every ornament had earned a spot. Whether it was true or not, we expected that each neighbor and friend was closely watching to make sure their ornaments had earned a place in our decorating scheme.

As the years passed, the neighbors came by not to thank my grandfather for removing snow but to see the Christmas decorations at the McCray house that had evolved and been added to for generations. Our house was a museum of Christmas treasures past and present. The Sunday before Christmas family dinner and open house was a very special part of our holiday tradition.

It had always been my job to hang the lights, but on this day I had a helper. Todd, who of course could not come up the ladder, stood below, headphones on under his stocking cap, and handed me the lights. As I strung them around the house, the sun hid behind patchy clouds and little independent flakes of snow occasionally fluttered to the ground. Although our house is modest, it takes me more than two hours to do the lights.

When Todd and I finished the outside lights, we went to the basement and started the trek up and down the stairs carrying boxes. My wife is very organized and each box is labeled with a destination. For Todd it was like rediscovering forgotten toys.

Mary Ann would spend hours with Todd over the coming weeks hanging and recounting the history of our Yuletide treasure trove.

As the holiday approached, Todd and I began to make a game out of the Christmas dog.

"We get the dog on the eighteenth and when do we return him?" I asked Todd.

"Dog goes back on the twenty-sixth."

"When does Christmas end, Todd?"

"Christmas ends on the twenty-sixth, Dad—and that's when the dog has to go back to the shelter."

I put my arm around Todd's shoulder and hugged him. "That's good, Todd. We're going to have fun with the Christmas dog, aren't we?"

With all of the work helping his mother to decorate the house and cleaning his own room, Todd was pleased to see Christmas week arrive. He removed at least six large trash sacks of junk from his room and I kept making him clean more while I had his attention. Neither his mother nor I dared to look into those sacks out of the sincerest fear of what had lurked in the dark folds of that boy's room. I'm sure he spent at least two full days on the project. When he thought it was clean, we had him mop the floor and wash the walls with warm soapy water. This might be our last opportunity to insist upon this level of cleanliness.

As I stood in the doorway and watched him work, I could hear Mary Ann laughing on the phone with one of her friends from Crossing Trails High School.

"I did not think I would ever see his room this clean. Not since the Lord fed five thousand with two fish and five loaves has anyone been able to make so much of so little. Todd can take one candy wrapper and in two hours manufacture an entire sack of trash. He can create clutter out of breeze and sunlight."

I turned back in Todd's direction as he said, "It's clean," holding a rag high in the air to signal the completion.

Wandering around the room grunting approval, I finally mustered the nerve to look under the bed. To my surprise, it was clean too. "This room is fit for a Christmas dog." He acknowledged his assent with a grin and I went back outside to work.

Todd probably had not slept much the last few nights leading up to December 18. He'd spent two weeks speculating to me about the kind, size, breed, and shape of the dog he wanted to adopt and this gave us both some opportunity to tease, which I gladly allowed.

"I think I want a big one," he said.

"Really," I said.

"Big like an elephant." Todd extended his arms as much as he could and still it was only slightly wider than his grin.

"An elephant would be real comfortable in your room. They like jungle."

"Not anymore, Dad. It's clean now."

"Considering all that junk you took out, maybe you could fit two elephants in there. Should we call the zoo and see if they have an elephant adoption program?"

"Dad, I don't want an elephant."

"Just a big dog. Right?"

"Of course, I could take three small ones instead."

"Perhaps," I fired back. "You could take one dog for a week or you could take three different dogs for one day each."

He stood there figuring for a few seconds and then smiled when he completed the math. "Nah, I think one big dog for a week is better."

When the eighteenth finally did arrive, Todd was at the breakfast table waiting for me, dressed and ready to go. I came down in my robe and slippers with a towel wrapped around my head, a rare sight for Todd.

"Mary Ann," I offered in my sickest and weakest voice, "I have a frightful headache—could be pneumonia. I'll have to spend the entire day in bed. We can only hope for a recovery before spring planting. You and Todd will have to do the chores for me till then."

She stood there with her hands on her hips and said, "Oh, George, quit teasing that boy. Get back up those stairs and change your clothes this minute!"

"I hurt too badly, Mary Ann." I tried to sniffle and hold back a few tears of pain. "I don't think I can walk." I stumbled into the living room and fainted on the couch. For extra effect, I stuck my one good leg vertically into the air and let it tremble with the last movements of life. My eyelids fluttered, my arms dropped limply to my sides, and I died on the spot.

Mary Ann followed me in and pulled the towel from around my head and said, "George, since you are so sick, maybe today would be a good day for Todd to practice driving the truck on his own. Can we have your keys?"

Springing back to life, I announced, "I'm feeling better. All I need is a good, hearty breakfast."

"Well, then, get in here and sit down and eat it before it gets cold," Mary Ann ordered.

At the table, I remembered my manners, and kindly commented on each and every bite of breakfast. "Mmmm, mmmm, Mary Ann, these are the finest pancakes you have ever made. Are there seconds? Thirds?"

"Same recipe for years now, George. You just eat 'em and quit talking about 'em."

"Anything different about this coffee? Sure tastes good."

"Nope and there is nothing different about this foot." She held her rigid right foot in the air in a menacing way. "Would you like to reacquaint yourself with it?"

I turned to Todd, who had sat through the entire meal wearing his hat, coat, and gloves, and said, "You about ready to go, son?"

"Yes. I am ready."

"Well, if you are ready, why are we sitting in this kitchen jawing with your mother? We have important work to do. Dog picking is today. Don't you remember that today is dog-picking day?"

He stood up and said, "Yes, we should go."

"Let me put on my best dog-picking clothes and then we'll leave."

I stood up from the table and before I could head upstairs to change, Todd gave me an enormous hug and the connection between the two of us seemed to run down through my toes.

Todd was generous with hugs and we did nothing to discourage them, even though they were sometimes offered at unexpected times and places. The school bus driver and the FedEx man both got used to them. There were other little social cues that Todd may have vaguely recognized but often ignored. Some of these Mary Ann worked hard to curb, like not leaving the bathroom door wide open so he could carry on a conversation with anyone within shouting distance. Other habits, like not keeping his room clean, we tolerated. Most boys stop holding their parents' hands when they turn nine or ten, but when we were alone and when he forgot just how old he was, Todd would grab Mary Ann's or my hand and walk along with us. This morning was special. It was not only a dog-picking day, but as we left the house for town, it was also a hugging and hand-holding day.

Walking toward the truck, I squeezed his hand gently.

My old brown Ford moved toward town at a pace that was too slow for Todd. Those size 12 red-sneakered feet tapped twice for each beat of the music that played on the truck's AM radio, and though he knew how long it took, he kept asking, "How much further, Dad?"

"At least another four or five days, Todd. You know what a long journey it is to town. We've got to cross the Rocky Mountains, pass through the Great Mojave Desert, go down one side and back up the other side of the Grand Canyon, and then loop all the way around Toledo." I paused and added, "And, 'cause I know you are in a hurry, I'm not factoring in a thing for tornadoes."

"Dad," he whined. "How much longer—really?"

"Ten minutes, son. Ten minutes."

Todd smiled contentedly, knowing just how close he was to the shelter.

"When do we take the dog back, Todd? Do you remember?"

"Yes, Dad, the dog goes back on the twenty-sixth. That's when Christmas ends."

"Very good. You know, if this goes well and if we all have fun and get the dog back to the shelter on time, maybe we could do it next year too. Would you like that?"

"Sure." Todd looked up at me with a smile. The last two weeks had given me time to adjust to the idea, but most of all I was pleased to be doing this for him.

The sign on the edge of town proudly proclaims WELCOME TO CROSSING TRAILS—WHERE THE OREGON, SANTA FE, AND CALIFORNIA TRAILS ALL MEET. There is only one stoplight in Crossing Trails, and it seemed to be unnecessary as we sat there alone waiting for the light to turn green.

A small police station about the size of a convenience store rests on one corner and the volunteer fire department is on another. Every year the two stations have a competition to see who can decorate their respective building with the most holiday flair. Perhaps because the fire station is manned by volunteers, over the last few years the town's Christmas Committee seemed partial to the cornerstone of their scheme: Santa at the helm of an antique horse-drawn fire engine. This year the police station countered with Santa's reindeer pulling an antique police car.

Main Street has seen little new construction over the years. All of the commercial structures, just to the ragged side of charming, are close to a hundred years old. Some of the buildings stubbornly cling to old wooden sidewalks cut from the durable oaks harvested from the nearby forests. Nearly all were decked out with holiday greenery and white Christmas lights.

Two blocks ahead and on the right side of the town square is the Cherokee County Courthouse. A bronze statue of a tired pioneer, hat in hand and staring west, stands at the base of the steps. An old gazebo commands the courthouse lawn and still serves as the home for the Cherokee County Volunteer Band, which would be performing their holiday program several times before Christmas, weather permitting.

Like many old things, the courthouse had remained antiquated long enough to become historic. A tall spire with a bell tower constructed of native limestone and brick rose high over the surrounding buildings. Judge Crawford, the county's only permanent judge, took a break in December from his duties.

In Crossing Trails, the farther you move away from the town square, the faster the charm wears off. Near the edge of town, after passing over the tracks for the old Atchison, Topeka, and Santa Fe Railway, there is a trailer park and an old gravel road that leads south to the county fishing lake.

We turned and followed the gravel past poorly kept and poorly constructed homes, punctuated by even more poorly kept yards, littered with worn-out cars and rusted swing sets. The less fortunate make their homes on the South Side. At one point this was good farm ground, but the water treatment plant, a trailer court, and cheap rental housing had changed all of that for the worse. If I remembered correctly, Hayley's grandparents lived on this ground when it was still farmed. Now the South Side and the county animal shelter were places that most people (and all animals) preferred to avoid.

As I came around the last bend in the gravel road, and the shelter was in view, Todd unhooked his seatbelt. Before I came to a full stop in the shelter's parking lot, marked with potholes like a mortar-littered battlefield, Todd threw open the truck door and headed toward the entrance. He moved quickly past an old Nissan pickup truck that Hayley drove. I recognized it as a car I often saw in town, usually with a few dogs in the back and another couple in the cab. The bumper sticker read, DOG ABUSERS SHOULD GET WHAT THEY GIVE.

There are several places that I prefer to not know too much about. Animal shelters are one of them. Our town's shelter, like most, was underfunded and crowded past capacity. Makeshift trailer annexes of critter cages filled with complaining felines were permanently parked next to the original building. The dingy yellow brick structure itself was discarded years ago by the sewer district. On warm days, when the wind came from the south, it became obvious why the county moved their administrative offices closer to town.

As soon as I had pushed the front door open, I realized that the interior of the shelter was only a slight improvement. The humans had given up their office space to make room for more animals and the reception area had become the administrative offices, so crammed with desks that one could barely pass without jostling papers or boxes that hung over the edges. Just past the reception area was the break room, where old reports and records, medicines, brochures, and books were stored. Against the wall of the break room was a worn-out countertop that the vet used for routine procedures and where a coffeemaker tried hard to crank out a pot of coffee one drip at a time.

Not seeing anyone in the front of the building, we moved through a swinging door, where we found dogs and considerable human activity.

As Todd and I walked into the large holding area,

I was immediately struck by how clean the staff managed to keep the building and the cages. It must have taken a considerable effort. One dog started barking at us and soon more chimed in, like a symphony building to a crescendo. Before long, the entire population of maybe thirty-five dogs was whipped into a frenzy of barks, whines, and howls. A woman clanged a dinner bowl on the side of a metal cage, a sound that seemed to distract them and bring a halt to most of the noise. I recognized Hayley as she walked toward us. Her name tag confirmed my suspicion. She wore her prematurely graying hair in a long braid and dressed in blue jeans and a dusty green jacket.

"Hello, Hayley. Nice to see you again. We're here to adopt a dog for Christmas."

She reached out and took Todd's big hand in hers. After she held it for a moment and he did not respond as most adults would, by returning the shake and offering some salutation, she tilted her head slightly and looked into Todd's big brown eyes. Her face showed genuine affection and kindness.

"I'm Hayley. It's nice to meet you, Todd. I remember you from the county fair." It was as if she knew to look past his disability and speak directly to the enthusiastic boy inside this strong young man.

"Yes, I was in 4-H."

"I remember how nicely you handled your animals. I recall a few blue ribbons safety-pinned to your shirt one year not too long ago, right?"

"Yes, sheep and cattle." Todd was very involved in 4-H, but unfortunately he was now too old to participate. It had been a great confidence builder for him.

"Todd, I know you are an old hand with animals, so look over all of the dogs and then we'll decide together if there is a good fit for you and your family. The unadoptable dogs are quarantined. So, just look around and let me know if you need some help or have any questions." She reached out and held Todd's forearm for a moment, as if she wanted to say something else, but instead she just turned and walked away, busily moving from cage to cage—doing what, I was not sure.

Over the years, I had learned that you could tell a lot about a person simply based on the way they related to Todd. I had a good feeling about Hayley.

This was a very important decision for my son and I did not want to rush him. After finding a bench, I attempted to read a newspaper that someone had left behind while Todd walked up and down the rows of cages to find just the right companion for Christmas. The floor had recently been washed and the smell of chlorine bleach hung in the air along with various animal odors. My ears were filled with the sounds of whines, barks, and metal dog bowls scraping the concrete floor. I watched Todd, part man, part boy, move slowly up and down the aisles.

He seemed determined to give each animal a fair audition. After ten minutes, I decided to join him. Dog picking looked like fun. Besides that, I was vaguely curious about the dogs. The stiffness that was stubbornly rooted in my right leg was barely noticeable as I got up from the bench and walked along with Todd. He stopped at each cage and made mental notes that he occasionally shared with me.

"This one reminds me of Trudy. She is happy to see me." Trudy belonged to my son Jonathan and was Todd's favorite old dog. She was a Border collie with a tinge of German shepherd thrown into the mix. When she was a puppy, Jonathan would bring her out to the farm. She loved to help Todd move the sheep out of the back pasture and into the barnyard, where they were safe from the coyotes, bobcats, and foxes.

"Could be a sheep herder extraordinaire!" I said.

Todd moved slowly to the next cage to inspect a floppy-eared dog that wouldn't bother to amble over and greet us. She was liver-colored with white splotches on her chest and front legs, with the distinct black muzzle of a coonhound.

"She's quiet," Todd observed.

"Yep." I read out loud from the tag at the top of her cage. "The shelter named her Sally. This says she is an eight-year-old female coonhound and spaniel mix. Spayed. Can sit and roll over on command." I turned to Todd and said, "Hey, that dog takes orders better than some of my children."

Todd rolled his eyes at me. At this rate we would be here for a month, so I returned to the bench and the day-old newspaper that was about to become cage liner.

After wading through the sports and weather sections,

I glanced up. Todd had progressed past only two more cages. He looked so much in his element. It occurred to me that if there were angels for animals, then surely Todd was one. I realized that some dog was going to be very lucky. Hayley worked her way back to check on Todd and seemed to like the way he studied each animal. She followed along and the two of them worked as a team in this most important selection. She didn't try to push him toward one of the less adoptable dogs. Instead, she tried to give explanations for every dog's condition.

As they stopped at each cage, Hayley encouraged Todd to get a closer look. My guess was that Hayley was spending more time with Todd than she did with the other visitors to the shelter.

"This is Baron. He appears to be a German short-haired pointer. He's lived in a cage most of his life. His owner thought that because he was a hunting dog, it would ruin him to run about the yard. He needs to be socialized. You know, spend more time around people. He could be a good pet, but he'll need a very patient and kind owner to teach him to trust humans again."

She opened the cage door. "He's scared," Todd said as he wrapped his arms around the trembling dog. Almost immediately, the dog settled down and began to wag his tail, sensing that he was safe and in good hands.

Hayley looked at the tag on the door and said, "He's only been here four days. It takes some dogs longer than others to become comfortable. He seems to have taken to you right away. Dogs are good judges of character."

"Hayley, why do some of the dogs seem excited to see me and others don't?"

"That's a good question. Some dogs are still stuck on their old owners. They aren't ready yet to accept a new family or friend. Every dog in here has a perfect human match. There's not a dog in here that won't act excited when the right person comes along."

"How come those dogs are separated?" He pointed to an area separated from where they were by a chain-link fence with a gate and a sign that said do not enter.

"They're in quarantine, not suitable for adoption."

"What's quarantine?" he asked.

"There are state laws about dogs that bite. They have to be isolated to make sure they do not have rabies."

Todd walked over to the fence and peered into the quarantine pens. "Why do those dogs all look the same?"

Hayley's expression darkened. "Most are pit bulls that the sheriff had to bring in because they have been mistreated. How a man treats a dog, Todd, says a lot about what's in his heart."

Before he could ask any more questions, Hayley led Todd in a happier direction, toward a safer dog. "This big girl we call Pork Chop, because she is a little overweight." Pork Chop was a mixed-breed big black dog.

"Her owner came in to claim her last week, and when we told him there was a fifty-dollar boarding fee, he told us that he was going out to his truck to get a check. We waited for him, but he just drove off and never came back."

Todd stared at her in disbelief. "Why didn't he come

and get his dog? She was waiting for him. Was there something wrong with that man?"

"I'd say so, Todd. I'd say something seriously wrong. Shame of it is that large black dogs, like Pork Chop, are the hardest to place with new owners. We call it the 'big black dog syndrome.'"

"Why's that?" Todd asked.

"Because there are so many of them; supply and demand."

Hayley reached the next cage and said, "Now, what is different about this dog?"

Todd stared and said, "He's little."

"That's right. Did you notice that he is the only little dog in the shelter?"

Todd looked around at the cages and asked, "Why is he the only one?"

"Well, we call them 'squat-and-pee dogs.' They're house dogs. They are let out briefly, they squat, pee, and come back inside. Large dogs are left outside, often for hours. They break out of fences and end up here."

"What kind is he?" Todd asked.

"He's a Jack Russell mix."

"I like 'squat-and-pee dog' better!" I chimed in from my perch on the bench.

Todd frowned at my attempt at humor and then stopped in front of the only empty cage in the shelter and asked, "What happened to that one?"

Hayley smiled. "Probably out with a handler for a walk or grooming."

"Grooming?"

"We do lots of things, Todd, to help the animals be adopted. You might notice that we never allow their waste to stay in their cages. We've learned that people will walk right by a cage that has been fouled and that's not fair to the dog, is it?"

"No." Todd shook his head.

"We also have learned that people won't adopt a dog that is too scared. So we work a great deal with frightened dogs so that they welcome visitors. We all know that people pick dogs based on how they look. Polly, for instance, was here for thirty-nine days. Forty days is a very important date for these dogs. They really need to be adopted by then. When Polly was still here after thirty-five, we were worried. She was a very happy and friendly dog, so we called a lady here in town, a volunteer groomer. She came in and gave Polly a haircut, a shampoo, and bought her a brand-new collar with a pink ribbon on it. She did a great job. Yesterday was Polly's thirty-ninth day and . . ."—she grabbed Todd's arm excitedly—"someone adopted her this morning! So, Polly is at her new home."

I was hoping that Todd would not ask the significance of forty days and was pleased that Hayley did not come right out and say what happened to these dogs if they did not find a home for them. Todd would have been troubled by the ugly truth. The concept troubled me too. I got up from the bench again and quietly followed behind Todd and Hayley for another half hour of detailed dog inspections.

It was approaching the lunch hour before they had looked at all the dogs and Todd heard all their stories. I was surprised that he had not yet made his selection. I wasn't sure if he had not found the right dog or if he just wanted to take them all.

"Do you want to see one more?" Hayley asked.

She led us into an area at the very back of the shelter where a few empty cages sat. The only occupied cage held a large black lab retriever mix. Another "big black dog problem," it appeared.

Hayley offered her comments. "He's an older dog. You can tell by the gray around his muzzle. He's quiet, not a barker. We don't allow the dogs to be adopted for the first three days. This gives the owner a chance to claim their pet if it is just lost, but after the third day, the dog becomes the property of the shelter. Starting today, he's ours."

"What's his name?" I heard Todd ask as Hayley opened the cage door.

She looked around the door for information, but finding none, she shrugged her shoulders. "Don't know, I guess he just showed up. They do that sometimes. He hasn't been here long enough for us to give him a name."

Todd seemed to hesitate. I had a good feeling about this dog. He sat, patiently aware, without jumping, barking, or whining, like many of the other dogs did when the cage door opened. He seemed focused, ready to receive a command, but his wagging tail showed that he was also pleased to see Todd.

Perhaps I was becoming a little bored by the selection process or I felt sorry for him because he was new to the shelter. I walked toward Todd and put my hand on his arm to get his attention. "Should we look him over?"

Todd didn't say no, so Hayley had him out of the cage in an instant. She gave the command "Sit," and he did so. The dog waited quietly while Todd ran his fingers through the gray and black hair on the nape of his neck. Then Todd stooped down so that he was at the dog's eye level and stared into his face for a few moments. He had warm green eyes that showed a certain patient wisdom.

After Todd sized him up, Hayley placed a choke chain around the dog's neck. He suddenly became excited, as if he knew he had been chosen. She snapped a leash on the collar and led him a few feet in one direction and then a few feet back the other way. He did not act like an animal that had spent much time in a cage. Hayley then issued several commands accompanied by a gesture. First, she held her palm outward, like a traffic cop directing a stop, and then she slowly bent her wrist so her fingertips pointed down toward the floor and again issued the command "Sit." The dog sat. Then she pushed the air down like she was cramming trash into a bag and said, "Down." The dog slid down onto his stomach. She said, "Stay," dropped the leash, and walked away. After she had taken ten steps, she turned to look back. He had not budged.

"He minds well, though he seems to have some age-related stiffness in his haunches."

Todd bent down, petted the dog, and ran his hands over his ribs. "He's thin. Is he eating?"

"He's eating. I bet he's been on the road for a while and missed a few meals."

Todd parted his fur and found a few rough spots, including a cut that had only recently scabbed over. He motioned to Hayley to look at the wound.

She kneeled down for a closer look. "We'll put something on it." She then looked approvingly at Todd. He had obviously noticed something important that even she had missed.

Todd stood up, folded his arms across his chest as if he were a discriminating and seasoned buyer of fine purebreds, and asked me, "What do you think, Dad?"

I walked around the dog twice, noticing four legs, a tail, and all the other required appendages. "He looks excellent to me," I offered.

Todd grinned happily and pointed confidently at the animal. "We'll take him." Finally, the dog jumped up from his resting spot, as if on command, and edged toward the exit. Hayley grabbed the leash and held him in place.

I did not waste any time in confirming the terms of our arrangement. "When do we bring him back, Todd?"

"We bring him back on the twenty-sixth, Dad. That's when Christmas ends." I looked to Hayley for reassurance and she smiled and shook her head approvingly.

Todd and Mary Ann had gone into town a few days earlier and had used some of Todd's allowance money to purchase a leash and collar. Given the time of the year, Mary Ann suggested a green collar and a red leash. They had selected a medium-sized collar, which Todd pulled out of his coat pocket and easily slipped around the dog's neck. Hayley shut the cage door behind us and Todd led the dog back into the reception area on the festive-looking red leash.

Passing all the other dogs on the way out, I felt a little sorry that they were not adopted for Christmas too. There was a fleeting moment when I considered taking two, but my reputation had to be considered, so I moved on. We filled out some paperwork and Hayley put some ointment on the cut.

After thanking her, we left the shelter with our new friend. The crisp winter wind caught my breath, but I managed to ask, "Do you want to name him?"

"Already did," Todd said to my surprise as he hurried toward the truck.

"What?"

"I named him *Christmas*." Todd opened the truck door and Christmas instantly jumped in. Todd climbed in next to the dog and I got in behind the wheel, oddly at ease with this warm furry presence comfortably wedged between my son and me. As I started the ignition, the radio came to life, a Christmas song filling the cold Kansas air.

I looked at Todd and the dog and said, "That's a good name. That's a real good name."

In the truck on the way home, the dog was well behaved. I suspected that it was not his first ride in a pickup truck. But for the occasional wag of his tail, he did not fidget or move around, nor whine or growl. Todd massaged the dog's muscles and ran his hands through his coat. This must have felt good, for Christmas turned around several times and gave Todd an approving lick. I couldn't resist reaching over and patting him a few times myself. He seemed very content with us.

"Where do you think we should keep Christmas this week?" I asked Todd.

Todd looked at me, surprised. "In my room."

"I was thinking maybe we should put him in the chicken coop to guard the hens. How about that?"

"Nah, Dad, chickens don't need a guard."

"Well, how about at the bottom of the silo? I have seen some rats down there and I bet he could keep 'em out of there."

"Nah, Dad, I think my room works."

"You did clean it up, didn't you, Todd?"

"Six sacks. I took out six sacks."

"That'll make enough room for him, won't it? Now, you're sure you don't want that elephant?"

Todd laughed at the idea. "Nope. I like Christmas."

As we passed back through Crossing Trails, I noticed a trickle of Christmas shoppers exiting various stores with wrapped presents or shopping bags in hand. There was a movement by the local chamber of commerce to keep shoppers in town, but I wondered if their campaign was working. Once on the highway, making our way back to the farm, it occurred to me that there had been many times when I just did not know what to get Todd for Christmas. As he sat beside me with that dog, I knew that this year was different.

When we arrived home, Mary Ann met us at the back door. "What took so long? I was beginning to worry about you two."

"Dog picking is hard work. It takes time." Mary Ann knew that Todd could be very deliberate on matters that were important to him, so she dropped the subject as the three of us came in out of the cold, through the back porch door and into the kitchen.

Todd led the dog around in circles. Christmas appeared to be just as well trained and obedient for us as he was for Hayley. He heeled appropriately, and when Todd stopped, he promptly sat down beside him and waited for the next cue. Todd had apparently paid close attention to Hayley and repeated the same series of commands for his mother's benefit.

Mary Ann carried on like she had just witnessed

the construction of the Eighth Wonder of the World. "George, look how the dog minds. Look how Todd can work with him. Isn't it amazing!"

"Incredible," I muttered.

Mary Ann leaned over so that she could look directly into Christmas's face and exclaimed, "He has green eyes. I love dogs with green eyes."

"He was the best one at the shelter," Todd said, giving Christmas a pat and removing the leash. The dog's tail thumped the floor as he wagged it, a sound that would become familiar in the coming week.

"Todd, that dog could not have been at the shelter. He is perfect."

"Mom, can I tell you about the shelter?"

"Why, of course, sweetie. Tell me all about it."

Todd was as animated as I had seen him in years. He grabbed his mother's hand and led her, the dog right behind them, to the kitchen table, where the two of them sat, with Christmas at their feet. Todd told his mother all about the shelter. He described virtually every dog, while Mary Ann patiently listened. I leaned against the wall and just observed, experiencing the whole trip again, this time through Todd's eyes.

While they talked, I opened doors and rummaged through kitchen cabinets until I found two old steel bowls shoved in the very back as if waiting for me to unearth them all these years later: Tucker's old dog dishes. Somehow I felt comfort and not sadness.

I ran some water from the tap into one bowl and put it

under the table for Christmas. I put some of the dog food that Todd and Mary Ann had purchased in the other bowl and set it next to the water. Christmas, not wanting to be rude, gently removed a few morsels from the bowl and quietly nibbled away while Todd and Mary Ann gossiped about his canine cousins at the shelter.

In our hall closet I found an old blanket on a shelf and I placed it on the kitchen floor. Christmas approached and pawed until all was situated properly, as dogs will do. Once it was acceptable, he lay down on his new bed. Leaning against the door frame, I listened to Todd recount the remainder of the day's adventure to his mother. They were so absorbed in conversation that I don't think they'd noticed me playing innkeeper.

Fifteen minutes passed with only an occasional pause for breath. I finally interrupted. "I offered to get him an elephant, but he passed."

"Oh, George, let him tell his story."

After all the events had been thoroughly reported, Todd and Mary Ann gave Christmas a tour of our small home. Apparently this approval process worked both ways and they wanted to be sure that Christmas found our accommodations to his liking. They moved out of the kitchen into Todd's room and the guest room, through the dining room, and finally to the living room, which stretched across the entire front of our home. Against the interior wall of the living room is a fireplace that warms our house.

Todd, dragging the dog's blanket along, stopped within range of the radiant heat cast from the fire. He spread the blanket out, marking their territory, and sat down on the floor. Christmas stretched out and ordered up a canine massage that Todd gladly administered, starting with his paws and finishing with just the right amount of therapeutic belly rubbing. Christmas yawned and Todd lay down beside him for a lazy rest by the fire. It seemed that our weary traveler had found a comfortable place and a good friend.

When Christmas woke from his afternoon snooze, he made his way through the kitchen to the back door and let out one small bark as if he had done it a million times. Mary Ann let him out and we were all pleased that Christmas was not shy about communicating his needs to us—one less worry about having a dog in the house.

By the next morning, a warm front had moved in and the snow was melting fast beneath a blue sky crowded with large scattered clouds. Several geese were honking loudly as they made their way from our lake and into our fields for a day of foraging for the bits of sorghum, corn, and oats that the combine generously left behind.

Todd and Christmas were still asleep while Mary Ann and I ate breakfast. My experience with sleepovers told me that last night might have been more about talking than sleeping. I left Mary Ann humming at the kitchen sink when I left to do my chores.

After feeding the stock, I turned and saw the two of them, Todd and Christmas, ambling toward me.

"Good morning," Todd said.

"How's that dog?"

"He's fine." Todd slipped through the rails of the corral and started to inspect the cattle. Christmas started to follow him in. Not wanting him to spook the herd, I said, "Christmas, sit." I used the same hand signal that Hayley used and he went straight to his haunches.

Todd grinned at me in his lopsided way. "Good dog picker, aren't I?"

"Indeed, you are a fine dog picker." I went over and scratched the dog's head and his tail wagged excitedly. I softly praised him, "Good boy, Christmas." After Todd left the corral, I said, "Okay, Christmas, good boy, you can go now."

He spun a few circles and stood by Todd. "Can I go to the creek with the dog?"

"Sure."

"Can I drive the truck down?"

It was a treat for Todd to drive the truck, even though his mother insisted that he keep the transmission in first gear. I fished my car keys out of my pocket and handed them over. "You just drive slowly or your mom will have me sleeping in the barn."

Todd opened the truck door. Christmas hopped in and once again settled easily on the middle of the bench seat. Todd started the engine and headed ever so slowly south toward Kill Creek. The creek always fascinated him.

For some reason, as I watched them leave, it occurred to me that I was about Todd's age when Tucker died. How different Todd's early adult life was from mine.

These thoughts made me grateful that I wasn't saying

good-bye to my son as he boarded a military bus, bidding this dog a final farewell. Todd would never have to know that returning home was only the first part of a difficult journey back. My Vietnam memories remain painful, but I've grown better at working my way through the resentment.

It's important to have a few choice spots for sitting and thinking, places that resonate with good memories and ample privacy. The whole idea of watching a son you love go off to war sent me straight to my favorite sitting spot at the back of the barn, furnished with a three-legged milking stool that my great-grandfather hewed from an oak tree right here on this farm.

Considering the unpleasant memories of war service was something that the army psychologist encouraged us to do. Even after all these years, with very little effort, I can still close my eyes and hear bomb blasts, the rapid fire of the M-16s, the heavy thuds of a .45-caliber pistol, the shouts, the pleas, the orders, choppers, F-4s dropping napalm, and against it all—insects, a dull roar of crickets, gnats, mosquitoes, and flies.

In the middle of winter, I could imagine the oppressive damp jungle heat. After enough remembering, I opened my eyes and tried to think of happier memories from that time in my life.

Mary Ann wrote me every day. Her letters are in a box on the top shelf of my closet. I tried to break up with her before leaving. I told her that she was too young to be sitting around waiting for me to come back, if I ever did. Because she was two years older than me, I kidded her that she had better act fast before her marrying years were a faded memory.

She would have none of it. After all the teasing about robbing the cradle, she was not giving up on me. When it was time for us to break up, she would let me know. Mary Ann said she would be there for me then and always.

We were married six months after I got back and she has been true to her word ever since.

My leg was stiff, so I got up to take a look at Tucker's old dog collar that hung on the wall. Turning to go inside for lunch, I heard the Ford truck grinding slowly toward the house in first gear. I felt better, grateful to be right there on the farm with my son. I was so pleased that Todd was not a young man going off to war. Little did I know that day how close I was to finally completing my journey home.

The barn door flew open. Todd was shouting, "Dad, guess what Christmas and I found! Cat tracks at the creek that were as big as my hands!" He held his big paws up in the air.

"Those would be very big prints. I don't think bobcats are that big and there hasn't been a cougar around here in years."

"They sure looked like big cat prints to me, Dad."

I thought a minute. "When the snow melts, it plays tricks on you and it makes prints seem two or three times larger than their actual size." I laughed. "Did you see any giant raccoons down there?"

Todd thought about it. "No giant raccoons. I guess you're right. It was just a bobcat."

"Makes sense to me."

Many years ago, my grandfather told me that when he was a young man out hunting, he heard that strange grunting noise deer make when they are startled. He turned and saw a cougar chase a doe into the forest. Just a few years back, another man I know, a lawyer in town, claimed to have seen a big cat flash across the eighth hole of the local golf course just as the sun was setting.

I put little confidence in these sightings for several reasons. Sooner or later most wild animals in these parts end up tangling with a car and losing. I had never seen or heard of that happening to a cougar in our area. Also, bobcats are much bigger than people think and they move so quickly that they could easily be mistaken for a larger cat.

Still there was one thing that made me wonder. It had been four years ago and I couldn't explain it then, so I forgot about it until now. A cow and a newborn calf got out through our fence. Two miles south of us are nearly a thousand acres of privately owned timber, left untouched for generations, if not centuries. I rode my mare, following the cattle tracks deep into the timber, until I came to a small creek.

The creek bed was damp and there were occasional pools of water collecting gnats and mosquitoes. There was not much of a trail and I had to constantly push spiderwebs out of my face to make progress. The cow and calf had stopped to drink. Given the volume of tracks, they had lingered there for several hours, perhaps all night. Cows have cloven hooves and leave distinct prints. I saw strange tracks around the edge of the pool. I got down off the horse for a closer look. There appeared to be cat prints the size of my hand stamped in the mud.

Not wanting to add my name to the list of local crackpots who swore to mountain lion sightings, I never said a thing. Later that morning, I found the missing cow and calf unharmed and forgot about the whole incident.

There was little risk in being careful, so I cautioned Todd as he walked away, "Just the same, maybe you and Christmas should stay away from the creek for a few days. I'll check on those tracks later."

Todd shrugged his shoulders. "Sure, Dad, but that cougar is no match for Christmas."

"You're wrong there. No dog can take a cougar."

Todd and Christmas left the barn and I walked slowly up to the house behind them. Christmas circled back several times, apparently wondering why I was so slow. When Todd wasn't looking, I crouched down and he kissed my face and wagged his tail. Todd was a fine dog picker.

On the days leading up to the holiday, I tried to put the war and memories of Tucker and Good Charlie aside, but it wasn't easy. Several times Mary Ann would stop and ask me, "Are you all right?"

"Yes," I told her, but she knew when I was struggling with those memories.

"Is it the dog?"

"No," I answered, though we both knew I was lying.

On Saturday, the day before our holiday open house, the temperatures were still moderate but the wind speed had increased. Because the breeze was blowing from the south, we would continue to enjoy warmer than normal weather. After Todd, Christmas, and I finished the morning chores, I drove the tractor down to the back field to check on the mystery tracks Todd had seen a few days earlier.

As I headed south toward Kill Creek, the wind blew even harder and I had to pull my jacket tightly around me and put on my gloves. Most of the snow had melted off the ground and the fields were wet but not yet muddy. Some green shoots of grass sporadically peeked up, but most of the fields had put on winter browns, tans, and grays.

I did not hurry the tractor along and instead enjoyed the time outdoors to think.

On the television that morning the political pundits were jawing about the latest war and I started to wonder why I could never make sense out of these debates. Behind me I pulled an old yellow and green John Deere manure spreader that cast cattle waste into the meadow—nature's fertilizer—and it occurred to me that these talking heads were spouting the same stuff I was spreading. They debated war like it could be right or wrong and like they were somehow uniquely positioned to know the difference. On the microscopic level of one soldier, I knew that wars seldom make sense, and maybe that's why I struggled listening to their dialogues.

Slowing the tractor down, I crossed over a culvert and then passed through a wooded hedgerow where I had to protect my head from low-hanging branches. A pair of red foxes sauntered out of the woods and through the meadow. I pushed in the clutch of the tractor and watched. Like most foxes, they were unbothered by a mere human. After they passed out of sight, sliding the throttle down a notch, I let out the clutch and continued toward the creek, my mind returning to the war debates.

There was another tragedy of war that was never discussed or even acknowledged and this one had bothered me a great deal over the years. Thousands of dogs served in Vietnam and saved countless lives, including my own. No awards or medals were ever given to these brave and loyal dogs. It was as if it did not matter when a dog sacrificed his life.

Few of these war dogs survived and the ones that did were callously abandoned. It had to be traumatizing for the remaining soldiers to evacuate and leave behind a friend that would lay down his life, not just once but every day. Each time I thought about it, I became hurt and angry.

The creek was in sight, and I saw an owl fly just over the treetops and land in a giant sycamore that stood at one side of the creek crossing. I stopped the tractor just short of the creek and sat. I could smell the distant odor of a wood fire, perhaps my own. This area of our farm never stopped being beautiful to me. It was a good place for putting life into perspective. I could hear the water moving gently through the riverbed, not like a roaring Colorado mountain stream teeming with trout and gold dust but like a river that takes its time and can say a lot if you have the patience to listen, which is exactly what I did. My mood lifted thanks to its wise counsel.

I turned the tractor off and applied the emergency brake, climbed down, and then looked for tracks. There were plenty of them. Raccoons, birds, rabbits, size 12 Converse tennis shoes, and a Christmas dog, but I did not see any big cat prints. So, I got back on the tractor and headed home, with the transmission in low gear.

Twice later that day, when Todd left Christmas alone for a few minutes, the dog wandered down to the barnyard and found me. He came over and nudged me, sliding his head under my hand, as if to say, "Pet me."

Wanting to see if he would follow commands for me like he had done for Hayley, I used this time to practice—sit, stay, and roll over—with him. I even got him to fetch and bring me an old tennis ball on command. He was very obedient and I had the sense that this dog, just like Good Charlie or Tucker, would give everything asked of him. Kneeling down, I held Christmas's face close to mine and felt his warm breath and soft ears. "You're a keeper," I said, without realizing the irony of my words.

I liked the smell of this animal. All of the outdoor scents that I recognized from our farm seemed to waltz freely through his fur, distilled and mixed into a nice natural aroma that was the outdoors I loved.

Remembering and missing my other old canine friends, I hugged Christmas extra hard. He seemed to understand. He rested his muzzle on my shoulder and pressed his cold nose against my ear as if to say he was very happy to be with us. When I released him, Christmas ambled over and picked up his ball and dropped it by my feet.

"You're pretty direct, aren't you?" I tossed the ball as far as I could and he chased after it. Good Charlie liked to play fetch too, although he preferred a Frisbee.

We buried Good Charlie in a graveyard by a small Buddhist monastery in the foothills near our base at Tan Son Nhut. When we told his story to the monks, they conferred among themselves for a few minutes and then concluded that Good Charlie was a reincarnated American war hero from our distant history. They seemed very pleased to have his presence with them and they promised to care for his grave. They undoubtedly meant it.

I have a couple of tangible reminders from those days of my life. One is a scar than runs from my buttocks down to my right knee like an ugly set of pink railroad tracks. The second is a damaged right leg, which, while keeping me on military disability pay, still throbs, aches, and causes me to move slower than I would like. Last, there is a purple heart in the top drawer of the dresser by my bed. Someday I plan on hanging that medal where it belongs—on Good Charlie's grave.

Christmas whined for me to attend to the ball he dropped at my feet and forced me away from my thoughts. I looked at him and said, "Well, old boy, taking you back may not be as easy as I thought, but a deal is a deal. Right?"

Christmas was sitting down and I took a wild guess and said, "Shake, boy, shake." Sure enough he held out his paw and we shook on it.

It was nice to have a dog around again and I remembered how special the friendship between members of the human and canine worlds can be. I tossed the ball toward the house and we both headed in for supper.

Mary Ann decided to make the evening meal an event. She set the table in the dining room with special Christmas dishes that our daughter had given us some years back. The table was covered with one of her favorite Christmas tablecloths, and red and green candles were arranged as a centerpiece.

After dinner, we helped Mary Ann clean up the dishes, a chore that Christmas cheerfully performed, licking up every last scrap of food. We spent the rest of the evening watching television in the living room warmed by the fire. Eventually, I shut off the lights and we headed up the old stairs for bed.

When the sun leaves the winter sky, temperatures

drop quickly. Even with the addition of insulation and central heat in the 1970s, our old house is still often cold, making pajamas and electric blankets necessary winter companions. That night, after I was in bed under the warm covers, Mary Ann felt especially good beside me. We could hear Todd muttering something to Christmas in his room downstairs.

"I think he likes that dog, George."

"You sure about that?" I asked.

"How about you, George—do you like the dog?"

"Oh, yeah, I suppose so. If you like the furry types, he'll do."

"You seemed better today."

"I felt better, much better."

"What was wrong, George?" she asked as she held my forearm.

"I had some thinking to do."

"You expected this, didn't you?" she asked.

"Yes, I suppose so." She rested her head on my shoulder and I said, "I want to thank you for something."

"What's that?"

"Have I told you enough just how much all of your letters meant to me?"

"You've told me a thousand times."

"I should have told you a million times. Thanks again, Mary Ann."

"I love you, George."

"I love you too. Good night."

Sunday, December 20, arrived and we readied for our family dinner and neighborhood open house. The scent of roasting ham and turkey wove its way down to the barnyard, making the swine and fowl nervous. Steam from the mashed potatoes condensed on the kitchen windows and coffee percolated in the old pot on the stove top. Several times during the day, I interrupted my work to inspect Mary Ann's efforts, using the taste method. My timing was good. Around two o'clock, I came in just as Mary Ann pulled sugar cookies in the shape of Christmas trees out of the oven. Oatmeal cookies were already cooling on the old oak countertop. Todd, Christmas, and I decided it was too much for Mary Ann to do all on her own.

We stacked the cookies we didn't eat on Christmas plates, set the table, and made last-minute adjustments to the lights and other decorations. Todd and I took showers and then the three males (two human and one canine) fell asleep for a brief winter's nap beneath an old quilt by the fire that crackled with the scent of pine and cedar logs. The rest of the afternoon, Todd and I did little more than add logs to the fire, make dog observations, and listen to the sound of rain falling hard and fast on the rooftop.

My children and their families began coming through the back door in the early evening hours. Only strangers ever came to the front door. The rain let up, but a gentle winter drizzle still fell. The melting snow and the newly fallen rain moved through a thousand little ditches, gullies, and rivulets. From the back porch, as I greeted my family, I could hear the water in Kill Creek rushing rapidly toward its confluence with the Kaw River.

As my children and grandchildren made their way in, quick hugs and kisses were exchanged and the house came alive with the sounds of holiday greetings. Coats, hats, and scarves were discarded as Todd pulled all family members to the front of the house to meet our honored guest, Christmas, basking by the heat of the fire.

This dog wasn't much into formal introductions and he stayed on his blanket, though he allowed head patting and scratching behind the ears. His wide bushy tail swept across the floor in a measured way that showed he sincerely enjoyed making each and every new acquaintance. After everyone arrived, we sat down to eat and to catch up on the latest family gossip.

At dinner, Todd again explained the Adopt a Dog for Christmas program to his extended family. Christmas rolled over onto his stomach and rested his head on his front paws. His ears perked up and he listened, as if he sensed he was the topic of conversation.

My daughter, Hannah, and my daughters-in-law all

thought it was about the sweetest thing they had ever heard. My sons just grinned and I suspected that they were thinking, *Dad sure got suckered on this one*.

As we passed plate after plate of food, each member of my family tossed glances in the dog's direction and offered some kind words of reassurance to Todd. "I'm sure he is the best dog at the shelter, maybe in the whole county." "You're sure a handsome old boy" was mixed in with a lot of "You're a good boy. Yes, you are."

Todd and I just smiled. We were, after all, very good dog pickers.

Christmas seemed to relish the praise, and with every passing compliment he inched his way off the blanket and scooted ever closer to the table. Eventually, he just got up and joined us, perched, as any dog with the least amount of intelligence would be, directly beneath the dining room table and within easy reach of socked feet that brushed across his fur and hands that "accidentally" dropped bits of tasty dinner.

There was one aspect of the Adopt a Dog for Christmas program that had been overlooked in our explanation and I wanted to clear it up. In a matter-of-fact way, I asked, "Now, don't forget, Todd, when does Christmas end?"

Todd looked down at his plate and repeated, "Christmas ends on the twenty-sixth. That's when he has to go home to the shelter."

I should have known better. This was the wrong time to bring it up and the idea of returning Christmas to the shelter put a chill in the air. There were scowls on the prettier faces at the table. My sons were looking at me in disbelief, even disapproval. Anxiety was welling up in my chest again. The awkward silence that lingered in the air told me that I had a problem on my hands.

I was trying to do something nice for Todd and this dog, and now if I didn't keep him, it would be me and not Christmas who would be crated and sent back to the shelter. I didn't know what to do.

Sitting there silently, I allowed the others to carry on the conversation, which seemed inevitably to make its way back to Christmas. Suddenly I felt as if I were on the outside looking in.

Our canine guest ambled around the dinner table for pats on the head, kind words, scraps of meat, and other delicacies. I just rolled my eyes. There didn't seem to be any effort to teach him table manners. Every woman at the table took her respective turn at adoration. My daughter, Hannah, a recently divorced accountant with no children of her own, started it. She held Christmas's head in her hands and began talking in a way that made me sink even lower in my chair, with my arms folded across my chest.

"Christmas, I do believe you are the most handsome and kind dog I have ever known." Christmas accepted praise in a very dignified manner, as if he had much experience with adoration. Hannah continued, "Why in the world would anyone put you in a shelter?" She looked up to me and asked again, incredulously, "Why was he in the shelter?"

"No one knows for sure. They said he just showed up." I tried to change the subject away from the dog. "Say, Hannah, I have a question on my taxes this year."

"Dad, I bet the Adopt a Dog for Christmas expenses are deductible. Do you think anybody has checked to make sure he has had all of his shots? Maybe you should do that for him. I bet the vet would come out tomorrow if you called now."

Then the boys took their turn talking to the dog. They were having a great deal of fun and I was sure it was at my expense. My oldest son, Jonathan, a finish carpenter married to his high school sweetheart, had three boys of his own. Being the oldest, he undoubtedly felt it was his duty to make sure the boys were not outdone by their sister.

"Well, old boy, this could be your last Christmas in front of a warm fire. Who knows where you'll be next year? Why don't you just take this turkey and go eat it. I've got lots of turkey dinners left in *my* life." Jonathan handed Christmas a large cut of dark meat and the dog ambled back to the fireplace.

I wondered if the dog would be ordering up room service anytime soon. They were all having a great deal of fun, but I was not laughing.

Thomas, the youngest of my three older boys, speculated with a wide grin and intermittent bursts of laughter that at Christmas's age any change of environment could be stressful. "Dad, be careful moving the poor dog back to the animal shelter. It's not that comfortable in the back of your old truck. Maybe you could put a mattress in the truck bed for him."

Ryan, the middle of these three older boys, was blessed with a quiet nature. He felt the need to emphasize each of his siblings' observations only with a wide grin. His eyes twinkled in amusement and I just kept squirming in my chair.

Maybe it was my imagination, but it seemed that each time the subject of Christmas came up, every man, woman, and child looked at me. Todd, of course, understood none of the subtleties of the conversation, but was generally pleased that his dog was commanding so much attention.

About the time the bigger eaters were going into the kitchen for seconds, Todd excused himself from the table, leaving half a plate of food unfinished. Christmas followed him to the edge of the dining room. "Look, everybody," Todd said. With Christmas by his side, he began to issue orders. "Sit!" The dog sat. Todd continued with the commands for shake, lie down, and stay. In each case, Christmas gladly complied. When he said "Stay" and walked toward the fireplace, the audience could stand it no more and broke into a raucous applause. Todd then allowed Christmas to come and sit beside him and feel the warmth of the fire.

After the two of them were comfortably situated, Todd turned on his radio, put on his headphones, and began singing his own versions of Christmas songs, loud and off-key.

Christmas tilted his head back and started to howl. Thankfully, we were in the privacy of our home, because the laughter was uncontrolled as Todd's older siblings had to restrain themselves from falling out of their chairs.

After the laughter died down, Mary Ann changed the mood by mounting her first open assault on my scantily fortified position. She said, in a voice I knew to be short on negotiation, "I can't remember when Todd has found something he has enjoyed more than taking care of this dog. He has been very responsible and those two have a special bond."

I foolishly dug in my heels. "Yes," I said. "And when does Christmas end?"

There was a long pause. Mary Ann folded her napkin and rather resolutely placed it back on the table, as if to signal that she was upping the ante. I had the distinct feeling that my wartime ally was about to abandon me. "George, I've heard the reverend say that we should act with generosity and kindness every day and not just on Christmas!" She picked up her napkin and wiped her mouth firmly to remove any unkind words or thoughts that might reside on her lips. The uncomfortable feeling in my chest was growing worse.

Considering a response, but knowing none would work, I just hung my head and finished my dinner in silence. Perhaps I was beaten and there was no use in fighting it any longer. I was prepared to keep Christmas. In fact, I would have liked it. My fears of owning another dog seemed misplaced and I was enjoying his company. But there was another reason why Christmas needed to return to the shelter. Perhaps the most important reason was that my son and I made a deal and I wanted him to stick to it. I wanted Todd to learn to be more like an adult and less like a child. Adults keep their promises, even when they become inconvenient. Adults have to learn that things can be good without being forever.

Everybody seemed to be missing another important point. For the Adopt a Dog for Christmas program to work, families should not feel pressured to keep the animals. If I kept Christmas this year, I would not be back to the shelter next year or any other year.

With dinner behind us, we cleaned off the table, washed the dishes, and began answering the knocks on the back door as the parade of old friends, family, and neighbors made their annual visit with candy, cookies, pies, cakes, and small wrapped presents.

My grandfather's duties as county road maintainer had ended decades ago, so these visits were rooted in tradition alone. The wives seemed to lead this parade and behind them followed their husbands with their hands in their pockets. This was a Christmas ritual that I could have done without this year.

It wasn't the train under the tree or the doll in the cradle that brought them to the front room. It was Todd tugging on their shirtsleeves and insisting that they visit Christmas.

Jonathan showed no mercy for my condition and led

the rural masses to the throne. "I want you to see something really special, Hank. This is Christmas, *Todd's* dog." He looked up at me and grinned.

Hank was an eighty-eight-year-old dairy farmer and someone whom I often looked up to as the father I had lost. He was sharp, fit, and worth a lot of money. His family farm was one of the oldest and most successful in this part of Kansas. Hank inherited a strong work ethic and a proud, determined outlook on life. A shrewd businessman, he had no time for an animal that did not turn a profit. Hank carried a soft spot for Todd and always took the time to show some interest in his life. It did not surprise me in the least that he too would make a big fuss over Christmas. Hank slowly bent over and scratched the dog's belly with his long wrinkled fingers as Todd explained for the umpteenth time the details of the shelter's program.

Hank patiently waited for Todd to finish. He removed the unlit cigar that was ever present in the corner of his mouth and then said, with the authority and wisdom that only age can bestow, "This is one fine animal." All the heads in the room nodded in agreement. Todd smiled.

Hank must have noticed that I was not joining in and said, "Why, what is wrong, George? Don't you like Christmas?"

Todd, bless his heart, came to my rescue. "No, Hank, Dad likes Christmas. Dad helped me get Christmas. He helped me pick him out from all those dogs needing a place to go for the holidays."

Something that Todd said turned over in my head until it stuck. I rubbed my chin and the idea hit me square between the eyes. Hallelujah, salvation had come. I changed my perspective and stopped seeing myself as the villain. Todd was right; this was my program as much as it was his. I just needed to get with it.

Walking over to Christmas, I commented, "One of the best dogs I've ever seen, Hank. He is a dandy. Shame of it is . . . he isn't ours. Like Todd said, the county shelter loans them out over the holidays." I paused a moment and added, "You know, Hank, I've got the phone number in the kitchen. They're open till noon Christmas Eve; I bet you could adopt a dog for Christmas too!"

Hank acted as if he had touched a hot stove. He sprang to his feet, quickly backed away from Christmas, grabbed his wife's arm, and all but shouted, "No! You know we're way too old for dogs. Jean, we have other stops to make. We had best be moving."

"It's no bother, Hank. It will just take me a minute to grab the number." I started to leave the room when I looked over at Hank's wife and Mary Ann.

Mary Ann's countenance was angelic. She looked upon me with eyes that welled with tears. Her voice quivered as she said, "George, this is just the most wonderful thing you are doing for these dogs."

Jean pulled away from her husband of sixty-four years and walked toward me, beaming. "Of course, George, we would love to adopt a pet too. This is a terrific program that you and Todd are supporting."

She turned to Hank, who had become agitated and stiff. His tired face suddenly showed every bit of its eighty-eight years. "Well, honey, I think this is a wonderful idea too, but at our age?" He grabbed Jean's arm as if to plead his case. Jean peeled Hank off and froze him solid with a glare. Defeated, he looked down and muttered, "Yes, Jean, let's get the number. I suppose a dog for the holidays might make things merrier."

I put my arm around Hank and offered a consoling pat to the back. "You know, Hank, I bet that boy of mine would help you pick one out."

I looked around the room for Todd, but he wasn't anywhere to be seen. Each of his brothers seemed to be smirking. They knew exactly what I had done to poor old Hank Fisher and they relished his misery. I did not like it. The boys were having far too much fun at the expense of my old friend. It occurred to me how to make a good idea even better.

"Hank," I said, "if every one of us in this room adopted a dog—or at least made a call or two to our friends—I bet we could clean out the shelter for Christmas. What do you think?"

Hank shifted his weight from one foot to the other and did not see where I was going.

"It's kind of like foster care for dogs. You give them a nice place to stay for a week or so, longer if you want, and that's a good thing for the dog, but some of the people will end up keeping the pets. Maybe not you or me. In fact, Todd and I have agreed that our dog will go back on the twenty-sixth. But many people will keep their dogs. That's why the program works. Just think how many fine foster homes could come from this house alone!"

The implication of my proposal slowly sunk in. Hank smiled. "You mean, George, not just you and me adopt a dog for Christmas, but every family should. Jonathan, Hannah, Ryan, Thomas, all of them."

My older sons all stared at me in disbelief.

"That's right!" I said.

The bait was set. There was not one but three hard strikes as my lovely daughters-in-law buzzed about the room proclaiming, "What a wonderful idea. Can we have the phone number too?"

Soon everyone was making arrangements for their very own Christmas dog. In the background a cacophony of grandchildren's voices pleaded, "Yes, Daddy. Please, Daddy. Can we, Dad?" They buzzed about me for advice and information on dog picking, all of which I generously dispensed.

Not wanting to leave a skimpy margin for victory, I scanned the room again and found the son who had offered the least mercy toward his poor father. "Jonathan, with three boys of your own, perhaps you should consider three dogs."

Hank immediately understood the magnitude of my catch. His eyes glimmered with mischief as he looked slowly down at the carpet and added in a most serious tone, "It's a bad thing for a boy to feel left out, particularly it being Christmas and all."

I must admit that at times it is hard for me to leave well enough alone, and this was one of those moments. "Jonathan, if you like," I asked in the most humble and sincere voice I could muster, "I could send the vet down the road to your place to make sure your three are up on their shots too."

By ten o'clock things were slowing down. We had pitched the Adopt a Dog for Christmas program to all the visitors at our holiday open house that night, suggesting that it be part of the holiday tradition in Cherokee County for families to take a dog in for a week and show it a little kindness. Todd was very supportive and never once showed the least hesitation when I explained that our dog too was just a guest.

I tried to imagine the conversations my older boys were having in their cars on the way home that night, certain that my grandchildren were carrying on incessantly about their Christmas dogs. While a small pang of guilt came over me, it inspired me the way the children shifted their focus so easily from what gifts they hoped to receive to what dog they could help.

They would probably discuss breeds, age, and temperament, and then everyone would agree that there was no finer dog at the shelter than Christmas. They would just do their best to choose a dog. For, after all, each animal deserved a home for the holidays. I could also hear each of my sons asking, "And when does Christmas end?"

What Todd had begun was turning out well. Getting the children and grandchildren to focus on something besides themselves seemed to make them happier and Christmas more meaningful for us all.

Todd had fallen asleep on the couch. Mary Ann was carrying the last tumblers of half-consumed soda to the kitchen. His stomach full, Christmas seemed settled in for the night. His back was to the fire and his four legs stretched out into the room. While I would have normally let the fire die out, I threw on two more logs and closed the protective fire screen. I patted Christmas on the head and bent down to address the vehicle of my newly bestowed sainthood. "Well, old boy, we had quite a day, didn't we? Do you have any idea what you and Todd started?"

Christmas tilted his head and opened his sleepy green eyes. He looked at me and I'll be darned if his black lips didn't curl back into a smile. His tail lazily began to sweep to and fro. I had to admit, he was a good old dog. "Well, good night, Christmas, we'll see you in the morning." I put a blanket over Todd and turned off the light.

"Mary Ann," I called out softly, "I'm going to bed."

"I'll be up in a few minutes, George," I heard her say as I headed up the stairs. She said my name pleasantly, with all of the love she held for me in full flower.

I brushed my teeth, hung my jeans on their hook, put my boots under the bed, turned out the light, got under the covers, and waited for Mary Ann. As I was just drifting off to sleep, I heard the steps. They came quicker than I expected and with a spryness that I thought was lost. My surprise did not stop there.

She leaped onto the bed. When I reached out to touch her in the darkness, I felt warm fur in my hands. It was Christmas. "What in the world are you doing up here, old boy?" His tail thumped rhythmically and he felt warm against my legs. Slipping back down into bed, I decided not to make him move. What did it matter if he rested there for the night? I would be true to the program and be the best dog host possible, even if it was for only a short period of time.

I had fallen asleep by the time Mary Ann came to bed. She nudged me awake.

"George?" she asked.

Coming out of my not-too-deep sleep, I leaned up on my elbow. "Yes, what is it, dear?"

"I'm worried about you."

"Why is that?" I asked.

"You seem to have made a friend here."

"So?"

"George, when does Christmas end?"

"On the twenty-sixth, of course. Why do you ask?"

She pulled the covers around her shoulders, giggled softly to herself, and rolled over to sleep.

The next morning, after I came in from doing my chores, I saw Todd on the phone in the kitchen as Mary Ann looked on.

"How many are left, Hayley?" he asked. Todd struggled with a pencil, numbering each line on a piece of paper from one through sixteen. "Wait a minute, I'm writing it down."

Todd slowly called the numbers out as he went. "Twelve, thirteen." Hayley Donaldson waited on him with great patience. Todd was now painstakingly writing a description of a dog on each line. I looked over his shoulder as he wrote in his crooked scrawl on the first line, "Huskee, Shiperd Mix, six, geerl."

My expression reflected exasperation with Todd's spelling, but Mary Ann frowned and placed her finger over her lips as she shushed me.

Christmas, the apparent crew chief of this operation, was at Todd's feet, his tail sweeping across the floor in three-quarter time. You would have thought the dog had been born under our back porch. He was completely at home.

All I could do was shake my head. This was going to

take all morning and I was sure Hayley was plenty busy at the shelter. Finally, I couldn't take it anymore. "Here, Todd, let me talk." I gently pulled the phone away and said, "This is George, Hayley. Let me help you."

"You already have, Mr. McCray—more than you know! Our adoption program is going very well this year and we repeatedly hear 'The McCrays sent us over.' Now Todd tells me that you are going to find homes for *all* the dogs in the shelter for the holiday. We're so pleased. That's wonderful!"

"Hayley, we'll help, but I doubt we can find homes for all of them. There must be dozens left."

"With your family's help, we're down to twenty-eight, not counting quarantine."

"Go over what you have and we'll see what we can do, but we can't promise the shelter will be emptied out by Christmas."

Hayley went over the inventory of remaining adoptable dogs as I made out the list. After we hung up, I turned to Todd. "You think about where we might be able to place some dogs and I have some work to do."

After replacing a frayed electrical line to the heater on the stock tank, I came back inside for breakfast and to check on Todd's progress. He had several pieces of paper and was trying to match up the dogs with prospective placements. He was up to line 14. His writing was deteriorating, but still legible. "Collee mix, geel, 7 . . . Merk and Cary."

As I headed in to wash up for breakfast, I considered

putting a stop to this matchmaking. Perhaps this was getting out of hand. Having been placed in an uncomfortable position with this dog myself, why was I doing the same thing to my family and friends? I was also concerned that I was putting pressure on Todd. I looked in the mirror as I washed my hands and wondered what was the right thing to do. The man I saw didn't know either, but could smell sausage and biscuits cooking and coffee brewing. The sound of silverware and dishes being hurriedly placed on the table told me that breakfast was about ready.

After all these years of marriage, I still marveled at the way Mary Ann made breakfast come off the stove at the exact moment I turned the spigot off in that old sink.

We sat down to eat, but Todd ignored his food. He was back on the phone with Hayley, getting more details together on the dogs. It appeared that they were becoming friends.

"Yes, I named him Christmas. He's right here beneath my feet. We're going to find a home for each one."

"Todd!" I couldn't help interjecting. "Quit telling her that! We can't make that promise."

"I gotta go. My dad and I have lots of work to do." Todd hung up the receiver and smiled. I had never seen him happier. He wasn't feeling pressured—he was feeling the pure joy of doing the right thing. While I hadn't planned on spending my day finding temporary homes for dogs, my misgivings melted away as I, like Todd, caught the spirit of Christmas. I jumped right in.

"Hand me that list, Todd, and let's start matching

some dogs up. Mary Ann, you just call these people and tell them about their dog, and ask when they can pick it up. Don't give them an opportunity to object or even think about it."

I noticed signs of protest on her face and headed her off. "This is a family project. Mary Ann, we need your help. Todd, what do you think about Hank? I'm sure he hasn't picked out a dog yet. Let's make it easy for him. You know a dairy farmer doesn't need a dog that barks a lot. Something older and steady would suit Hank best."

Todd looked up and down the list until he saw the perfect match for Hank. He scribbled Hank's name beside an entry for Sally. "Good choice?" he asked, flashing the list in front of my face.

"I remember that lazy old coonhound. She wouldn't even get up and walk over to see us. That's a perfect choice for old Hank. None better. What we need now is a closer. Somebody who can make the deal happen, someone with unparalleled powers of persuasion, like a debate coach. Do you know anyone who will not accept *no* for an answer?"

"You mean Mom?"

"Perfect. She's the one!" I turned abruptly to my wife and said, "Mary Ann, call Hank's wife and tell her it's a black and tan coonhound, female, twelve years old, likes all cows, but prefers Holsteins."

Mary Ann, it seemed, was also getting into the spirit. She moved toward the phone and resolutely began to dial the Fishers' number.

"Jean, this is Mary Ann. How are you this morning? Beautiful day, isn't it? Is Hank done with his milking? Sure glad you came by yesterday. Say, Jean, George and Todd were just talking to the shelter and I guess they have a coon dog over there named Sally that still needs a home." She paused and then went for the sale. "Are you and Hank still interested?"

There was a long pause and Todd and I began to wonder.

"Well, Jean, I'm sure George and Todd could pick her up for you and probably take her back too."

There was another pause and I moved closer to Mary Ann so I could hear the other end of the conversation. I could barely make out Jean's voice. It was backpedaling at its worst: "We don't have any dog food and we're going to be gone an awful lot of Christmas Day and Hank is worried about a strange dog bothering his cows."

I whispered to Mary Ann, "We'll buy the dog food."

She pushed me away and turned her back to me. For some reason, like all wives, Mary Ann did not like me talking to her while she was on the phone.

"Well, Jean, I do understand, you and Hank being at that point in your life. If you talk to Hank and he changes his mind, just give us a call. Merry Christmas."

Todd looked up at me, stupefied. "Dad, I don't understand. Hank changed his mind. Why wouldn't Hank want a dog for a few days?"

There may not have been an answer that Todd would accept. It wouldn't dawn on him that most of us tire of giving. "I don't know, son. Maybe he has too many cows." I knew that response was a fill-in-the-blank for most of us. If it wasn't too many cows, it was too many kids, too much work, or too many problems.

Although it was a hard lesson to learn, Todd was seeing for himself that there is seldom room at our own inn for others.

There were two more calls that did not go well, either. I was beginning to wonder if this family project was going to work. Something inside me told me to leave it alone for now, but Todd would have none of that.

"Jonathan will take the dogs. You call him. I know he will."

I called the number and spoke with my daughter-in-law.

"Karen, this is George. We sure enjoyed seeing you and the boys last night. I hope you had a good time."

"Oh, George, we had a great time. The kids are still buzzing around here talking about the Christmas dog."

"Really?" I said, hoping she would volunteer more information without me having to ask.

"Yes. In fact, the boys and Jonathan are on their way to the shelter as we speak."

"Say, Karen, would you mind repeating that to Todd? He's right here and I think he would like to hear it too."

"Sure," she said and I passed the receiver.

The two of them spoke for a few moments and Todd was clearly pleased by his big brother's commitment.

Another call revealed that my daughter, Hannah, had

apparently spent the morning sneaking a rather skittish German short-haired pointer named Baron from his cage and up into her apartment, where pets were not allowed. She was certain, however, that this rule did not apply to temporary houseguests. Being a well-educated accountant, she knows all about rules and contracts. Todd and I were sure she was right.

By December 22 our family members had taken twelve dogs. Our neighbors and friends had taken several more, but there were still seventeen dogs left in the shelter and we were out of prospects.

Todd didn't seem worried. He grabbed the phone book and said he had a call or two to make. I left him alone as he headed to the barn. He returned an hour later with a big smile on his face and, though uncertain, I suspected that he convinced either the governor or the state legislature to adopt the remaining inhabitants of the Cherokee County Animal Shelter. The next vehicle that turned into our drive that day solved the mystery.

Around two-thirty that afternoon, a television van found its way, with Todd's help, to our rural home. I had seen it at the courthouse before with a big "5" on the side and the satellite antenna on top. At first, I thought it was lost or there had been an accident on the highway not far from our house, but then a woman I recognized as an anchor from channel 5 came to the front door.

Todd yelled out, "Someone must be selling something!"

"No, it's a television truck."

"Oh, that's for me," Todd said calmly.

It was then that I realized what Todd had been doing on the phone. We all went to the front door and welcomed our local celebrity with anxious glances. She introduced herself as Brenda Lewis and asked for Todd, who immediately stepped up and held out his hand.

She smiled at him. "It's nice to meet you in person, Todd. The station manager and I enjoyed talking with you this morning and we decided to follow your suggestion and do a story on the Adopt a Dog for Christmas program. Can we come in and talk with you about it?"

"Yes, come in, please."

We sat on the sofa, by the fire. Brenda Lewis talked to Todd and shook Christmas's paw and then asked me if I could turn up the volume on the Nat King Cole Christmas music Mary Ann had been listening to. Motioning to the cameraman, she began to tell her audience all about Adopt a Dog for Christmas. The camera panned to our family and Christmas on the sofa as she described Todd's efforts. She told her viewers that the shelter was staying open late that night and would be open tomorrow morning until noon. As she walked to the end of the living room, the cameraman followed her and pointed the camera at all of the decorations in our house. She finished by saying in her best anchor voice, "Let's all do what we can so Todd's dream can come true. Please adopt a dog for Christmas!"

The television crew shook our hands, told us the story would air at six o'clock and ten o'clock, and left. Naturally, we called everyone we knew to tell them that Todd would be on the news. Todd called Hayley at the shelter; she couldn't believe her ears. The day seemed to drag on slowly as we carefully checked our watches to make sure we did not miss Todd's marketing efforts. Finally, at six pm, Todd, Christmas, Mary Ann, and I all piled on the sofa and watched Brenda Lewis on the evening news. From that day forward, Todd became a great fan of channel 5.

Around seven o'clock, after dinner, Jonathan and his kids arrived to show us their dogs. My grandsons were as excited as I had ever seen them. Everyone had watched the news and was kidding Todd about being a television celebrity. He seemed quiet and I thought something was bothering him. It's not often that a young man like Todd can make a big difference in even one little corner of the world. The ten o'clock segment was the same as the six o'clock. Mary Ann and I went to bed excited and proud that our son and his adopted dog were now both famous.

Christmas Eve arrived and chores still needed to be done. I came in through the back door. Todd was sprawled out on the kitchen floor, with Christmas snuggled up beside him. His headphones were on and his eyes were closed. I waited a few minutes, took off my hat and gloves, sat down at the kitchen table, and said loud enough for him to hear, "Good morning, Todd. Missed you for chores today. What are you doing?"

He took his headphones off, stood up, and sat down

with me at the table without saying a word. He folded his hands in his lap.

"What's wrong, Todd? Do you feel all right?"

"Yeah, I was just wondering if all the other dogs were adopted."

"Me too. Let's call Hayley and find out."

I waited for several rings but there was no answer. Had they decided to close early? I was about to hang up when Hayley, out of breath, answered the phone.

"Cherokee County Animal Shelter, Hayley speaking."

"Hayley, this is George and Todd."

"George, we placed *all* the remaining dogs this morning! It's been chaos. Our phones have been ringing off the hook. This friend of yours, the dairy farmer . . ."

"You mean Hank?" I interrupted. Todd had heard Hayley's news and was beaming.

"That's him. He was the first one in line this morning when we opened the doors. He took two!"

Todd pumped the air with his fist and yelled out to his mother, "Hank took two dogs! We did it! Every dog in the shelter is gone!" Christmas began to bark excitedly as Mary Ann came rushing in. She, Todd, and Christmas did a little victory dance.

"Thanks for everything, George. You and Todd did a good deed for our dogs."

Feeling a little embarrassed, I wanted Hayley to know that I had nothing to do with it. I called out to Todd in a voice Hayley could hear, "You did a good job, Todd."

I was going to wish Hayley a merry Christmas when she spoke again, but with a slightly disappointed tone. "Well, George, I said we found a place for all the dogs we had, but that's not quite right. We still have one in quarantine. A female. You don't have to tell Todd. I can come back tomorrow and feed her. It's okay. I don't want him to think he let us down. I know he tried so hard to find a home for all of the dogs."

"Can you stay open for another hour?" I asked.

"There is something you should know before you head down here, George."

"What?"

"She is about to have puppies."

We could see deer in the meadow beyond the house and hear a hoot owl's cry from the barnyard. But what I remember most about that afternoon was the exciting chill that lingered in the air beneath a cloudless sky. Something special was happening in our corner of the universe. Mary Ann, Todd, Christmas, and I were all crammed into the cab of my truck. We were headed to the shelter to get the last unadopted dog in Cherokee County, Kansas. I called Jonathan and he agreed to come out with his boys and help fix up a place in the barn for our newest guest. They had been planning to come for dinner and to open presents, but now they showed up early and got to work. As we left, they were dragging heat lamps out of the garage and rummaging through the house for old blankets and bowls.

"Maybe we should just get into the shelter business," I joked as we pulled out of our driveway. Todd seemed a little too pleased with that idea, so I had to add, "I'm kidding. Shelters don't get paid for keeping dogs. They are not a money-making business."

He looked confused, so I tried to explain. "They are

like a charity. There is no one to pay for keeping the dogs. The dogs don't have owners to make payments."

He still looked puzzled. Before I realized it, I'd gone too far. "The dogs don't have homes. That's why they are at the shelter. Do you understand?"

Todd was quiet. I thought Hayley had explained this to him before, but the only thing that sunk in was that the shelter kept lots of dogs. Until now, he had not quite figured out how or why the dogs got there. Finally, as he sorted it out in his mind, he asked, "Why don't the dogs have owners?"

Trying again to help him understand, I said, "It's hard to say. Some people buy a dog and it just doesn't work out. Some people have to spend lots of time taking care of themselves and don't have anything left to share with an animal. You're not like that, though, are you?"

"No," he said slowly.

"I admire that about you, Todd." It was then that I knew what made someone an animal lover.

"Dad, what will happen to Christmas when we take him back?"

"He'll stay at the shelter until a very special person is willing to make Christmas a permanent part of his life."

"How long do you think that it will take?"

"The good ones go quickly, Todd. Maybe you could help Hayley find a home for him or, if you miss him, you can always go into town and visit."

Todd didn't say a word and I had no way of knowing if what I had said to him made any sense, or if it had been wise to suggest he visit Christmas after we returned him.

When we arrived, Hayley was pleased to see us, but surprised by the size of our entourage. She led us quickly into the shelter and down an empty corridor of cages. There was an eerie ghost-town feeling in the air. At the far end of the rows, we found the most recent addition and last remaining guest of the county animal shelter, a female dachshund the shelter employees named Ruthie.

Mary Ann opened the cage door. Her maternal instincts were ramped up to full power. She scooped up Ruthie before Todd and I could make an introduction. Ruthie eagerly greeted Mary Ann's face with her cold nose and it was clear that these two were going to be pals. We filled out the obligatory paperwork, bid Hayley a merry Christmas, and were quickly back on the road.

Todd and Christmas were the first victims of Mary Ann's newly found friendship with Ruthie. They were displaced to the back of the truck, where they huddled beneath a blanket to protect them from the chilly air as we headed home. Ruthie sat on Mary Ann's lap with a minimal amount of fidgeting.

Mary Ann and I hummed along with the Christmas tunes that played on the radio and we both felt truly happy. Mary Ann's hand reached over to touch my cheek and then rested gently on Ruthie. This was a Christmas Eve to remember.

As I turned the truck into our driveway, we could see activity in the barn and knew that Jonathan and the kids were preparing for our newest Christmas guest. Driving past the house, I went through an open gate and directly into the barnyard. Mary Ann cradled Ruthie protectively as we got out of the truck and walked to the barn.

"Hello!" Jonathan called out as we opened the barn door. "Come see what we've done."

One of the large box stalls that had housed Dick and Doc, the draft horses that pulled the maintainer years ago, was now our makeshift maternity ward. Within it, they had made a box with two-by-twelve boards and lined it with straw. A heat lamp hung from the rafters and some old towels were in the corner. Jonathan brought out a lawn chair from the garage, where he remained perched while his boys hammered in a few more nails. Mary Ann stepped over the sides of the box and gently set Ruthie on the bed of towels.

We had hosted many animal births on this farm and had learned to respect nature as a good midwife. We provided our moms privacy and they did the rest. Christmas jumped over the boards, sniffed Ruthie, and then curled down beside her, gently nudging her face and ears with his nose. She would have none of it. She growled and Christmas wisely backed off. However comfortable with humans Ruthie may have been, she wanted no part of an unknown male dog, at least at this point.

Mary Ann scolded the poor dog. "You men just don't know when to keep your distance, do you?"

Once our guest was settled to Todd's and Mary Ann's satisfaction, we headed back to the house for a family dinner. We ate quickly, as all of us were more concerned with Ruthie than with having another helping of mashed potatoes. After dinner, Nurse Mary Ann led the procession back down to the nursery for another inspection. She made the men stand in the cold night air while she went in with Jonathan's wife, Karen. When they came out of the barn, Jonathan's youngest son, Jeremy, looked up behind eager eyes. "Grandma, can we open presents now?"

Mary Ann lifted Jeremy up and held him close. "It's time," she announced, glancing back at the barn door. "Shut the door," she called out as she carried Jeremy back to the house.

I don't remember any of the presents that I gave or received that year. Truth was I seldom gave or received anything that was truly needed. It was after eight PM by the time all the presents were opened and the children were loaded back into the car.

After Jonathan and his family left, I snapped the red lead onto Christmas's green collar and took him outside and waited patiently for him to do his business. We watched as Todd and Mary Ann went down to the barn to check once again on Ruthie. Christmas seemed strangely agitated, restless. He pulled on his leash and whined, and barked once or twice in the direction of the woods that flanked Kill Creek. I suspected that there were deer in the nearby meadow.

Todd and Mary Ann joined me and reported that Ruthie was resting comfortably. Walking to the house,

Christmas pulled, and though he came along, he stopped in the doorway, turned toward the barn, and barked again, not happy about what was left behind.

"What's wrong, Christmas?" I asked. "Isn't the Hilton good enough for you anymore?" We were apparently too exhausted to notice the open barn door.

I was in the deepest of sleep when a different kind of Christmas clatter woke me late in the night. It was not Santa on the roof. It was a Christmas dog barking and throwing himself at the back door with the full force of his body. Todd was screaming, "Dad, Dad, something is wrong with Christmas!" Dogs have a wide variety of barks. Some barks are meant to warn, others to intimidate, but not this bark. It was a higher-pitched bark that seemed to be highly agitated and concerned. Trying to focus, I listened more closely and could make out Ruthie's high-pitched bark. Something or someone was in the barn and that couldn't be good.

Mary Ann and I both pulled on our robes and I decided to take no chances. My grandfather was right. It was good to have a gun in the house. I rummaged through the bottom of the closet and found the ancient rifle I had hoped I would never need. I chambered a round, grabbed an extra bullet, and headed down the stairs as fast as I could on a leg that was still cold and stiff.

By the time I got to the door, Todd had opened it and Christmas streaked out with more speed than I could have imagined. He stretched into full flight. It seemed as if his feet did not bother touching the ground. I followed behind, moving as fast as I could, but unable to match the dog's quick exit. Mary Ann was yelling behind us all, "Be careful!"

Ruthie was barking more urgently from the barn. Then there was snarling, hissing, and an awful racket of unfamiliar sounds. "Todd!" I hollered. "Don't you dare go into that barn!"

Christmas did not hesitate. As he shot into the barn, his barks became even more intense before turning into snarls. Within seconds, there was a sound I had heard only a few times in my life. It was the unmistakable din of animal warriors locked in a life-or-death battle. The noise was horrific and unyielding. The sounds suggested that nothing could possibly be living in that barn within a very few short moments. Would Todd know to stay out of a fight like this? He still had not reached the barn. I had to do something quickly.

I raised my rifle and fired into the air, hoping to frighten away this intruder or maybe scare Todd enough to slow him down. The old rifle has quite a kick to it and the shot caused an immediate ringing in my ear. I ejected the spent cartridge and chambered the one remaining round. Though I had not fired a gun since 1969, the motions came easily to me, without thinking.

Just as Todd came to the barn door, swinging open in the wind, a flash of brown exploded from the door and nearly knocked him over. I could not believe my eyes. It was a full-grown cougar making a run for it. Todd was right. It was a darn big cat and it moved with a grace and power that I had never witnessed in man or animal.

Christmas was after him with the zeal born of centuries of breeding. He barked and Todd screamed and all three of them were headed across the barnyard. The big cat came to the fence and, instead of leaping over, spun around and faced Christmas as he closed in.

A motion detector caused the barn's floodlights to turn on and I could see the cat hissing and pawing at the air as Christmas danced from side to side, forward and backward, with a menacing growl. The cat would approach and Christmas would back off. When the cat retreated slightly, Christmas would again lunge forward, only to be rebuffed again. The cat was growing more aggressive and suddenly it crouched and leaped forward to close the gap. With one giant swipe, he smacked Christmas across the chest with his right paw. Christmas was flicked like a fly from a tabletop and tossed five feet through the air. He rolled back onto his feet and angrily attacked again, oblivious to the size and skill of his foe.

While I hoped that Todd would know better than to get in the middle of a fight like this, amid the excitement, I was not sure. It was with him, therefore, that my worry remained. Leaning against the barn for support, I trained the gun sight on the big cat. He was fifty yards out and it would be a difficult shot, particularly with Todd and Christmas moving in and out of my line of fire.

"Todd," I yelled. "Get to the ground so I can shoot the rifle." He must have been too excited, for he kept going. Disaster was only moments away and I had to take a chance on one shot. My mind sifted through the options quickly. It came across my mind that the easiest shot would be to Todd's leg. It just might save his life. I also thought about the dog. I was sure that the cat would leave on his own but for the attacking dog. The cat was the hardest shot of the three, but I knew it was the only one I could live with myself for taking. I again tried to put the cat in the sight, but he was still moving too quickly. I had no confidence in my ability to make that shot, particularly with such an old rifle. Wounding the animal could make things worse. By eliminating his ability to run away, he would be forced to stand and fight.

The shot needed to be a clean kill. I needed another option and came up with it. I did not like it, but I could not think of anything else to do.

Aiming, I slowly squeezed the trigger. The old .30-06 jumped in my arms and the recoil threw me back. The crack rang out over Cherokee County like an explosion. Todd froze, pulled back into reality. The bullet struck the gravel in the few feet between the cougar and the dog. Rocks and stones spewed up into the faces of both beasts. I lowered the rifle.

I knew I had only an instant while the dog's concentration was broken and I yelled at the top of my lungs, "Christmas."

When he turned in my direction, I then screamed the one order we had practiced the last several days. "Sit!" I pushed the air down with the palm of my hand.

Christmas looked at me, and while he did not obey the command, he was distracted. The big cat took advantage of the lull, turned, gathered his strength, and leaped over the fence.

Christmas, seeing the escape, ran along the fence line, searching for an opening. Todd and I yelled at him, but it was no use. He squeezed through and, with the yelps of a hound, set out in the darkness after the cat.

Quickly both animals passed through the meadow, out of the range of our lights, and into the surrounding forest. I figured the cat would leave Christmas far behind in no time.

"Todd, are you okay? Let's check the barn." He hesitated, staring at the fence where Christmas had disappeared, but turned and came back toward me. I was panting and out of breath before I got to the barn door. Mary Ann was at my elbow as I turned on the inside light. We were scared to death for Ruthie. She was huddled in the corner. Mary Ann cautiously approached her motionless body. Not having the nerve to look, I stayed back.

Mary Ann let out an excited scream. "Three of them!"

Ruthie had managed to give birth to three puppies that were suckling beside her.

"Three puppies," I repeated.

Before we could head back to bed, Christmas ambled back to the barn, where we had remained with Ruthie, as if he had been on a casual midnight stroll. Despite the swat he'd taken from the cougar, remarkably, he was unharmed except for a few scratches.

Todd put his arms around the dog's neck. "That was a big cat, Dad! Not too big for Christmas, though, was it?"

"Nope. I guess you were right, Todd. No cat is too big for Christmas."

Mary Ann turned to me. "I've had enough excitement for one night. Let's leave Ruthie to be with her puppies. Morning will be here soon enough."

Before walking back to the house, we checked and rechecked to make sure the barn door was closed.

Todd headed immediately to bed. Mary Ann and I fell into the two big stuffed chairs that flank the fireplace, our hearts still beating from the excitement. Christmas also seemed unsettled. He sat between us and pawed at my knee. "So, you want to be petted?" I asked. "I guess you deserve it. You are one amazing dog." He let out a little whimper and then settled down to sleep.

The next day brought us a holiday to remember. I was a little late with the chores, but Todd, Mary Ann, and I made hourly visits to the barn to check on Ruthie and the puppies. None of the scratches the big cat inflicted on Christmas was serious, but still Todd dabbed the cuts with iodine. Hayley called from her house and insisted on driving out to the farm to see the litter. Upon her arrival, Todd showed her each puppy and recounted last night's heroics. I was not sure whether she was more impressed with Todd's ability to handle animals or Christmas's ability to handle cougars.

She waited for the right moment and then pulled me aside and whispered, "George, after Christmas, would you please call me? I'd like to discuss Todd with you. We might have a job for him at the shelter. We have an opening, but I've been slow to fill it. I've been waiting for the right person to apply. I think I may have found him."

"I can't think of a nicer Christmas present for Todd," I said. While nodding in agreement, I decided to not say anything to Todd or his mother until after the twenty-sixth. I wanted to deal with the issue of returning Christmas first.

Later that morning, the channel 5 news truck pulled up to do a follow-up story on the puppies and the Adopt a Dog for Christmas program. Brenda Lewis took a picture of Todd, Mary Ann, and me, each of us holding a puppy, with Christmas and Ruthie looking on like proud parents. It now sits in a frame on our mantel.

When the news crew was finished with us, they turned down the road to do a segment on Hank. It seemed that he was doing just fine with his two dogs.

Christmas Day was thankfully calm. Two of my grandchildren phoned Todd several times to pass on the anecdotal happenings of their adopted Christmas dogs. Todd, in turn, updated them on our excitement. It seemed that notwithstanding my efforts, we had been added to the list of local crackpots claiming to have seen a cougar but having absolutely no proof except for the temporary iodine stains on Christmas's fur.

For lunch, Mary Ann warmed up leftovers and then we relaxed for the rest of the day, doing little more than feeling the winter sun as it poured through the window, putting logs on the fire, and enjoying our four-legged guests. We were all tired from the previous day's excitement and allowed ourselves to nap, with our dog curled up beside us.

That night we rested our heads on pillows and let the bed take over the job of supporting our tired bodies. Mary Ann leaned over, kissed me softly on the cheek, and said, "Merry Christmas, George."

I held her tightly, not only because I loved her dearly

but also because I wanted to hold the moment—my most memorable Christmas. "Merry Christmas, Mary Ann."

"George?" she asked softly. "What are you going to do with Christmas tomorrow?"

I took her hand, massaging her fingers gently, and told her truthfully, "I don't know." There was nothing I wanted more than to just tell Todd that Christmas was staying, but that still did not sit right with me. At that particular moment, I couldn't explain that what I wanted to give Todd was a gift more important than a dog. I didn't know how to explain that the gift with the most love cannot always be wrapped or delivered. I didn't know if Mary Ann could accept that some of the best gifts for Todd would not be given but withheld. I knew exactly what I should do; I just didn't know how to do it. Nor did I particularly want to do it. There was no doubt in my mind that letting him keep the dog would be the easiest thing to do.

It was one of those confounding times when I did not know whether the bigger man held his ground or just let go and admitted he was wrong.

On December 26 I awoke to a bright, clear day with frost on the ground. Todd was already in the barn when I went out to do the chores. Christmas was with him. Sitting in the lawn chair, Todd held a tiny puppy in his hands. He, Christmas, Ruthie, and the puppies had all come together on our small farm. For a moment they were family. I didn't have the strength to tell them that it couldn't last. I turned around and went back to the house before any of them noticed me watching from the door.

After breakfast, Todd came to me. "I called Hayley. She is going to come out and help us with the puppies and Ruthie."

I looked over the top of my newspaper. "That's good, Todd."

"Dad?"

"Yes, Todd." I was bracing for what was coming next.

"About Christmas . . ." he started.

"Yes?"

To my surprise, and in a matter-of-fact way, he plunged ahead. "It's the twenty-sixth and we have to take him back. That's the way the program works. You take the dogs back on the twenty-sixth."

I looked to Mary Ann, suspecting she was losing the fight against her tears. A few small ones rolled down her cheeks. I thought it would be Todd crying.

Things like this never happen in any one instant, but right there, I knew that Todd had taken a giant leap toward becoming a man. He had learned something so important: He kept his word, even when he could make no sense out of the commitment. Putting my arms around Todd, I said, "That's right, son. That's how the program works. It's a good program too. Isn't it?"

Later that morning, Hayley arrived to pick up Ruthie and the puppies and Todd left me to help her. She didn't say anything about taking Christmas and we didn't mention it either. I stayed away, still cursing myself, uncertain of my decision and feeling a little bit sorry for myself. It happened again. I was attached to this dog and now I was going to lose him, just like Tucker and Charlie. Alone in the barn, I sat on the milking stool and stewed. There was still no good answer.

When I got back to the house, Todd was waiting for me. He was sitting on the porch in his tattered blue jeans and red tennis shoes, listening to his radio. He was humming softly to Christmas tunes. When I walked up to him, he just smiled, patted Christmas on the head, snapped the green leash onto his red collar, and headed out to the truck. Christmas did not complain or resist. He jumped into the cab and the two of them waited patiently while I fumbled for my keys, trying to come up with some rational way to avoid this heartbreak.

It was a very long ride into town that morning. Todd did not once ask me to reconsider our agreement to return Christmas. He just sat patiently, with his head-phones on, one arm wrapped protectively around Christmas.

Today was December 26 and, as promised, Christmas was going back to the shelter. I was never more proud of Todd, nor more irritated with myself. Todd was on the road to becoming an adult. I wasn't so sure what road I was on. When we arrived at the shelter, Todd jumped out of the truck and Christmas followed, but when I hesitated, Todd peered into the truck. "Don't worry, I'll take Christmas inside for you."

Todd slammed the truck door shut and headed toward

the entrance. When Todd opened the front door of the shelter, Christmas stopped, turned, and looked back at me. I leaned across the seat and reached for the passenger door. I wanted to open it, to call them back, to put an end to this. Again, I tried to toughen up. I had asked Todd to be a man and I would not take this accomplishment away from him, no matter how hard it was on me. So, I just sat, waited, and felt miserable. After a few minutes, Hayley and Todd came out together. Hayley came around to the driver's side, and I rolled the window down.

She patted my arm and said, "Don't worry, Mr. McCray, we'll take good care of him."

"Thanks," was all I could say. I looked over at Todd. He already had his headphones on, retreating into his own world. Forcing myself, I put the truck in reverse and headed home.

There must have been ten times when I started to think about places to turn around and go back and get that dog, but I kept the truck heading west until I saw our farm on the horizon. In a few days we would all feel better.

Mary Ann tried to be patient with me. She knew I was trying my hardest to do what was best for Todd and not just what was easy, but for the next few days, it might have been warmer outside than standing beside the arctic blast formerly known as my wife. Todd called Hayley and checked on Christmas and Ruthie several times a day and learned that they were fine.

On December 29, Hayley called and asked for me. I assumed she was calling about the job she had mentioned, but I didn't want to get my hopes up for Todd.

"So," I said, "I hear that Christmas is doing well."

"He is indeed. I just wanted to thank you and your family for all you did. The program was a huge success this year. I think all of the families had such a good time with their guests. Over half the families kept their dogs, which means we aren't so cramped."

"Over half kept their dogs?" I repeated, stunned. "Really? But I thought most everyone brought their dogs back. I thought that was how the program worked."

"Of course, we don't want anyone to keep a dog they don't want, but if a family likes the dog and meets our requirements for pet ownership, then we are pleased to place it."

I was silent as her words sunk in. In my determination to teach Todd a lesson, it hadn't occurred to me that most people would keep their dogs. This seemed to make returning Christmas to the shelter even worse. Finally, I just said, "I guess I had it all wrong."

"No, there is no right or wrong, George. Just what works for your family. By the way, we are thinking about adding cats to the program next year!"

"Humm," I muttered.

"Say, George, I wanted to talk to you about the job at the shelter. We would like to offer Todd the position. It doesn't pay much, but I bet he would really like it. He's so good with animals. They trust him. What do you think?"

What I thought was, *I must be dreaming.* I was so happy for Todd and pleased that someone besides his mother and me could recognize just how much he had to offer. I had always hoped that Todd would someday have a real job and some normalcy in his life. I wanted to scream for joy, but I just collected myself and smiled at Mary Ann, who had initially answered the phone and stayed in the kitchen. She looked at me, puzzled, and could sense my excitement. I whispered to her, "The shelter is offering Todd a job." Again, poor Mary Ann was crying.

"When can he start?" I asked Hayley.

"Is Monday morning too soon?"

"What time?"

"Seven forty-five should work. The shelter opens at eight o'clock."

"We'll be there, Hayley! And thanks so much."

"George, just one more thing . . ."

"Yes, Hayley?"

"There have been two families wanting to adopt Christmas. One claims that he's their dog who had apparently wandered off months ago. They said that they recognized him from the news story that was picked up in other parts of the state. I told them that Christmas was on hold for a few days because the adoptive families always get first dibs. Should I let him go?"

"Hayley, let me think on it," I said, my elation for Todd turning to something else. I still did not know what to do.

"I'll wait until closing time today, five PM, but no longer."

"Thanks for everything. Mary Ann and I are so pleased and we think that there isn't a soul in the universe that could do a better job with the shelter's dogs than Todd. You can count on it. You will not be disappointed."

"I'm sure you are right, George."

"Hayley, I'll get back to you on the dog."

"No problem."

When I hung up the receiver I was so excited I hardly knew what to do. Mary Ann and I danced around the room until I felt the need to say, "I told you so."

She dropped her embrace. "What do you mean by that?"

"Trying to teach Todd to be like an adult has paid off. Bringing the dog back. That's what I mean. It all turned out right."

"George McCray, don't you dare try to take one bit of credit for this. This is all Todd's doing. You're still an old fool for not keeping that dog."

I suspected she was right, but of course there is nothing more infuriating than being married to someone who is right, which caused me to lash out. "Well, I sure hope the shelter doesn't need someone to climb more than two rungs high on a ladder or to drive a truck out of first gear."

As soon as the words were out of my mouth, I knew the comment was unfair. Rightly so, Mary Ann stormed out of the kitchen.

Not to be overshadowed by her indignation, I slammed the back door and looked around the barnyard for Todd. He was probably out exploring, for he was nowhere to be found. I decided to get in the truck and visit Hank. He would be so excited for Todd. Besides, Hank often had a way of making sense out of things that were too troubling for the milk stool.

Hank was down at his barn doing what farmers spend most of their time doing: fixing the machinery that is supposed to make their lives easier. A lot of wisdom can pass while holding a wrench for Hank. He was replacing some worn sprockets on a hay elevator and chomping on the unlit stub of a cigar when I found him. He spat occasionally and laughed as I recounted the adventure of the cougar.

"Cougar?" he asked suspiciously.

It seemed that his coonhound had worked out just fine. He did return the other dog, concluding that one was enough. He told me that Sally was the best equipment purchase he had made in years. Free. I then turned to the subject of Todd.

"It's like this, Hank. I want Todd to be responsible more than I want him to have a dog. With this job at the shelter, he'll be around dogs all day."

"Makes sense, George. Would you hand me that can of WD-40?"

I passed him the can and he sprayed the solvent on a frozen three-quarter-inch nut that would not budge. I continued. "Todd getting this job is a big step in the right direction. Me caving in seems like the wrong way to go."

Hank grunted and the nut came loose from the bolt. "Sounds like you're trying to convince yourself of something. What are you so worried about?"

I looked at him with surprise and he knew he was going to have to say more to make his point. I pressed him. "What do you mean?"

"Are you sure this is not more about you and less about Todd than you think?"

"What?" I asked again, still confused.

"Maybe I'm wrong, George, but Todd having this dog or not having this dog isn't going to make an iota of difference in the long run. At least not to Todd." He looked me straight in the eye. "Getting the dog would be good for you, George."

"How's that?"

"George, you spend your life taking care of things. That's a farmer's life. You take care of fences, animals, equipment, and plants. You nurture and bring things to life. Like your dad and your grandfather before you, you're a good farmer, a good father, and a good husband." He chuckled and then added, "And a darn good neighbor. The problem is, George, that you've become so comfortable giving to others that you forgot how to let something or someone give back to you. For some reason it makes you uncomfortable. Ever since you've come back from that war, George, you don't want anyone doing anything for you. Why is that?"

Hank might as well have struck me on the side of my head with that wrench he was holding. "Honestly, Hank, I never thought this had a thing to do with me."

Hank grunted and spat a little more cigar out onto the barn floor. "Would you hand me that wire brush over there?" He handed me the wrench and took the brush. "George, this has everything to do with you and absolutely nothing to do with Todd. Get that through your head." He spat out one more bit of tobacco. "But, I suppose I could be wrong."

We both knew he was right. I stayed a little longer handing Hank tools and watching his breath condense in the cool winter air. I handed him another brush, a mallet, and a screwdriver. Finally, I knew that I needed to go home.

"Sure you don't want to stay for a cup of coffee?" he asked.

"No. Thanks. I have some dog business to attend to."

He clasped my arm. "Good for you, George."

As I drove back to the house, I made up my mind. I needed a way to fix everything without compromising and without teaching Todd a lesson I did not want him to learn. Hank's words gave me the inspiration I needed.

When I got back to the house, Todd was sitting on the back porch. His radio was playing and his hands were pushed deep into his coat pockets. My legs ached as I got out of the truck and slowly made my way over to him.

I sat down beside him. "Son, would you take off your earphones for a minute?"

"Sure, Dad."

"Hayley called."

"I know I have a job. Start Monday."

He smiled at me and started to put his headphones back on.

"Todd, would you please keep your headphones off? I was thinking, with you having a job of your own now, things might get a little lonely around here for me."

"Yeah, you're losing your helper, aren't you?"

"Are you okay with that?"

"Sure," he said. "The shelter pays better than you." He then started to put his headphones back on again.

I reached out and grabbed his wrist. "Todd, you know

how I have always thought dogs don't work out well for me?"

"Yeah," he said.

"After Christmas, I don't think that anymore."

Todd smiled. "I am a good dog picker, aren't I?"

"I was thinking maybe I need a dog too. A new helper. What do you think?"

"Sure," he said, "but only if you clean your room first." He chuckled and I playfully punched his arm.

"Todd, I was thinking maybe Christmas would be a good dog for me. What do you think?"

He looked at me with a very blank face. I think he was too frozen with excitement to show any expression. He jumped up. "I'll get the leash! You get the keys!"

"I'll get the collar too!" I pushed open the back door and looked for Mary Ann. She was brutalizing some poor, defenseless biscuit dough with a rolling pin. I had a feeling that those little protrusions in the mound of dough were substituting for my own facial features.

She turned to me and curtly asked, "What?"

Todd pushed in behind me and stuck his head in between my arms so I could hold him in a headlock. I gently spun him around so he could see his mother. "Tell your mom what we decided."

"Dad needs a dog, Mom, 'cause I got a job and can't help with the chores as much."

Mary Ann looked skeptically at us both and tried to figure out what we were up to. "Really?" she asked. "And when did that happen?"

"Just now," Todd said.

I tightened my grip slightly with my right hand and then rubbed a few of Todd's ribs and asked, "How good can you tell Mom what dog we're getting when I am tickling you like this?" I strummed his ribs like an old guitar.

Todd laughed and squirmed and said, "Dad wants Christmas, Mom. He is going to be Dad's dog now."

For the second time in a day, Mary Ann was crying, but this time she was in my arms and I could feel her sweet kisses. "Oh, George, you finally understand that it was you that needed the dog, don't you?"

"Yeah, it was me."

"Well, what are you doing just standing here? Get to town!"

I took a long drink of water from a tin cup that I kept by the sink, grinned at Mary Ann, and then pushed Todd out the door.

Mr. Conner considered it unlikely that the dog on the television was Jake, but he would never forgive himself if he did not make the one-hour drive over to Cherokee County to find out. His children and grandchildren told him that they knew Jake when they saw Jake. Mr. Conner told the children that Cherokee County was more than sixty miles away and that dogs did not typically roam that far from home. Mr. Conner's children swore up and down that it had to be Jake. He was inclined to attribute the Jake sighting to wishful thinking. For, after all, he told them, there are more than a few big black dogs around. But to satisfy his own curiosity, he decided to check it out. Besides, he concluded, the worst-case scenario was a quiet drive in the country.

Conner smiled and thought about the old dog. It sounded like Jake's business was serious this time. He had managed to get himself on television as the champion of a noble cause. What other dog could do that? He wondered about Jake's new family and why they brought him back to the shelter. The shelter manager told him that the family that kept the dog over Christmas had a few things to work out before they made a final adoption decision. If they did not want Jake, then he could claim the dog after the shelter officially closed at five PM. Hayley said he could show up anytime after five but before five-thirty, while the staff was feeding the animals and preparing to close for the night.

According to Hayley, yet another family was interested in Jake too, but if the dog was Jake, as former owners they would have a higher priority. Mr. Conner checked his watch. He was early. He did not mind. This way, he would have a chance to see if it was Jake, and if it wasn't, he could turn around and be home before the traffic was bad.

Mr. Conner pulled up behind an old brown Ford pickup truck that was moving way too slowly, put on his blinker, and passed it. He marveled at the distances between homes and wondered how these rural inhabitants got by without a grocery store, video store, coffee shop, laundry, or deli within easy driving distance.

Around four-thirty, Conner pulled into the Cherokee County seat, a small town called Crossing Trails. He had to chuckle when he saw that the main street was actually called Main Street.

Conner fumbled for the directions and quickly determined that he needed to pass through the square and turn south on Prairie Center Road. When the light turned green, he pulled forward and tried to make out the worn street signs. When he found Prairie Center, he turned right, and within forty yards the pavement turned to gravel. He checked his watch again. It was 4:40. He followed the gravel road past a less-than-spectacular neighborhood until he finally came upon an old building that was clearly marked as the Cherokee County Animal Shelter.

It was time to find out about this dog. Conner collected his wallet and car keys, walked to the front door, opened it, and then looked around for assistance in a reception area that had been taken over by outdated office furniture. Seeing no one around, he pushed past a swinging door and into the animal holding area. Two shelter employees seemed to be in a heated discussion. Conner approached them and waited for a pause to interrupt.

Todd, you drive to town this time," I said as I handed Todd the keys to the truck. "Now that you have a job, you need to get more driving practice in, so you can take yourself to work. I can't be running you in every day."

"Are you sure?" he asked.

"Why not? Now that you are a high-salaried government employee, maybe you'll make enough money to have a car of your own."

"Do we have to stay in first gear the whole way?"

"Nah, as soon as we get over the hill where your mom can't see, shift into second."

I probably did not pick the best time for driving practice, but I was so ready for Todd to start growing up that I rushed things when I should have known better. Sure, I had let Todd drive on the highway a few times before. Over his mother's objections, he earned his learner's permit a few years ago, but had never received his unrestricted license. But concentrating on the dog business and concentrating on his driving business at the same time was presenting a few problems. More than once,

I had to reach over and make sure he did not stray over into the other lane.

"Todd, I think we are going to have to do some practicing."

"You think so, Dad?" he asked.

"It's real important, Todd, that you stay right in your lane."

"Somebody is behind me, Dad." I turned around and looked. Sure enough, a red Ford decided to use the highway that day too. I waved him around us and he passed, disappearing ahead of us. He had out-of-county tags and probably wondered why in the world we were driving so slowly.

When we got to Crossing Trails, Todd did a real nice job at the stoplight and then turned down the road to the shelter.

"You're doing just fine, Todd. I think you are a good driver. Very safe. Your mom would be very proud of you and so am I."

"Never had an accident," he proudly noted.

Stifling my laughter, I said, "Yep, you're pitching a perfect game so far. Let's keep it up, okay?"

There were only a few cars in the lot, but two things seemed out of place. The red Ford that passed us on the highway was now sitting in the lot, and someone had placed one of those large construction trailers on the edge of the property.

Todd had no problem parking my truck. It was 4:45, so we made it in plenty of time. We walked through the front door of the shelter. We saw no one around, so we headed back to the animal holding area. We could see Hayley and Jennifer, a part-time employee, discussing something that must have been unpleasant for they looked and sounded tense. An older man stood beside them saying nothing. He did not look pleased either. We approached down the center aisle.

"What do you mean he got out?" Hayley asked.

"I told you the fence needed fixing yesterday," Jennifer answered.

"Yeah, and I thought you were going to take care of it!"

"With the holiday, it was hard to find anyone who would come out to fix it."

Jennifer and Hayley saw Todd approaching and Jennifer started to cry before taking off down the hall.

I had a suspicion that it was not good. "What happened?" I asked Hayley.

"There was a weak spot in the fence. I guess Christmas squeezed out. He's gone."

Under the circumstances, I wondered why they were just standing around. "Did you call him? Maybe we can get in the truck and find him."

Hayley shook her head. "Jennifer was so upset, she has been out calling and looking for him since two-thirty. She was afraid to even tell me. He's been gone for hours now. He could be anywhere."

The stranger pushed forward, holding something up. "Excuse me, but is this the missing dog?"

All three of us peered at a photo that he held in his hand. It sure looked like Christmas to me.

"That's Christmas," Todd said immediately.

The man let out a deep sigh. "When he lived with us, we called him Jake. We learned very early on that no fence could hold that dog. When Jake wanted to go, Jake went."

"Jake?" I repeated.

"That was his name when he lived with us." The stranger held out his hand. "Bill Conner."

I shook his hand and introduced myself and Todd. "We adopted him for Christmas and just came in to get him for good. We didn't know he was yours."

"Jake is a bit of a wanderer. I think he goes where he wants to go. When he lived with us he would be gone for a few days, doing Jake business, and then just unexpectedly return."

"He wasn't that way with us," Todd said quickly. "I mean, he stuck around."

Bill Conner put his hands in his pockets and looked at Todd. "As far as him being my dog, nobody owns Jake. Sooner or later, Jake goes where he wants to go. You can't just pick Jake out and think you own him. Jake has to pick you out. That's the way it works with him. It may be that Jake's business is over with both of our families." Bill Conner smiled and shrugged his shoulders as if to say that he was accepting a reality even if he did not like it. "Jake has new Jake business."

We were all silent for a moment until Todd spoke up,

seeming slightly offended. "Christmas was a good dog for us."

I considered that to be an enormous understatement.

"I can't tell you how sorry I am," Hayley said. "If Christmas shows up here, I'll call you both and we'll see what we can work out."

Todd reached out and put his hand on Hayley's shoulder and spoke once more as if to reassure us all. "Don't worry. Christmas can take care of himself."

We pulled out of the shelter parking lot to a light snow shower. It was too warm for the snow to stick, but the gray sky set an appropriate backdrop for my disappointment. Todd seemed to know from my silence that I was upset and bothered. He kept saying, "Don't worry, Dad. Christmas will be fine." I was amazed that Todd seemed to be handling this better than me.

When we turned into our driveway after a long and silent trip home, Mary Ann was waiting for us. I dreaded telling her, but when I got out of the truck she just gave me a big hug and said, "I'm sorry, George."

"How did you know?"

"I called the shelter. I wanted to remind you to buy more dog food. I talked to Hayley and she told me."

"It's all right. It's probably for the best," I said. I got the collar, the leash, and the yellow tennis ball out of the back of the truck. "I guess we won't need these anymore." I tossed them on the ground and walked off toward the barnyard.

Todd started to follow me until Mary Ann called him back. "Todd, why don't you come to the house with me. I think your dad needs a little time to think."

I went into the barn and found the milking stool waiting in my thinking spot.

Mary Ann was right. I had been a fool about this dog. I handled the whole thing poorly. What happened was exactly what I feared, but it was my own fault this time. It was like authoring your own worst nightmare. Everybody has something they aren't very good at and I guess dog relationships just don't work for me. I stared at Tucker's old collar hanging on the wall and resolved to toss it into a trash can. I was done with dogs. This time for good.

If Bill Conner was right about this dog, then it might not have mattered. He was destined to drift off anyway. It sounded like he was going to go where he wanted to go. I admired the dog for his independence, but I found it hard to believe that he would have wandered off from this farm. From the beginning, he seemed so comfortable with us and us with him.

I exhaled deeply. On top of everything else, my leg was throbbing in pain. I shifted my weight and tried to get more comfortable when I heard something. *Pong. . . . pong . . . pong.* I was still a little goosey about that cougar, so I tensed up. Before I could place the sound, a yellow tennis ball rolled right up to the foot that was connected to the end of my aching right leg. I was ready to pick it up and throw it right back at Todd.

I turned toward the barn door to throw, but it wasn't Todd. Standing there in the door frame, with the last remnant of sunlight to his back and snowflakes falling over him like a thousand tiny paratroopers, was a dog named Christmas. His tail was wagging and you would have thought that he never left us. I yelled, "Come here, boy! Come on now!" He hesitated for just a second, but then bounded toward me.

Rising off the milk stool when he jumped, I was knocked back onto my own haunches. He was so glad to see me. I hugged him and buried my face in his winter cold, winter clean fur. For a moment, I'm sure my grin was wider than Todd's grin on a spring-painting day, a creek-exploring day, or a radio-listening day. I could not wait to show *my* dog to my son.

Grunting, my stiff leg hindering my ability to stand, I asked, "You want to play catch?" Christmas was wagging his tail. He had clearly chosen us just like we chose him. With all of my strength, I let the ball sail through the barn door and out into the cold winter air. He barked twice and scampered off into the barnyard.

With a second effort, I stood, remembering that for many years my grandfather hung the stool on a nail along the wall. I picked the stool up and turned it over. There was still an old piece of leather strap nailed to the underside. I found the nail and hung the stool up by its strap before heading inside to share my good news with Mary Ann and Todd. I was hoping that it would be a long time before I would need that stool again.

I headed for the back door, yelling, "Mary Ann, Todd, get out here, now!"

Christmas raced around the corner with the ball in

his mouth. I tossed the ball again and Christmas disappeared around the side of the barn, out of view.

Mary Ann and Todd opened the door and nearly fell out onto the porch with worry. "What's wrong?" Mary Ann asked.

"I just figured out how to get Christmas back."

"How?" Todd asked.

"It's easy. I'll just throw the ball and he'll fetch it."

"What?" Mary Ann asked.

On cue, Christmas roared around the corner with the ball in his mouth and bounded up onto the porch. I shrugged my shoulders. "See. It worked."

Christmas was home, this time for good. Todd and Mary Ann's reunion with him was no less exciting than my own, although Mary Ann could not resist tugging his ears gently and scolding him for running away. "And to not even leave a note. Shame on you!"

After things settled down, I made a call to Hank, letting him know that it all worked out and to thank him for helping me to set things straight. I got another surprise.

"George," he said, with the confidence I always admired, "I'm not getting any younger, you know."

"I hadn't noticed."

"It's time for me to be thinking about the mark I leave with this life. I just want you to know that I sent a construction company out to the Cherokee County Animal Shelter. That place is a disgrace, but it won't be when I'm done with it."

"Nope, Hank, when you do something, it's done right."
So, that explained the construction company trailer in the
shelter parking lot. Hank was wasting no time making
things right for the dogs of Cherokee County.

Later that night, sitting in front of the dying embers of
my fire, I put my newspaper down and closed my eyes.
I reached out and stroked my dog's fur, listening with
pleasure as his tail thumped the floor. I thought I could
almost hear Mary Ann chuckle and say, "And George,
when does Christmas end?"

I smiled to myself while still petting the dog, and then
whispered to my wife, to my children, and to the whole
world, "As long as we can still make room at the inn,
Christmas never ends."

During the week of October 17, 2002, a mountain lion was killed on the highway near Kansas City. An expert concluded that it had never lived in captivity. There continue to be numerous sightings in the area.

CHRISTMAS

with Tucker

To my grandparents

Chester and Maurine Richardson.

Like all great grandparents,

they finished up where my parents left off.

With one paw in the wild and another scratching at the door of humanity, dogs are caught in an awkward spot. It misses the mark to describe a dog as just an animal. We recognize that our pets can be both beasts and evolved life-forms keenly attuned to human needs. Country dogs may be more appreciated for their animal nature—hunting, herding, and guarding—while city dogs are cherished for their humanlike ability to expertly deliver companionship and unbridled affection.

From time to time, for a lucky few of us, we come across a dog that seems to move naturally back and forth from one world to the other. Such a dog can howl at the distant coyote, hunt for his own food, refuse to back down from a charging adversary, and run hours on end with equal glee under snow or sun. In an animal like this, we respect the sheer aliveness that radiates from his eyes. And, when the day's work is done, he'll lay down by our feet, content. For this dog, you know that there is nowhere he would rather be than with you. This dog is complete in both worlds. He models for us how to simultaneously be good and alive—animal and angel.

Frank Thorne owned this kind of dog. He received the four-year-old Irish setter in exchange for repairs he made to an old tractor. The owner of the broken-down machine had inherited the tractor and the dog from his grandfather. He kept a picture in his wallet of the old man standing beside that proud setter, taken after one of their weekend hunting trips. The snapshot was good enough—he had no room for a dog.

Thorne was too sick, too broken, and too mired in personal problems to know the value of his bargain. The setter spent most of his days tied up outside on a chain attached to a giant steel corkscrew that tightened into a clay loam, binding him to the ground like concrete.

Tethered, he could only watch wild turkeys amble across the meadow, roosting to a setting sun, or rabbits venture from their winter thicket as snow danced across Thorne's barnyard. The dog yearned to experience all that was outside the radius of his twenty-four-foot circle.

From time to time, when Thorne had better days, he would take the dog for rides in the truck, long jaunts along the banks of Kill Creek, or just let him into his modest, run-down house to enjoy warm evenings by the fire that glowed in an old pot-bellied stove. Thorne was a lonely man incapable of realizing a friendship with the dog or anything else.

Not long after his arrival, the dog saw a boy walking across the field to the west. He pulled on the chain, whined, and pulled again. His tail wagged, but there was no give. In the late afternoons, before Thorne returned home, he could hear a school bus full of children stop at the top of the hill. The same boy he had seen walking through the fields was on the bus, too.

He saw or heard the boy almost every day until June. As the summer progressed, the boy ventured out less frequently. By August, he did not come out at all. When he heard the boy in the yard, the dog could tell that the boy's energy was different. There was less laughter on the hill.

Things grew worse with the man, too.

Thorne stopped leaving the house and a putrid odor seeped from his pores. The dog knew the smell. He recognized it from his previous owner, who ran a tavern near the city. October turned to November and Thorne became less attentive to the dog's needs. The setter lost weight and the sheen vanished from his red coat. As hunger set in, his disposition naturally deteriorated. He paced nervously.

One day in November, around 3:00 P.M., though it was still some distance away, he could hear Thorne's truck rapidly approaching home. There was another sound farther in the distance that caused pain in the dog's ears. He whined and tried to bury his head between his paws as it grew nearer. It was the sound of sirens.

Impervious to his own discomfort, he wagged his tail excitedly as Thorne's truck screeched on its brakes and turned wildly into the driveway. The truck fishtailed to a stop not ten feet from the dog's run.

The dog did not know what to expect from this tall, gaunt man. In the past, he was affectionate and seemed to value the dog, but lately his master treated him like an inconvenient responsibility. Thorne stumbled out of the truck and, without bothering to shut the door, fell to the ground. This is the position from which humans often play with dogs, so the dog grew *excited and ached for a greeting, some acknowledgment of his existence, but there was none. Instead, Thorne pulled himself up, brushed the dirt from his clothes, and made sure the package he so carefully clutched in his hands was still intact.*

The pain in the dog's ears grew more severe as the sirens grew closer, but still all he wanted was to be with the man. He ran excitedly at the end of the chain and barked for attention.

It was still early in the afternoon, but not too early for the ubiquitous bottle in the brown paper sack, the bottle that held the scent that the dog now associated with his master. Thorne gripped the sack in his left hand like a lion trainer clutches the whip that separates him from certain death. The red setter whined again and even let out a little yelp, but Thorne still ignored him. Instead, he walked into the house and slammed the front door behind him.

Soon more cars pulled into the driveway; two of them carried the painful siren. The noise ended when the drivers turned off their engines, got out of their cars, and approached the master's house.

The dog was confused. It was rare for other people to enter his area. The strangers' voices seemed nervous and there was a scent in the air that he associated with danger. The dog barked furiously and pulled at the chain.

The uniformed men talked to the dog. They said that they would not hurt him, but still they stayed well away from his run as they approached the house, and he could sense their aggressive postures. He was prepared to lay down his life to defend Thorne from this strange new threat.

The men banged on Thorne's old front door. The dog des-

perately threw all of his weight at the chain, but still it did not give.

A few moments later, one of the men led his master out of the house in handcuffs, locked behind his back. The dog sniffed the air to assess the potential for danger. There was no odor of blood, but the smell of alcohol, stale and sour, clung to his master. Thorne's head hung down as he walked toward the cars. He said nothing to his dog as he was shoved into the patrol car.

An older man had arrived at the scene and he spoke to the uniformed men in a voice that the dog recognized; he had heard it before from the top of the hill. There was no fear in this one.

The old man went to his truck and pulled out a half-eaten bologna sandwich and tossed it to the dog, eyeing him from a safe distance as the setter devoured the human food. The man approached him, and the dog hunkered down in fear—still uncomfortable with a stranger entering his space. It was not difficult for the dog to trust the old man, who spoke in a deep, soothing tone and brought him food when no one else had. Tired, and exhausted from trying to take care of his master, he rested on the ground. When the man reached out to pet him, he calmed to his touch and rolled onto his back in a submissive gesture.

The old man stood and looked west. The sky was darkening. A difficult winter would soon be upon them.

Most barns double as family museums. The vertical beams are riddled with the nails and hooks that hold history. Pieces of harness, rusted tools, license plates from old trucks, or a calendar from a bygone era—they all tell a story. It is the task of the curator to pick the right exhibits, to find the single pieces that sum up the entirety of a people, a place, or a time long past.

From the window of our old wooden barn, I could see my son, Todd, throwing the ball to our dog, a mature black Lab he'd named Christmas. The engines of both his truck and my wife's car were warming up. Todd's breath was condensing in the cold winter air. We were all preparing for another day's work. For myself, I had an unusual task, one that I had embarked on nearly fifty years ago. It was time to finish it.

I lifted Tucker's leather collar off a hook, the letters of his name faded but still visible. At six o'clock, one of our family's most important museum patrons was scheduled to visit. I wanted to put together that one exhibit that would make the past clear, not just for me but for her, too. To do so, I had to go back to a cold wintery place where I had been reluctant to travel. If I was to assume the curator's role, I had no choice.

Everyone has a winter like that one. A place and time that changes us forever. A place and time when the wind blew so cold that the memories still hurt. It was now time to walk straight through that hurt and excavate an important piece of my life. For her, I would do this work.

The sound of gravel crunched in the driveway as Todd and Mary Ann each pulled out, leaving me alone on our farm. I would have the entire day to focus on my project. It seemed that I had been way too busy the last few decades, often doing unimportant things, to take the time to do something this important. Now the work had to be done.

With the collar in my hand, I walked toward the house. Once inside, I collected the other pieces that would form the exhibit: an old tin cup from the kitchen window-sill; from the top shelf of a closet, a stack of letters carefully banded together and arranged chronologically, and a tattered puzzle box with hundreds of rattling pieces. I poured myself a cup of coffee, threw a few hickory logs on the fire, and settled into my old rust-colored corduroy recliner, the treasures assembled on my lap. This spot had always been a good place to think, to explore a few crevices and crannies and, if things went well, rejoin parts of myself that had been split apart.

I picked up the tin cup and closed my eyes, waiting until I could feel the steely cold of that winter of 1962 blow across my face and hear the faint rumble of the old truck as it labored up McCray's Hill. . . .

The truck door creaked open and then slammed shut. The old man walked through the back kitchen door and took off his hat, exposing gray hair cut short. He had high, flat cheeks that were tanned in the summer from hours spent working outside, a Roman nose slightly large but proud, and a complexion that was surprisingly immune from wrinkles for his seventy-two years.

He was an inattentive shaver who apparently believed that using a razor on alternate days was good enough. His eyes were as blue as the Kansas sky and as sharp as a red-tailed hawk.

There was not a suggestion of fat on his frame, which was steeled by work too hard to imagine by today's standards. After fourteen-hour days in the barns and fields, he moved stiffly. The no-nonsense look on his face was as constant as the cuts, bruises, and scrapes on his body.

Now he gently kissed on the cheek the tall, white-haired woman standing at the kitchen sink, and filled an old tin measuring cup with the cool rainwater drawn from their cistern. He tilted his grizzled head back, drained the cup empty, and then let out a long "Ahhh." He repeated this ritual several times a day during their nearly fifty-year marriage. It unfailingly brought a contented smile to her face.

Standing there together by the sink on that early-winter afternoon, they appeared a perfectly matched team, ready to plow through the prairie sod that had sustained generations of McCrays. She was lithe, beautiful, and wore one of her ubiquitous flowered dresses, beneath which radiated a calm goodness that was a wellspring of comfort to all who knew her.

In the summer months, he might fill and empty the tin cup four or five times before his thirst was quenched. Any water that remained at the bottom of the cup he would unceremoniously pitch out the kitchen window onto his wife's jewel-toned flowers, the blossoms of which she chose for one purpose alone: the nectar that best attracted her beloved hummingbirds.

But that day, one cup full of water was enough. Grandpa Bo set the cup down, clutched Grandma Cora's elbow, and pulled her close to him.

In a secretive way, from behind my book, I watched them from my reading spot on the living room sofa. For several months now, I had been hiding behind, or perhaps *in*, my books. That afternoon, I had to leave Tarzan stranded in a tree, so that I could pick up a few words of the conversation between my grandparents, two of the people I loved most in the world and whose house I'd shared every day of my thirteen years.

My grandmother's voice seemed surprised. "Not again. Oh, no. Bo, I'm so disappointed." After letting out a pained sigh, she continued, "I shouldn't be surprised, though, given his state of mind. The poor fellow practically had to raise himself with those parents of his, and he's lost more than he's gained in this life—so many jobs, his marriage, and now a friend."

There was a silence and I could not hear their words until her much louder "You what?"

His baritone voice reassured her. "Don't be upset, Cora. This can work out."

"I'm just shocked, that's all. I never thought . . . Are you sure?"

He grunted. "I stopped being sure of anything on June 15, 1962."

When I heard that date, a sinking feeling came over me. Like December 7, 1941, it was one of a half-dozen dates our family would never forget. After putting my book down, I got up and walked into the kitchen. The talk stopped when I entered the room.

They both looked at me expectantly, so I invented a question. "Grandpa, did you sell the cows?"

"Yes, I sold them, and had lunch at the Ox. Saw Hank Fisher and his wife." He hesitated and then just spat it out. "And I made a stop on the way and brought home a dog."

"A dog!" I had always wanted a puppy and I could barely believe my ears.

"It's not exactly what you think, George, so don't get excited."

"What do you mean?" I asked.

"He's not a puppy and you don't get to keep him. Frank Thorne has himself in a bad spot again. He has to leave his farm for a while. He was your dad's friend and he's our neighbor, so I guess it's up to us to help him out. I'd appreciate your help."

"You mean that mean-looking red dog that he keeps tied up in front of the house? The one that barks like a devil every time my school bus goes by?"

"That's the one."

My idea of a good dog was a friendly puppy. I let my feelings be known in a simple and direct way. "I don't think I want to take care of Thorne's dog."

Bo McCray had the same simple, direct communication style. "You'll do it anyway."

I looked to my grandmother for support, and she stared hard at me in a way that signaled this issue was not up for discussion. "All right, then, where is he?" I asked.

With a tinge of annoyance, Grandpa set his battered tin cup down on the countertop. "In the truck," he answered, pointing toward the back door. "And if he has a name, Thorne didn't mention it."

The old truck was typically parked in the implement barn, but this afternoon it had been left in the gravel driveway close to our farmhouse, so I walked out the back door, without another word. I stopped and stared at the truck for a moment, not sure what to expect and having no idea of the value of the cargo in the hold.

As I let the kitchen door slam behind me, it occurred to me that, like an elephant or a giraffe, a dog was foreign to the McCray farm. The adult words, spoken frequently by my father and by my grandfather, too, came rushing back to me. *Dairy cattle and dogs don't mix, George. Quit asking for a puppy.*

For years I grumbled about it, as any kid would, but like hot days in February, I accepted that dogs were not part of the McCray landscape.

Now this no-name dog was sitting in the truck and I didn't know what to make of it. Part of me was excited, but there were other, unsettling feelings, too. At that point in my life, I needed the world to be arranged according to rules that I could count on, even when those rules were unpopular.

In my life, the one rule that children counted on most had been broken: *parents don't leave their children.* That rule I considered inviolate. For me, there was an obvious corollary, too: *a boy doesn't lose his dad in a tractor accident on a hot summer afternoon.* My father, John Mangum Mc-Cray, was here one morning as he had always been, ate breakfast, went outside to work, and by that afternoon, was gone forever.

Now this *dairy cattle and dogs don't mix* rule was being broken, too. Deep down, I was sure that I would never be allowed to have a dog, and though I resented it, it was still one of the rules that I counted on to keep my crumbling universe in order. It was somehow frightening to see this rule broken. Which rule was going to be broken next? What had I done wrong to be the only kid in my school who had lost a parent? I felt as if I were being punished, but I didn't understand why. Somehow, my father's death spoke some dark truth about me. Surely, good kids didn't lose their dads—only the unworthy and the undeserving are so fated. What had I done?

There was more swirling around in my mind, too. I put my hand on the stock gate release and hesitated before pulling the latch. Surprises had lost their appeal. I just didn't know what to do or how to feel about this most recent unplanned event. The latch release needed oil and it creaked as I opened the rear stock gate. I made a note to myself to squirt some oil on the hinge.

Standing in the truck bed, hesitant but with his tail wagging, was a beauty of a dog. I had never seen Thorne's dog up close. Though he seemed thin and needed cleaning up, he had long red hair and looked to be an Irish setter. I opened the door fully and reassured him. "It's okay, boy. I won't hurt you. Come on, jump on down."

He took very little coaxing. He ran at me full speed and jumped. Surprised, I scrambled backward and fell onto my backside. Instinctively, I raised my arms over my head to protect my face from an attack.

This assault was not, however, of a violent nature. In fact, it was more a matter of his smothering me with affectionate kisses and trying to nuzzle me to my feet. The dog put his cool, wet nose to my face as if we were the closest of friends, cruelly separated but now reunited. I laughed and pushed him away gently. "Enough!"

It was no use; he was back on me, demanding attention. I got up and took a few steps, hoping to gain some separation, but he chased after me, nipping playfully at my feet. He seemed to take great pleasure in knocking me to the ground so he could jump back on me and pummel me with canine attention.

Trying a different tactic, I just froze. He backed a few feet away from me and started barking, demanding that I play with him. I started to run away, hoping he would chase after me, but he was so excited that he set out circling the house at full speed, his big, floppy, red ears going up and down as he bounded by me. I wondered if doggie Christmas had arrived early for this pooch.

After two quick loops around the house, he decided to return his focus to running circles around me like an Indian war party, substituting yelps and excited high-pitched barks for war cries. I decided to take the offense and dove on top of him, knocking him down. Before he could recover, I jumped up and ran off. He rolled over, and we began a long game of tag, now both of us circling around the yard at a furious pace.

We wrestled, ran, and played for nearly an hour, until finally the sun began to set. The dog seemed to have endless energy, so eventually I just collapsed on the ground and covered my face with my arms. He rested his head on my chest while I tried to catch my breath.

The back porch door slammed as Grandpa walked out and calmly petted the dog as he rested by my side. He shaped a homemade collar and leash by making a slipknot in an old length of rope and looped it around his neck. "Come on, boy," he said reassuringly.

The dog followed my grandpa obediently. He was a totally different creature now—alert, quiet, and respectful—like he was working and not playing. Grandpa walked him around the yard for a few minutes. Then he led the dog toward me as if to reintroduce us.

They stopped a few feet away from me and, as he was apt to do, Grandpa summed up the dog and my life in a few sentences. "He's a bit older for a *puppy*, but he has great potential. You can practice with this dog for a month or so. Maybe, after Christmas, when you go to Minnesota, your mom will let you get a dog of your own."

"I'm not sure if I want to go to Minnesota."

"Your mother misses you. She needs you."

My dad wasn't the only rule breaker. My mom had "left" me, too—albeit with my blessing—moving off the farm at summer's end to be near her parents in Minnesota. My sisters were both in college there and Mom, wrapped in grief, simply couldn't bear to be on the farm without my dad. Back in August, when she decided we should move, I asked her if I could stay for a while longer.

I understood that she needed to get a new start on life, but I just wasn't ready to leave. I asked to stay on the farm until Christmas, and she reluctantly agreed. It had seemed so simple, but I was beginning to realize that the plan had grown complicated as each passing day made me question what "home" really meant.

"Don't put me in the middle of this, George."

I took the homemade leash away from him. "The truck gate needs oil. I'll do it."

"Dinner will be ready soon," he said, as if he were relieved to change the subject, too. "It's going to turn cold tonight. After you oil the hinge, you had better plug the heaters into the stock tanks or your chickens won't have water. By the end of the week, it could start snowing, too." He looked down at our new charge. "When you're finished, please put Frank's dog on the back porch, where he can stay warm."

He started to turn away, so I caught his attention. "Grandpa?"

"Yes," he said, turning back to me.

"I don't think Mr. Thorne deserves a dog if he is going to just tie it up all day."

Grandpa paused for a few seconds, considering his words. "I don't know about that. All I know is that Thorne is gone for now. So I did him a favor. Maybe I shouldn't have, but I did what I thought I had to do."

He stood there for a few moments longer, alternating

glances between me and the dog. He seemed lost in thought. Finally, he turned away and walked toward the back porch of our old house, but not before issuing one last instruction. "George, if it snows on Friday, as much as they say it might, I'll need you to help with the morning milking while I run the road maintainer. Can you do that?"

Shrugging my shoulders, I said, "Sure, I guess," and walked off to do my work.

Our family owned and operated McCray's Dairy, which would have passed to my father had he lived, and then on to me. Dairy farming sounds almost picturesque to city dwellers, but in reality it was a combination of some of the hardest things about farming. Keeping cows fed and watered was a giant task—and that was before you even got to the milking part.

In the summer months, the cows foraged in the meadows around our farm for their own food, but to produce maximum quantities of milk, we also provided our small herd with grain year-round. The grain had to be grown, harvested, and stored. During the summer, we also put up large amounts of hay, which is just grass—cut, dried, and put into bales, which can be fed to the cows during the winter months when the fields are fallow.

Watering a herd of cattle is no small task, either. It is essential that dairy cows have lots of water available to them. Each cow drinks between twenty-five and fifty gallons of water a day, depending on the weather. On a hot August day, even a small herd of dairy cattle would need a thousand gallons.

Unfortunately, in the 1960s, rural water service was

almost unheard-of in Kansas. Farmers had to find their own sources. We had two: our lake, which was really just a big three-acre pond, and the rainwater that trickled down through the roof gutters and that was stored in large underground concrete cisterns. When the cisterns ran out, which they often did, we had to buy water in town and then haul it to the farm.

Nobody should have to work this hard, but Grandpa, like most small farmers, had a second job to bring in cash. When he wasn't farming, milking cows, or attending to his old pair of Clydesdale horses, Dick and Dock, he was one of three county-road maintainers: he graded gravel and repaired potholes in the summer, and was charged with keeping the snow off the roads in the winter. Grading and farming went together well. There was more farmwork in the summer and less grading to do. In the winter—when there was less farmwork—there was typically more grading. Because it was not as physically demanding, grading was a good job for my grandfather to retire into. At least, that had been the plan until that day in June.

He used a big piece of equipment that most people would describe today as a grader, but back then it was called a "maintainer." He even had an official county designation, "Senior Road Maintainer," but some people called him The Maintainer, or Big Bo McCray. To me, he was usually just Grandpa.

When I came home from school, I had a specific list

of chores that I had to do before dinner. My sisters had their lists, too, but when they left for college, a lot of their work fell to me. First, I had to find and chase stragglers up to the barn. Once all the cattle were near the barn, I shut a big steel gate that separated the barnyard from the meadows and fields that surrounded our farm. I put their grain in feed troughs, and made sure water was available for them while each cow waited her turn to be milked. Electric pumps moved the water out of the cistern and into large aluminum tanks we kept by the barn.

While Grandpa and my dad did the milking, I fed and cared for the remainder of the stock we owned, which included pigs, chickens, and horses. I also was expected to clean out Dick and Dock's stalls. Fortunately, their stalls opened out into an open-air paddock, where they spent most of their time and left most of their messes.

The morning milking was a whole different matter. The steps were the same, but they had to be performed in the dark; the process started at 4:30 A.M. I doubted if I could brush my teeth at that hour, let alone function as part of the milking crew.

I had been exempt from that chore so that I could be attentive at school. No one realistically expected any kid to get up at that hour. Now it looked to me like another rule that I thought I could count on was going straight out the window. It knocked me even more off balance. Most likely my grandfather and I were struggling with the same problem. How in the world were we going to get all of this done without my father's help? For him, the answer was simple. We would work harder. For me, it was not so easy.

On the surface, I felt some resentment at being charged with extra work, but the problem wasn't just the morning milking. As I walked out to the garage to grab the oilcan from the toolbox, the feelings festered.

After oiling the hinge and checking on my chickens, I stood by the back door and stared south out into the meadow, watching the few remaining leaves of autumn fall from an old oak tree and float to the ground like little yellow paratroopers. Fall was over; winter was beginning.

The wind blew harder and I had to button my coat. I stood there trying to figure out what it was beyond the wind that was bothering me.

There was still a melancholy feeling fueled by my grandfather's simple request to help with the work that needed to be done. I sat down on the back porch steps and petted Thorne's dog. Running my fingers through his fur gave me some comfort.

As adults, we forget these confused teenage years. After we've addressed a problem or a feeling a dozen times, resolution becomes second nature. But at barely thirteen, it was all new and still very confusing. Most of us don't get it right the first time. I was no exception. Destiny compelled me to try on the wrong attitude. Knowing how the wrong attitude fits and feels is often the first step in recognizing a better one when it comes along.

At that young age, I could see only so far. Until we mature and develop the ability to get perspective on our problems, we're left in an inevitably selfish and superficial place. That's what makes those teen years so hard.

What was on the surface, staring hard at me that afternoon, was a big question of fairness. First off, I had lost my dad. He was the person I looked to more than any other to show me the path through life. He was the sentinel rock at the top of the hill from which I could take my bearing even in the stormiest of weather. More than anyone else's, when I tripped and started to fall, it was his strong arms that picked me up.

On a deeper level, though I didn't want to admit it, part of me was just plain scared. My grandfather expected me to do adult work—I already worked harder in one day after school than most of my city friends did in a month—and I was still not quite ready to give up being a boy.

I began thinking about how hard my life had been on that farm. And now it was going to get worse.

Maybe it was grieving, maybe it was sulking, or maybe it was just being a teenager and needing to get over my self-pity. Justified or not, I didn't think it was fair that I had to do my own work plus half of my dad's, too. And now, with Thorne in jail, I had to take care of this dog. I wondered if there was a limit to what was expected of me and if I had a say in a darned thing. No one asked me; I was just told what to do.

Sitting there on that back porch, petting Thorne's dog, I

felt none of it made sense anymore. My mom was right—this farm life was hard—and things would be much easier for me in Minnesota.

Mom had told me on several occasions that if I changed my mind and did not want to wait out the rest of the fall school term before joining her, she would send me a bus ticket. That was starting to make sense to me. Who could blame me for wanting to spend time with my own mother?

The thought of being with her again caused something in my mind to click into place, like the tumbler on a combination lock, and I was able to go a little bit deeper into the problem. Being so caught up in my feelings of loss for my father, I failed to realize how much I was missing my mom and my sisters, too.

Minnesota was starting to tug on me just as it must have tugged on her.

The dog rested his head on my leg and finally seemed tired. After getting up, I turned my back on a vivid sunset and went inside, disgruntled and confused. Did I love the farm? Was it the last connection to my father and a lifestyle I had valued? Was it my future or just part of my past—another fatality in a barrage of rules that were no longer applicable? Leaving Thorne's dog on the back porch, I opened the kitchen door, went to the sink to wash my hands, and sat down with my grandparents for dinner.

CHAPTER 5

"G eorge, you've been awfully quiet tonight. Is everything all right?"

"Yes, I think so, Grandma."

I tried to gather enough courage to bring up the subject of the morning milking. "I was wondering how I can do the morning milking and get ready for school at the same time."

Grandpa set down his fork and gave me a sly smile. "Good question."

I pushed the point. "I don't know if I can make it all work."

"Sure you can, George."

"How?"

"Same way I did when I was your age."

"How was that?" I asked again.

"It's easy, George."

"Really?"

"Sure it is, son." He leaned back in his chair and pulled his suspenders out away from his chest, and then rested his giant hand on my shoulder and smiled. "You have to get up early. Getting up early is good for you. I've been doing it for nearly seventy years. These snow days aren't likely to happen more than forty or fifty times this winter."

He gave a little grin and I knew he was teasing me. "Not really, George. It's mostly just big snowstorms that can take a few days at a time to clear. You can do that, can't you?"

Truth was, I wasn't sure I could do it or wanted to do it. I resisted the impulse to say "It'll be hard to help with the morning milking from Minnesota" when the thought of leaving the farm and my grandparents behind became even more upsetting. That would be a very hollow victory for me. I lost my composure and tears formed in the corners of my eyes.

I just stood up and walked out of the kitchen. The sound of a chair being pushed away from the table suggested what I already knew. My grandmother would be following right behind me.

I turned around to face her and she clutched my arm. "George, we'll get up and do the chores together. It'll be all right."

I felt like a little boy and was angry with myself for losing control. At the same time, I needed some comforting and was glad to get it. I wanted to be like my father and grandfather, capable of so much, without a word of complaint along the way. I just did not know how to do it.

"Thanks, Grandma, but I've been thinking. . . ."

She looked at me patiently. "Yes?"

I tried to swallow my words as soon as they came out. "Maybe it's time for me to go to Minnesota."

There was a very brief flash of pain in her eyes and then she smiled in an accepting way. "We're all mad, and sad, and frustrated, and it just comes boiling over sometimes. It happens to all of us." She took my hand and with more love than I could imagine existing in any one person, said, "George, if you want to be with your mother in Minnesota now, we'll make it happen. You go read for a while and relax. Make a decision when you're feeling better. We wouldn't want you to stay here if it isn't where you want to be."

She patted me on the back and I retreated to my living-room fort: a brown sofa with the fireplace on one side and a stack of my library books on the other. I tried to rid my mind of the problem by escaping into a book. Somewhere between the beginning and the end of the story I was trying to lose myself in, another realization surfaced. There were only three members of McCray's Dairy before it lost its strongest partner. My grandfather was struggling hard to take up the slack. If I left, it would be down to a team of one. It would be pretty lonely for him and I didn't want to let him down. I wondered if Grandpa could run the dairy without me and doubted he could afford to hire anyone else.

Decades later, I would constantly tell my son to re-move his ever-present headphones so that I could speak to him. I sounded like a broken record—"Todd, take those things off so you can hear me." When I was thirteen, the constant refrain was "George, please put your book down and come in here and talk to us."

At the sound of Grandma Cora's voice, I shook myself into the present and walked into the kitchen. She was finishing cleaning up from dinner and Grandpa was still reading the paper. Without looking up, he asked his question.

"Is this nameless dog of Thorne's any good?"

"Sure."

"What's he like?"

"Well, he seems all tuckered out right now."

With the water running as she washed the dishes, my grandmother misheard my answer, with interesting results.

"Well," she chimed in brightly. "Tucker is a very nice name for a dog."

My grandfather looked up from his paper and smiled

at me. Neither of us saw any reason to correct her. So I just went along. "Good a name as any."

"I want to see this Tucker for myself," she said, drying her hands on her apron. She held open the back porch door. "Why don't you come and show him to me?"

I stayed on her heels, curious to know what she'd make of the dog. She knelt beside the setter, who opened his eyes and gave her a trusting look as she gently massaged his ears.

My grandfather got up from the table and joined us. He smiled as she conversed with the dog.

"Tucker, you are a fine dog."

It took less than five minutes. Tucker could say goodbye to the back porch and hello to inside living quarters.

"George, please take Tucker inside right now where we can properly care for him." She followed me into the house and pushed a pile of scraps into a steel bowl. Tucker did not bother to chew much of anything; he just gulped it down. When he finished, he settled down beside Grandma, who'd joined my grandfather at the table, and stretched his paws out in a contented way. She continued to scratch his ears and pet his red coat, praising him for no discernable reason, though she used his new name every chance she could, as if to teach it to him. "Sweet Tucker, nice boy. . . . Tucker, you're going to like it here. . . . Are you still hungry, Tucker?"

Retreating again to the sofa, I left Grandpa in the kitchen reading the paper. Occasionally, he would look over at Grandma with a raised eyebrow as she kept up her patter with Tucker.

It was getting close to bedtime when what remained of my living-room reading time was again interrupted. My grandmother was still in the kitchen, now carrying on an intense conversation with my grandfather that was quickly losing the casual tone that I could naturally tune out while reading. The rising volume of her voice reflected her agitation.

"All of those years of John wanting a dog and you were so stubborn about it—now you bring home a dog. How did you think it was going to make me feel?"

"The dog needed a home. What else was I to do? Besides, I thought it would do George some good."

"George is going to Minnesota and that dog is going back to Frank's when he gets out of jail. How is that going to work?"

"Not so loud, Cora, he'll hear us."

Soon there were muffled sobs from the kitchen.

"Do you want me to find another place for the dog?"

"Bo, it's not that."

"Then what?" he asked.

I heard her let out a long, low moan. "When I glance at our little George, I see John. It makes me want to bust inside." She tried to hold back her tears, but she just sobbed. "Oh, Bo, even the smallest things trigger memories and make me think of John. First we lost him, and soon enough we're going to lose George, too. He may not even last here till Christmas—he just told me so. Nothing is going to be right on this farm."

"Don't say that, Cora."

"What else am I to think? My insides have been chopped to pieces. I don't understand. How do you stay so calm?"

My grandfather let out his own long sigh and spoke in a determined way. "It's like this, Cora. We can't afford an avalanche. For now, that's all I am trying to do."

"What do you mean, Bo?"

"One loss triggers another, and another, and before you know it, the whole family is busted apart at the bottom of the hill. Just a pile of rubble."

Unable to resist, I peeked, unnoticed, into the kitchen. My grandmother's head was buried in my grandfather's massive chest. She hugged him tighter. "I know," she told him sorrowfully.

"We can't let that happen. I've got to stay tough—for you, for George, and for the whole family."

"You're my granite. You've always been. Nothing ever has and nothing ever will knock us down from the top of McCray's Hill."

He pulled her closer. "I won't let it." He plucked four or five pins from her hair, loosening it from its knot and letting it fall down her shoulders, the way she wore it at night. He ran his fingers through it in a comforting gesture.

"What am I going to do? I can't go on like this anymore."

"It's November. You'll do what we do every year."

"What's that?" she asked.

"After you make the best Thanksgiving dinner in Cherokee County, you'll waste weeks of time putting up all of your Christmas decorations, just like you always do."

"How can I do that, alone, without John and Sarah helping me? You know how much they loved Christmas. The girls were always the first ones to drag the decorations out of the basement and string the lights. Now they are all gone."

"I'll help you. George is still here. We'll do it, somehow."

"I'm sorry, but right now Christmas seems frivolous."

He held her cheeks in his hands. "You've got more substance than any person I know. There is nothing frivolous about keeping our traditions alive. It may be just what we need to stay propped up. I need you to do it."

I crept upstairs, not wanting to disturb them and feeling vaguely guilty for listening in and watching them. It was only November, but it was cold getting ready for bed. Tucker followed me up the steps and sniffed about my room. I pulled a blanket down from the top closet shelf and put it on the floor. He stared at it and then leapt up onto my bed, apparently not that interested in cold oak floor planks. After shutting off the light and situating Tucker at the foot of the bed, I pulled the covers over my head and tried to get warm. The "Minnesota" debate continued to rage in my head. It was easy to picture my mother near a cozy fire, resettled in the beloved hometown she'd always missed, laughing with family and old friends and enjoying the evening in front of a television, something no one around here seemed to think we needed. I loved my McCray grandparents deeply, but I had fond memories of the Peterson side of my family, too.

My mother's parents lived in a grand house near Minneapolis that was not only equipped with a television but also filled with cousins and an endless parade of friends and neighbors. It was a wonderful place where we had spent several joy-filled summers. Now my mom deserved and needed that love and support. I just didn't know about myself.

When she met my father after the war, moving to a farm had been a compromise for a city girl who'd fallen in love with a country boy. Though she went willingly, the farm no longer made sense, not for her. The McCray farm was now merely a painful collection of reminders. She agreed I could manage for a few months without her, safe in my grandparents' care, while she resettled our family in Minnesota. After Christmas, which she and my sisters would spend on the farm, I would go back with her to start fresh, too.

For me, though, moving away from the farm seemed like a betrayal of my father. I thought perhaps I'd get over that feeling, but as the weeks and months passed, I could not let it go. There was part of me that hung on to a hope: if I just had enough patience, my dad might still walk right through that back kitchen door. For after all, he had been doing it every day of my entire life. He would be laughing with Grandpa Bo. On his face would hang the outdoors, punctuated with little bits of grease, grass, and dust cemented to his face by sweat and sun. He would be tired, but it was farm-tired: sore muscles, sun-bleached hair, and the ever-present assortment of scrapes and bruises that marked one day of simple toil.

Through it all, over the years, no one ever looked more alive to me than my father when he came home at the end of the day. If it happened, if this was all just really one long, cruel dream, I wanted to be there when the screen door slammed shut and he walked back into our lives.

So I stayed and waited and pretended that maybe tomorrow would be that day. My mother made it clear that she had not wanted to leave me behind, but she understood and allowed that I needed a few more months on that farm. So, in early September and with my full approval, she packed the car and drove off.

With my father gone, my mother moved to start over, my sisters away at college, and my grandparents lost in each other's arms, I was not sure where that left me, but I did know that I felt very much alone on top of that windswept hill.

Before long I could hear, like sand blowing hard against glass, the sound of little bits of snow and sleet tapping out a haunting rhythm on the windowpane. Tucker sneaked up from the foot of the bed and squeezed into the space between me and the wall. He felt warm and comforting.

Tucker's ascent from the back porch and into our home was now complete, but my work was just beginning. Very soon, things would begin to change.

T ucker needs his breakfast, too," my grandmother said as she set his bowl on the kitchen floor. He lapped up his food with vigor while we looked on.

"He eats more than George!"

"Very funny, Grandma."

My grandfather stood near the kitchen window, surveying the yard. "All we got was a dusting." He then turned his attention to a quick study of the dog. "He looks better. Food and a comb can do wonders for man and beast alike."

It took only moments for me to recognize what a good dog Thorne had stumbled on to. As I got ready for school that morning, it was clear that both my grandparents had reached the same conclusion.

No one in the house could pass the dog without petting him and making some favorable remark about either his appearance or his friendly demeanor. When I got out of bed that morning, I almost tripped over him. He had spent the rest of the night on the floor, at my bedside. Having a dog felt so normal, if not necessary—it was as if the McCray family had suddenly discovered the benefits of running water.

Looking back on it now, Tucker was the only living creature in our house who wasn't feeling sad, and perhaps that's why he established himself so easily in our hearts and minds. When he wagged his tail and acted content, he reminded us how happiness looked and joy felt. We sensed that there was a huge absence in our lives, and though Tucker couldn't fill it, his presence hinted, gave us some hope, that those vast empty spaces might someday be full again.

On Thursday afternoon, after dropping my lunch pail and books in the house, I trudged around the farm, doing my chores with Tucker by my side. It had been a while since I strayed far from the barnyard, and I thought today would be a good day to do some exploring. Grandpa caught up to us and seemed to have a new project in mind for us.

"Hold him for a second." He slipped a bit of twine around Tucker's neck and roughly measured its diameter, tying a small knot in the twine and stuffing it into his pocket. "I've got some leather scraps around the shop. I'll make him a collar. Do you want to help?"

"Nah, I think I'll take him for a good long walk down to the creek."

Grandpa reached into his jacket and pulled out a letter. "I almost forgot. This is from your mother." He handed the slim envelope to me, along with the rope we were still using for a leash. "You better take this, too. Just in case he tries to run off. Don't let him in the barn when I'm milking. I don't want him spooking the cows."

"I won't. Thanks, Grandpa."

I pocketed the rope and the letter. I wondered if he'd speculated on its contents and how he felt knowing that I'd told Grandma I might want to leave the farm before year's end. I knew that my grandfather, like Grandma, wanted me to feel that I would always have a home with them. I didn't want to hurt him in any way.

As Tucker and I walked away from our homestead, the late-afternoon sun reflected off his brushed coat in hues of deep burnt pumpkin and cinnamon that reminded me of autumn. The clouds hung low in the sky and made the blue space above us seem closer, yet still immense. It was brisk for November, but bearable with a sunny and gentle breeze that carried a musty timber smell up from the creek.

As we walked out of the barnyard, we passed by Dick and Dock. Both of the giant beasts were resting their heads on the top rail of their corral. Tucker ambled over to investigate the pair, but when he got too close, they kicked up their heels and disappeared into the barn.

"Come on, Tucker, let's go."

We headed east along the path that went past Thorne's cabin. At the edge of the fence line, we turned south, through the hayfields, and down to Kill Creek. Once we crossed under the fence, I slipped the rope around his neck so we could practice working on the leash.

When we got to the creek, I released Tucker and skipped stones. While I counted skips, Tucker sank down to his eyeballs in the creek, holding his head just above the water and lapping up cool drinks of the murky water with his tongue.

While resting in a little patch of grass by the bank, I watched the dog play in the water and tried to take in the pleasing aroma of the wild onions that were the last remaining bits of plant life tenacious enough to stand up to the advancing march of winter.

I pulled the envelope from my pocket, removed the letter, and started to read:

Dear George,

Everyone misses you terribly, but I'm at the top of the list! I like my new job and still can't believe how much they are paying me . . . three times what I made working for the telephone company when I was a teenager. I am enclosing a few pictures of your new house and your bedroom that I thought you might like to look at so they will feel more familiar to you when you get home. The house is only 5 minutes away from Grandad and Grandma Peterson! They spend lots of time over here and can't wait to see you. How are things there on the farm? I'm sure your grandparents are glad to have you around and I know they will miss you very much when you leave. Please assure them that we will all come and visit as much as possible! Trisha and Hannah are still loving college life—especially since they're at Grandad's alma mater and he and your grandmother join them for all the football team's home games. They were both home for the weekend and insisted that we make

"George's Oatmeal Cookies." I told them I would not dare make them until we could share them with you.

Grandma and Grandad Peterson asked me to tell you "hi," too. We'll see you at Christmas. I can't wait . . . miss you so much. I'll try to call you before we leave so we can start planning, packing, etc.

Love,
Mom

p.s. When I come back to Kansas for Christmas, I am going to make you a whole sack of your cookies!

I folded up her letter and put it back in my pocket. The house in the picture seemed huge by our standards and my bedroom was already decorated with a football bedspread and bookshelves. I had always wanted bookshelves in my room.

When I turned to the north, a growing chill was in the air. The sky was going from blue to gray and puffs of darker clouds were rolling in on the horizon. With each gust of wind, the few leaves that remained on the trees were letting go, accepting their place. Unfortunately, I had no such clear convictions. Kansas. Minnesota. Minnesota. Kansas. Where was my resting place?

The dog's nose was deep in a mouse run and his tail wagged rhythmically. I wondered how dogs sensed or thought about *home* and if Tucker might have something to teach me on the subject.

"Tucker, come on. It's time to walk back."

CHAPTER 8

S now day!" my grandfather yelled, his voice booming up the staircase.

Nowadays, when children hear grown-ups say "snow day" they rejoice because it means school is canceled, and they can sleep in and dream of a day spent sledding or building snow forts. But back then, those two words meant something entirely different in our house. It did not necessarily mean that I had no school. What it did mean, I did not especially want to hear at 4:30 on a Friday morning.

Tucker liked bunking with me, and I was happy to have a warm furry thing near me in the early-morning hours. He seemed ready to do his part to make sure I got up on time. Try as I might, he was hard to ignore. Once he heard my grandfather's call, he began yawning, scratching, and stretching.

Already my grandmother was brewing coffee, and when its aroma mixed with that of fried potatoes, eggs, and bacon, it was a strong call to draw me out of bed, though I remained huddled in a cocoon of warm covers for a few more precious minutes.

There was an additional sound on that November

morning: the powerful, deep rumble of the diesel engine on the maintainer as it first turned over. As the engine smoothed out, the muffled coughs of that old steel dragon gave way to a roar that was out of place on a cold winter morning.

I could hear my grandfather put the throttle into idle, allowing the engine to warm up; he often let it warm up for a good half hour, especially on very cold mornings. The cab door slammed shut. Grandpa was on his way to the house to make sure I was moving around. There was no need to pull back the curtain from the window; I knew what I'd see outside—snow.

Tucker, now wide awake, sensed that some action was afoot. He pricked his velvety red ears as if to say, "What is this 'snow day' stuff?"

The back kitchen door slammed and Grandpa yelled up the stairs a second time, "Snow day!" I was more than wide awake now, knowing that I'd have to take over my father's responsibilities and do the morning milking, so that Grandpa had adequate time to do his job, too—all before I caught the bus and put in a full day at school.

Tucker jumped off the bed, sensing the work that needed to be done, and looked at me. I thought I heard him say, "Let's go. Don't you know? It's a snow day."

"Not you, too! Okay, okay!" Between my grandfather's calls and Tucker's coaxing, I somehow moved past the adolescent brooding and resentment that had gripped me when Grandpa Bo first laid out the extra morning chores. Egged on by Tucker, I felt the tasks now more of a challenge than an unjust imposition, and I would rise to them—even if I was rising very slowly in this cold weather.

Forcing myself out of bed, I pulled my jeans over the long underwear that kept me warm. All the while, Tucker circled around me impatiently. I scolded him. "Look, Tucker, I don't have fur like you. I have to wear this stuff. You'll just have to wait."

Peering downstairs through the floor grate that allowed the heat from the kitchen to flow up into my bedroom, and which also was our unofficial intercom system, I yelled to my grandfather, "I'll be there in a minute!"

Tucker and I spilled down the stairs and into the toasty kitchen, ready to work. My grandmother hugged me as if she had missed me terribly. Her affection chased away any lingering chill in the early-morning air. She had her winter clothes on and was ready to help out with the milking.

"Snow day," she repeated, holding me tightly. I ate quickly. Grandma Cora's cooking, like glowing embers in the pit of my stomach, sustained and warmed me for hours—if not a lifetime.

There were twenty impatient cows to milk and only two hours to do it before I had to be ready for school, so Grandma and I got to work in the predawn hours. First, my grandmother filled two buckets with hot water from the kitchen sink and mixed in the special soap we used on the cows' udders and teats to kill any bacteria that could contaminate the milk. I patted Tucker on the head and reminded him that this was the one chore for which he would have to stay behind.

We put on our boots and headed out the back door, each carrying one pail of hot, soapy water that steamed all the way down to the barn in a cold morning air that both assaulted and embraced us.

There were floodlights illuminating the barnyard, so we could see how hard it was snowing. Already, there were two or three inches on the ground.

After pulling off my warm mittens, I lifted the latch from the hook and slid open the south barn door. As I let in the first six cows, Grandma poured their feed into the troughs. There might not have been much variety in their diet, but still each cow eagerly made her way to the breakfast table. To get to the trough, each cow pushed her head straight through the milking stanchions, which I closed behind them so that they were securely in place.

We were lucky, or so my grandfather reminded me. As far as modern inventions went, a close third behind the wheel and indoor plumbing was the Babson Bros. automatic milking machine.

The milk from our cows went first into a large stainless-steel container that was attached to the machine. To the uninitiated, it looked like a giant steel urinal attached to a motor.

As I strapped the Babson Brothers' finest invention to each cow, my grandmother scrubbed away, preparing for milking. My father or grandfather could complete this series of tasks with effortless motions, but with freezing fingers, and less experience, I moved clumsily. It was 6:30 before Grandma and I could close the barn door and call the job finished.

By 7:15, on that Friday morning of our first snow day, I was cleaned up and standing out by the road, waiting for the bus. Far to the west, I could hear the distant roar of the maintainer vanquishing our first snowfall by pushing it to the shoulders that flanked the roads. If it had only snowed a little bit more I might have been able to avoid school. Winter was only just beginning to stretch her legs.

CHAPTER 9

W ake up, McCray!"

Mary Ann Stevens pushed me from across the aisle of the bus. She wore her hair in ponytails and though she was a year older was not too snooty about associating with a seventh-grader like me. I liked talking to her on the bus and she seemed to fill in where my sisters left off. She shook me again. "We're almost there."

I opened my eyes in disbelief. "Already?"

The bus had followed the highway and arrived at the Crossing Trails Central School, which housed grades one through twelve. The school was but several years old. Before the county schools consolidated in the late 1950s, I could remember my older sisters riding their ponies to a one-room schoolhouse that was only two miles from McCray's Hill.

The road to the school was clear that morning since the maintainer had blazed through the snow just an hour earlier. I had rested my head against the cold glass window and slept the entire way. My first snow day had worn me out.

As I stumbled out of the bus, Mary Ann continued

to tease me. "Sleepyhead, I was talking to you for fifteen minutes before I realized you were asleep."

"Did you say anything interesting—for a change?"

"You'll never know."

I teased her back. "Next time I have a hard time falling asleep, I know who to call."

I had assumed that my teacher, Mrs. Weeks, liked me. That morning I realized I was mistaken. I barely had my coat off when she excitedly made her morning announcements.

"Class, the lead part in our annual holiday all-school play goes to . . ."

She paused dramatically as all the girls commenced oohing and aahing, as if one were about to be crowned Princess of the Kansas Territory.

"George McCray," she said proudly. "You will play the part of our narrator, Santa Claus! Isn't that exciting?"

This was awful. I smiled politely and tried not to groan. Last week she had mentioned the play, and I figured I would get stuck doing something, like building the sets. But this? Memorizing lines would take time and work—on top of all my other newfound responsibilities. Her news was hardly cause for celebration. My male classmates snickered at my "good fortune" until she began casting them as assorted elves, reindeers, and angels, which was even more humiliating.

Mrs. Weeks must have assumed that because I loved to read, a major part in the school play would fit me nicely and add some much-needed cheer to the first Christmas without my father. If Dad had been around, he would have helped me with my lines, and my mother would have made me a costume and a long white beard. It certainly wouldn't be that way this year.

My teacher was right about one thing—I did love to read, and I was one of the best readers at Crossing Trails Central School, even better than some of the high school kids. Instead of having to read what Mrs. Weeks assigned, I was allowed to choose whatever appealed to me, from Zane Grey to Walter Farley, Dickens to Defoe. Reading was a passion that I'd inherited from my father.

Dad never went to college, but he was far from uneducated and was insistent that we take school seriously. He read paperback novels, from the classics to pulp detective novels, and loads of magazines, his favorites being *Popular Mechanics, Sports Illustrated, Time*, and *Scientific American*. He remembered what he read, too.

He bought us the *Encyclopaedia Britannica* from a silver-haired traveling salesman who drove a long black Buick, wore a striped suit with a red bow tie, and swore up and down that with these encyclopedias the McCray children were virtually assured of success in their chosen endeavors.

For three years, my father stayed up long nights reading all the volumes. His mind traveled over a wide range of subjects the following morning. At breakfast, the conversation was as likely to cover wheat prices and weather as the feeding habits of orangutans or the farming techniques on an Israeli kibbutz in the Negev desert. My sisters typically acted bored, but Mom would always say, "Hush, girls, it won't hurt you to learn something."

My father read stories to my sisters and me every night, even when the girls claimed to be too old. Mom would walk in and out of the room and simply smile. I think she enjoyed watching him read to us as much as we enjoyed being read to. He chose rollicking adventure tales, animal stories, classics, and even fairy tales that always seemed to be just right for all three of us. Those evening reading sessions were among the things I missed most about Dad.

Although it was hardly compensation for being cast in the play, Mrs. Weeks did give us a free period later that day, encouraging us to start learning our lines. But I decided to write to my mother. We had a lot of catching up to do.

Mom,

It's been a busy week. I have really been missing you. I'm just not so happy here on the farm, without you and Dad. I had to get up at 4:30 this morning to do the milking and Grandpa has LOTS of snow to clear. It's not that bad getting up so early, but I really don't like it that much. I'm taking care of Frank Thorne's dog. We named him Tucker—Mr. Thorne never named him anything, as far as we know—and I like him a lot. I got the part of Santa Claus in the school play. I hate that, but Eddie Sampson has it worse. He has to be an elf

and wear red tights. Happy Thanksgiving—ours will
be a quiet one, but we can't wait to have you here for
Christmas.

Love you and miss you so much,
George

Though I used the letter to let off steam about the
extra work, my goal was simply to let Mom know how
much I loved and missed her. I purposely stopped short
of telling her that I couldn't wait to move to Minnesota,
and that I was considering taking her up on that offer
of a bus ticket. Writing it down on paper felt like a real
commitment, and a reality I wasn't ready to confront.
Once again, I wondered fleetingly what would happen to
the McCray Dairy if I left it behind. How would it be for
Grandpa Bo and Grandma Cora to be alone on the farm?

On the bus ride home that afternoon, I tried to memorize my lines, but it was hard to concentrate. It occurred
to me that if I left Kansas before Christmas, I would get
out of having to play Santa. Somehow, though, the idea
of leaving just to avoid memorizing a bunch of words
didn't do much for me. The wind shook the bus and we
had to drive slowly to avoid the snow that drifted across
the county roads. I knew that my grandfather would be
out late into the night. I did not know that very soon he
would have a reluctant helper.

CHAPTER 10

Grandma, I can do the milking on my own today."

Complaining to my mother seemed to have purged some of my resentment. Besides, it was Saturday morning, so there was plenty of time.

"Thanks, George. I could use the rest." She sat down in her chair. Scratching Tucker behind the ears, she pulled him close to her. "Tucker and I will have a cup of coffee and wait for the sunrise."

When the work was done, I rested inside, but I quickly grew bored, so I bundled up to walk Tucker—the part of my dog-sitting responsibilities that I enjoyed the most. Tucker loved to walk, too—so much so that in the days to come, it would seem almost cruel to deny him his out-doors time. That Saturday we ventured to a place where we would return many times.

My family always called it Mack's Ground, though Mack was an early settler who had long since died. Decades earlier the land had passed into the hands of Mack's descendants, who lived in Texas and didn't pay much attention to their Kansas holdings. Tucker and I made it our private park.

Mack's Ground was a thousand acres of timber,

creeks, and secluded meadows that started out just east of Thorne's house and went on for several miles. They were mysterious and ancient acres. While Mack's collapsed old cabin was worth digging around in, my favorite place was Mack's Lake. It was bordered by forest and filled with bass below the water and ducks above. The lake was built by the WPA in the 1930s. The banks were lined with stones, which made it perfect for fishing.

My grandfather told me that lots of lakes were built in that period just to keep men busy. As a young man, in his spare time, he himself ran a crew of horses that worked on several local lakes, including Mack's Lake.

Tucker was eager to point a rabbit or a covey of quail, though I wasn't much of a hunter. Lighting out after a squirrel or a woodchuck was more fun for Tucker than any game of fetch I might devise.

The best part of our journey was always returning to the lake, and that was where we invariably ended our late-afternoon scouting missions. Tucker loved to play along the shore. It was not yet cold enough for ice to cover the lake, so I skipped stones across the surface of the clear water and watched clouds pass overhead like herds of galloping white stallions.

Thinking about the week's events as my rocks careened across the glassy lake, I made a mental note to tell my dad about the school play. And then I remembered. When I remembered, I just sat and felt very empty. The world seemed like such a big place, and I a very little occupant.

Thanksgiving came and went, and it was, indeed, a quiet one with just the three of us, Tucker, and too much food (most covered with Grandma's gravy). The snow had come and gone, but mid-December was now upon us, and the reprieve was not to last.

One afternoon as the snow was falling again, and Tucker and I ambled back to the house from Mack's Ground, I heard the phone ring. A few moments later my grandmother appeared on the back porch. "George, it's your mother on the phone. Long distance!"

After knocking the snow off my boots, I raced inside to take the call from Minnesota. Today, a long-distance phone call is commonplace, but in 1962 it was an event.

It seemed like a scene from my old life—Mom talking to me after I came in from an outdoor romp. The only difference was that now her voice seemed riddled with sadness.

"I got your letter. I sure miss seeing you, too, George."

"Thanks, Mom."

Sounding as if she'd been crying right before she'd called, she continued, "I haven't been feeling like such a good mother lately, running up here to Minnesota and letting you stay behind. I don't know what I was thinking."

"It's okay. I asked you to let me. Remember?"

"I thought that being with Grandma and Grandpa was what was best for you, but maybe not. I didn't want to pull you away from your grandparents and the farm before you were ready, but maybe you should come up here now and not wait for the fall term to end. What do you think?"

Her suggestion was in line with what I'd been thinking, but I hesitated. I wasn't ready to pick up and leave right now, and in that moment I resolved to stay as originally planned.

"Mom, it's only another few weeks until Christmas," I began.

"Can you wait that long, George?"

"Yes, I'm okay," I assured her, but clearly she was not.

"All right, then. I suppose I can wait, too. We'll have a fun Christmas together, then head home. Now, tell me about Frank Thorne's dog."

I was thrilled to change the subject and talk about Tucker.

"He's about the best dog in the world. Tucker goes everywhere with me, except school, and Grandma says he whines for an hour after I leave."

"He sounds wonderful. I can't wait to see him. Tell me something else . . . What do you want for Christmas?"

For the first time in my life, I had not thought about

it. I knew what I wanted, but no one could deliver that. "I don't care. Anything is fine."

"George, you're quiet today. Are you sure you're all right?" she asked.

"Sure, Mom, I guess so."

"Are you looking forward to the move?"

"Sure, Mom, I guess so."

"Is that all you know how to say?"

I laughed. "Sure, Mom, I guess so."

"All right, then, tell your grandparents hello and we'll see you soon. I love you, George."

"I love you too, Mom."

Not an hour later, the phone rang again. Grandpa was still out working, so the sheriff just left a message. Thorne was getting out of jail and his court date was a week off. My grandmother marked the hearing date and time on the calendar they kept by the phone.

I tried not to notice.

It was 9:00 P.M. before my grandfather parked the maintainer in the barnyard after going over the roads one last time and came inside for a belated dinner. With Grandma Cora's help, I'd finished the evening milking. Tucker detested being left behind, tied up on the back porch or left in the kitchen, but he had no choice in the matter. Dogs and dairy cattle don't mix.

"Still snowing," Grandpa substituted for a greeting, stating the obvious. Tucker met him at the kitchen entrance, tail wagging as if he was happy my grandfather had made it home safely. Grandpa bent down and drove his cold hands deep into Tucker's fur and pulled him close, allowing Tucker to nuzzle into the gray stubble that grew on his neck.

"How much snow?" I asked.

My grandfather stood up and looked across the room at me. His eyes seemed tired. "Eight inches total for the last two days, drifting deeper. How did the milking go?"

My grandmother answered for me. "Don't worry, Bo, George has it under control."

Because my grandfather was not a talker, starting a

conversation with him was no easy feat. Saying something like, "How 'bout them Yankees?" would get you little, if any, response. With my father gone, he talked even less. The good thing was that when Grandpa Bo did talk, he usually had something to say, and everyone in the room would drop what they were doing and listen carefully.

Now he said nothing for a long time. Finally, he just nodded his head up and down real slowly and said, "Good."

"Will we have school tomorrow?" I wondered aloud.

The first person my grandfather called after dinner was Mr. Bangs, the principal at Crossing Trails. Mr. Bangs always followed my grandfather's advice on whether or not the roads were safe for the school buses. Forget the person who could push some secret red button in the White House. As far as I was concerned, the most powerful individual in the world was my grandfather; he was the one man who could pick up the phone and say, "No school."

Even if I did have to do the morning milking by myself on a snow day, school closings and downed phone lines meant adventure and excitement for me. It was a fair trade. I would take Tucker to explore Mack's Ground in the snow. It would be easier to read tracks and it would be far more fun than memorizing lines for a school play.

"Grandpa," I began, thinking that a little guidance from me could be helpful, "think about how bad it would be if a school bus got stuck in the snow. All of those poor little first-graders—they couldn't walk through eighteen inches of snow without freezing to death."

He just grunted. "Appreciate your concern, George, but I said eight and not eighteen."

After reading and setting tomorrow's clothes next to the heating grate to warm, I climbed into bed and tried to fall asleep. Tucker would join me when he was ready. Through the floor grate, I could hear my grandparents talking in the kitchen. If I concentrated, I could follow the gist of their conversation.

"If it keeps up like this, there will be no ambulance or fire service for much of the county."

My grandmother's voice was full of concern. "People might need medicine. There could be families without food or electricity for weeks on end. We could lose heat. And without heat, water lines will freeze."

"More is coming, Cora. It could be the worst snow in fifty years."

I was listening, as children at that age are still apt to do, hoping to catch a word or two about something else that was on my mind.

For as long as my memory served, the biggest day of my life was Christmas. Although my mother had brought it up briefly on the phone, no one in this household had mentioned it to me and it was only two weeks away. I did not know how to feel about Christmas this year.

What I wanted was going to be hard to bring down the chimney. It was an important conclusion I reached that night when thinking about a Christmas wish list. How do you ask for your old life back? Why couldn't things be like they were when my father was with us and we all lived under the same roof?

Christmas, it seemed to me, wouldn't be any good this year. How could it be when you were thirteen years old and knew, just knew, you were not going to get what you wanted?

This thinking about what I wanted and how I was not going to get it brought about an unpleasant realization. We all come to it eventually, and we forget about how much it hurts the first time it sinks in. As painful as it is, it's probably the first and most important step in growing up.

I remember very clearly that it came to me that night. Not getting what you want for Christmas is really an introduction to one of those facts of life that adults must face.

There was this vague but growing conclusion settling in my young mind that life does not always bestow upon us everything we want or think we should have. We are forced to move away from hoping others will give us what we want, to a new place where we must discover how to find happiness on our own. Santa was the last vestige of youth where all of our wants are magically delivered by some *other*.

Once again, a rule I considered inviolate had been disregarded. Christmas would be anything but the best day of the year for me.

It was like being in the middle of a really great Zane Grey novel, and when I got to page 100, just as I victoriously led my mare over the top of a windswept hill after outwitting the bad guys, someone switched in fifty pages of the bleakest scenes by Charles Dickens and messed up my perfectly good life.

Why couldn't things just be the way they used to be? I'd reached that awkward moment when a child—on the brink of young adulthood—realizes that he is not the center of the universe and is entitled to very little in this life unless he goes out and gets it for himself. From my still childlike perspective, Christmas was doomed to failure because no one could give me what I wanted.

Tucker finally decided to come upstairs. He whined and wagged his tail, and I coaxed him up onto the bed. He was fully capable of jumping up on his own, but he usually held out until I gave him permission. "Come on, Tucker, you can do it."

His warm body helped make me feel safe and secure. I pulled him close to me, buried my face in his coat, and realized that all I could do was hunker down and get through the winter. I would just have to accept that things did not always turn out the way they should. Maybe that was the new rule.

We rested quietly, and right before I fell asleep, things got worse.

"Cora." I heard the words come up through the grate. "Yes?"

"George has done a great job with Tucker."

"I know."

"I'm proud of him."

"So am I."

It was quiet and then my grandfather's words came up like thick, dark smoke. "Tomorrow is Thorne's hearing. Assuming he's coming home, I suppose he'll want the dog back."

Grandma let out an exasperated sigh. "I suppose so."

Yeah, that was the new rule. Things don't always turn out the way they should. It made no sense to me that Frank Thorne—a man I still viewed as a loser—should have a great dog like Tucker, languishing on a chain, when I could give him a good home, where he would be loved and well cared for.

A good home—I just didn't know where it would be.

The next morning I heard the maintainer fire up, but no one was rushing me out of bed, yelling "Snow day! Snow day!"

This meant that my grandfather had decided that the roads were bad enough to necessitate school closing. I guess my concerned pitch for the first-graders of Cherokee County had found a receptive audience. Grandpa had no idea how long it would take to open up all of the side roads and county lanes. He just hoped that the snow would stop soon.

Although McCray's Dairy had been spared, power and phone lines were down elsewhere. Until the roads were cleared, service trucks could not make repairs.

There were only a few road maintainers in those days. My grandfather was responsible for clearing the entire southwestern section of the county, and he had to make the most of the hours he could work the maintainer before even worse weather or total fatigue set in. Now more than ever, he had to "get at it."

I was fine with trading the drudgery of a school day for a few extra hours of laborious milking. Besides, my grandmother allowed me to start an hour later. Lying in bed till the genteel hour of 5:30 made the milking chores seem tolerable. Throughout the task, I couldn't help but wonder how Thorne's hearing would go, or if it would be delayed because of the snow.

After the milking was finished, I came inside and tried practicing the lines from my play, with Tucker at my feet, and read my favorite books by the fire. The day passed quietly, though Grandma Cora and I listened anxiously for my grandfather's return as the light began to fade. He'd been home for lunch, but we hadn't seen him in several hours.

Finally, he returned, with Tucker greeting him once more as if to say, "Where were you? We were worried!" Still, neither of my grandparents had said anything all day about Thorne's hearing. At dinner, Grandpa announced that there would be several more snow days and at least another day, maybe two, of additional school closings. Ordinarily I would have rejoiced, but I was increasingly worried about Tucker's fate.

"Before you go to bed, George, I want to talk to you." It was coming. My grandfather was not the type to orchestrate a conversation, so I assumed it could not be good. I tried to stall as I washed up and brushed my teeth, knowing that the subject matter of our talk was predictable. I went downstairs near the warmth of the fire and waited for Grandpa to look up from his newspaper. He seemed to be stalling, too, and his eyes were pained.

"George, you've done a good job with Tucker."

"Thanks, Grandpa."

"I spoke with Thorne today. They had the hearing, even with this rotten weather, and he's out of jail and back home. He asked me to thank you and says he'll come around and fetch Tucker tomorrow."

A fury gathered up inside me that I had not expected. "That's not fair. Why should he get him back? He doesn't even know how to take care of that dog."

"We both know you're going to Minnesota. It's been good for you having Tucker around, but it's time to move on. You knew at the start he wasn't yours to keep, remember?"

"I could take him with me."

"It's pretty simple, George. Tucker is Thorne's dog."

With angry tears on my face, I stood up and walked out of the room. Once again, nothing seemed fair. Bit by bit, everything I loved was being taken away from me—Dad, my old life on the farm, Tucker. Bitterness and resentment rose up from some dark space in my mind and I did not know where to put it.

The following morning, after the milking was completed and with school still closed, I decided to spend the entire day with Tucker, back on Mack's Ground. The idea of running away with Tucker, before Thorne could fetch him, had come to me the minute I woke up and now, as I was closing the barn doors, it gripped me.

In my often still-childish mind, I envisioned fixing up Mack's old log cabin, hunting and fishing for food, and fashioning clothes from animal hides. However unrealistic my dream was, I spent the morning cleaning up the cabin and making a mental list of what I would need for repairs to my new home. By late morning, the wind started to blow the snow and the absurdity of what I was planning finally sank in. For starters, there was one glaring omission from my plan of frontier survival: heat.

By noon, I had given up on running away. I sat down to lunch with Grandma Cora and she asked me what I had been doing. Although I may not have had the courage to run away, I did muster the strength to talk about it.

"I was wondering if I really have to go to Minnesota. Maybe I could move into Mack's old cabin with Tucker and the two of us could live back there."

"How would that work?" she asked with no judgment in her voice.

"With Tucker, I could hunt and fish for my own food."

My grandmother wisely ignored the limitations of my plan and tried to get at what she perceived to be bothering me. "Are you tired of living here with us?"

"No. It's not that."

"You're at the age when young men start dreaming about being on their own. Do you think that's it?"

"Maybe."

"George, your grandfather and I love having you live here and we are going to miss you very much when you leave for Minnesota."

It surprised me the way it just came tumbling out like someone knocked over a glass of water. "I don't want to move to Minnesota, but I don't know where I want to go instead."

She was quiet for a long time and I knew she was carefully choosing her words. "Sometimes, all of us wake up and wish we were somewhere else. That's natural, too." She laughed and said, "When it's cold like this, I usually think about Florida."

She took my hand. "George, you know something we all learn sooner or later?"

"What?"

She then told me something that I always remembered years later with a chuckle.

"George, honey, you don't have to run very far to run away."

She smiled and pulled her hand back. "You know someday this farm was going to be your dad's place, and now, with him gone, it'll be yours. Of course, it's up to you to decide if you want it. No one is going to make you take it. And if you're worried about what'll happen to the McCray Dairy when you're in Minnesota, now don't you be. We'll manage."

I didn't say a thing, so she continued. "You love the dog, don't you?" She found the missing voice for my thoughts that I could not locate on my own.

"Yes."

"You're mad about having to give him back and things just don't seem very fair right now, do they?"

"No."

"I remember when your grandfather first brought him home and asked you to be responsible for him. You resented it, didn't you? It's funny how things change. A few weeks ago you thought it was unfair that you had to take care of Tucker, and now you think it's unfair that you can't do it."

"That was before . . ."

"Maybe you should talk to Frank Thorne. Maybe the two of you could work something out. Who knows, maybe he would let you keep Tucker until you left. It's only a few weeks. He might not mind if you took him for walks after school. I bet there are options here you haven't even thought about."

"You want me to talk to Frank Thorne?"

"Sure, why not?"

"I don't like Frank Thorne." That was my way of *not* saying that I was uneasy around the man. More than once, I'd heard my dad say, "Frank likes his privacy." And, there were all of those stories about the Thorne family—how his grandfather had been little more than a horse thief, his dad a shiftless gambler.

"Why, I've known Frank Thorne since he was a baby. Did you know that Frank and your dad used to be friends in high school?"

"I guess."

"Just because he has a drinking problem, that doesn't make him a bad man."

Before I could think much more about it, the subject of Christmas came up. She stood, walked over to the kitchen window, put her plate in the sink, and turned back to me.

"George, what would you like for Christmas this year?"

I squirmed a little and realized that I did not want to answer her question. "I don't know, Grandma. What do you want?"

"I've never known you to be without a Christmas wish list. Surely there's something you want."

"I haven't been thinking much about it."

"George, you and I are having the same problem. It's

been awfully hard getting into the Christmas spirit this year. What are we going to do about it?"

She was right about that and we both knew it. "I don't think I want to have Christmas this year. Christmas is for little kids."

She put her hands on her hips and scolded me ever so slightly. "I am not a little kid and I still like Christmas."

"I don't know, Grandma."

"I know what will help us. Let's you and me cut down a tree this afternoon."

"Sure," I said halfheartedly, thinking how ruined this holiday already seemed. Why didn't Grandma just give up on Christmas? Before I could ask her, we were interrupted by the ringing of the telephone.

Grandma answered it. "Hello, Frank. . . . Sure, that'll work just fine. I think George would like to talk to you about the dog, too."

She hung up the phone. "Frank will come by tonight to pick up Tucker." I felt like someone had reached down my throat, grabbed my heart, and gave it a big yank. I went into the living room and just sat.

Knowing that it was coming did not make it any easier.

CHAPTER 15

Grandma did not tolerate my moping for long. She insisted that I bundle up and go with her to find a Christmas tree. In years past, this would have been fun. Today, it was a chore. Tucker tagged along for a while, but soon took out after a rabbit and decided to go on his own hunting expedition. He may have been a half mile off on Mack's Ground, but I was sure he could smell or hear us tromping along and would come bounding back when he was ready.

We pushed through the snow until we reached the woods that flank Kill Creek and where wild cedar trees grow like weeds after a summer rain.

Though it was snowing, it was not particularly cold. I carried a handsaw and we trudged along, with Grandma rejecting most of the specimens as too big, too small, or poorly shaped. She was ambling and enjoying the walk.

"George, you know this is going to be a hard Christmas for all of us."

"I know." Of course I knew.

She kept making excuses to hug me. "I sure do like school closings. I am going to miss you when you have to go back."

"I'm going to miss you, too."

"Let me tell you one thing that makes Christmas fun for me."

She had a big smile on her face and looked different all bundled up and walking outdoors. I could see a side of her that was playful and young and sad all at the same time.

"What's that, Grandma?" I stood with my hands on my hips and tried to catch my breath. Trudging through the snow was hard work. It amazed me that she kept up with so little effort.

"Thinking about that one special thing that someone might enjoy receiving that they did not even know they wanted. Like this Christmas tree, George; it might be just what you need—that one thing that gets you in the spirit."

She stopped and stared for a long awkward moment. Although I was not sure, I thought maybe she was trying not to cry. As she spoke, her words cracked in a few places. "I bet a perfect tree is just on the other side of the creek waiting on you."

"Do you think the ice is frozen enough for me to walk over?"

"I'm sure it'll be just fine. The water is shallow there. Go across and pick out the one you want. I'm getting a bit cold and may head back."

We had really not talked about how or why, but it seemed that Grandma Cora had led me right up to the west creek crossing. This was a place I had been avoiding.

As I walked over the ice and through the clearing in the woods that led to the meadow on the other side, I realized I was now standing in the place where Dad's accident occurred. I had been pushing the details out of my mind for months. Now, standing there in the meadow, I felt reality flowing over me and that day in June came blowing back in my face.

My mother was cleaning the kitchen and my grandmother was quietly working at her puzzle table. I was sorting through baseball cards on the living-room floor. My sisters were in town, working at their summer jobs.

Grandma Cora complained to me, "This one is the worst. The pieces are so small and the shapes irregular. I think your mom and your sisters have given up on it."

My mother yelled to us from the kitchen. "George, Cora, come in here. They're at it again!"

We had seen the hummingbird acrobatics many times before, but we wouldn't deny the combatants an audience.

Grandma and I joined my mother by the sink. Two male hummingbirds were fiercely attacking a third in an effort to drive him away from the flowers. They hovered, darted, dashed, and generally moved—horizontally and vertically—through the air with astonishing speed. Theirs was a well-thought-out battle plan. And as with all good plans, position on the battlefield was everything.

As we watched them zooming in and out of view, we saw my grandfather running up to the house, his face white. Instantly, we all knew that something was terribly wrong. When he threw open the back kitchen door, he hung his head as if he were pained to the bone, breathing hard. My grandmother took one look at him and ran to his arms. "What is it, Bo?"

He shook his head back and forth, as if to say no. "I'm so sorry, it's John, he's, he's . . ."

"What is it? What happened?" my mother pleaded, rapidly losing control.

My grandfather faced them both, his legendary strength drained away. "There's been an accident. The tractor flipped. John was killed—"

My grandmother screamed, and my mom buried her face in her hands, crying over and over again, "Oh, my God, no, not John!"

It was the worst day of my life in that house. It was as if the walls of our home, our lives, our very souls, just collapsed.

My father was cutting a field of alfalfa when it happened. The purple flowers attract bumblebees. He had been mowing near the bank of the creek when the tractor kicked up an entire nest. There were bites all over his body. He must have been fighting them off when he lost control of the tractor, which went over the creek embankment. He was thrown from the cab and hit his head on some rocks. He tumbled into the creek, and the tractor rolled over him, pinning him under the water.

My grandfather, wondering why the tractor had been quiet for so long, set out to check on his son. Good partners have a way of watching out for each other. It must have been terrible for him to have a vague worry change instantly into an unspeakable truth.

Six months after that day in June, I found myself standing in the same place my grandfather had found my father's body. It was a place I pretended did not exist—the place where all the rules were broken.

That running-away feeling came over me again. Suddenly hating everything about the farm that stole John McCray from me, I never wanted to see another field of hay, milk another cow, or touch another tractor. If I could, I would just get on the first bus for Minnesota and never look back. No one would blame me. The absolute finality of death was sinking into my young mind.

As much as it hurt, I accepted that my father was never going to walk through the back kitchen door again, no matter how long I hung around the McCray farm. There was no reason for me to stay here for another minute, thinking that he would.

Using the saw, I cut down the first tree I focused on, angrily hacking away at the trunk. When I finished, I grabbed the tree by the trunk and started to walk back toward the creek.

As quickly as the bitter resentment had welled up, it vanished. It was as if someone just pulled a plug and it all drained out onto the ground. In its place, there was nothing but loneliness.

Dropping the tree and plopping down in the snow, I had a long-overdue conversation with my dad. It was time to sort things out and tell him how I felt.

I love you, Dad, so much, and I miss you every minute of the day. I have this dog, Tucker, and he's been helping me out a lot. Well, he's not really mine but I sure wish he were. You'd like him, I bet. And I'm so grateful to have Grandma and Grandpa helping me out, too. But no matter how hard I try to stop feeling sad and lonely, I just can't help it. I try to stay busy—I'm doing the milking by myself on snow days, and I'm even in this stupid school play. But I don't know how to go about it all without you here. And I don't know if I should stay here or go to Minnesota. I miss you giving me advice. I miss you reading to me. And I'm really sorry for not doing all those chores when you asked.

"What are things like where you are, Dad?" I said out loud, with tears on my face. "Do you think I'll ever see you again? I sure hope so."

How I wanted his strong but gentle hand on my shoulder to tell me it would be all right and that all of these unbearable feelings would pass, and the world would operate by the rules again.

Listening hard, I was hoping for some sign. And then I remembered something he said to me many times before he died. He said that I should take the best parts from the men I admired the most in the world, add them all together, and then try to be that person. One thing I admired about both my dad and my grandfather was that when things went poorly, they always got back at it and tried again. They were both men who valued perseverance.

I realized that if he could talk to me today, that is what

he would tell me. I could hear his voice in my ears just as if he were standing there on the bank of the creek. And if I tried hard, I could feel his touch on my shoulder, too.

No matter how bad the roads, George, we just climb back up on the maintainer and try to clear the way. That's all we can do.

So, right there, I gathered my resolve, stood up, wiped the tears from my face, and made a resolution not to give up.

As I brushed the snow from my jeans, something moved at the top of the hill where we collect wild Easter lilies in the spring. I thought it was a deer, until I heard a bark and saw a dog running full speed after a rabbit. It was that big red Irish setter coming to join me.

Before long, Tucker's efforts were rewarded. A rabbit dangled from his jaws. He looked very proud and perhaps he sensed my sorrow, for he suddenly dropped his prize at my feet.

Some people might think it was an unimportant gift, but I knew that for Tucker, there was no greater offering. I had gotten my first and perhaps only Christmas present that year. He was trying to give me the most valuable thing that existed in his world. He was trying to make sure I stayed alive when doing so might mean he would go hungry.

I leaned over to scratch him behind his soft, floppy ears. "Thank you, Tucker. Thank you for being my friend."

It was time to go home, so I dragged the tree back across the creek. It was probably too big of a tree, particularly to haul a half mile back up to the house. But if Grandma was right and a tree was going to fix my Christmas, it was going to have to be a big one.

After I crossed the creek, I looked for my grandmother, thinking she might still be out walking, but she was gone. I could see her tracks leading back to the house. Seeing her solitary footprints, I sensed her own brand of sadness and was reminded of something my mother told me before she left. She said I mustn't ever forget that however hard it was for me to lose a father, and for her to lose a husband, it was just as hard for Grandma Cora and Grandpa Bo to lose their only child.

That night Grandma Cora put little bits of Tucker's rabbit in with the pot roast, and we offered him a plate of his own as our thanks for his sharing, and as a treat for his last dinner with us. After a brief discussion, with all of us trying hard to keep our emotions in check—even Grandpa—we'd decided that it was only right that Tucker should go back to his owner. After dinner, I think each of us said our private goodbyes to Tucker. All I could do was sit with him on the living-room floor, stroking his red coat and feeling the warmth of his body. I had no words for how I felt.

It was very cold and dark by the time Frank Thorne pulled into the driveway.

CHAPTER 16

Frank thorne was in his mid-forties, thin, and had a blond handlebar mustache that went well with his cowboy boots and hat. He smiled shyly as he stood at the back door, gingerly stepping into our warm house. Tucker looked at Thorne and wagged his tail, but he stayed at my side.

When my grandfather extended his arm to shake hands, Thorne had to pull his hands from his pockets. His fingers were stained with black grease. "Welcome home, Frank."

"It feels good to be back."

"Do you have any work laid out yet?"

"No. Not yet." He remembered that his hat was on and he hurriedly removed it. "Hopefully, I'll have something soon."

"Well, I might need some help on the maintainer, if this weather keeps up. You interested?"

Thorne paused. "I think I should have something come through any day now, but thanks for asking." He looked at me and continued, "George, I understand you've taken care of my dog for me."

"Yes, sir. I have."

"Well, thanks." He looked at Tucker, who was still waiting patiently at my side. "Come here, boy." Tucker wagged his tail and approached Thorne, but not before I gave him one final pat on his silky head. Thorne knelt down and petted the dog. "Good to see you, Red."

I could feel Tucker slipping away from me and I'm sure I sounded pretty desperate. "Mr. Thorne, I was wondering if you might sell me your dog?"

He looked at me dumbfounded. "Sorry, son, but I'm not looking to get rid of him." He slipped a chain around Tucker's neck. "Looks like you two have become pretty good friends, so you can come up and play with him anytime you want."

For the first time in my life, I wanted to rip the limbs straight off another human being. My face turned red as a pie apple. Grandma put her hand on my shoulder. "Well, thank you, Frank. I'm sure George would enjoy that. You take good care of yourself."

It was just more than I could stand, watching Thorne head out the back door with Tucker. My grandparents and I were silent as we listened to Thorne's truck pull out of our driveway. Suddenly, afraid I was going to say or do something I would regret later, I stormed out the back door. Once again, I had an overwhelming urge to run away from all this, but I had no destination. I simply stood in the dark, snowy yard, burning with anger despite the cold. I did my best to collect myself, for the sake of my grandparents, and after a while I went back inside. I still felt powerless and confused.

The next morning, when the bus drove by Thorne's house, I sunk down into my heavy winter jacket so Mary Ann wouldn't see the upset in my eyes. Tucker was tied up, resting beside Thorne's old brown truck, on a snowless patch of ground. I wanted to jump off the bus and take him, bring him *home*, but I knew that was impossible.

No matter how bad the roads, George, we just climb back up on the maintainer and try to clear the way. That's all we can do. I was trying to climb back up, but I just kept slipping. The path ahead was growing harder to follow.

CHAPTER 17

That afternoon, I got off the bus at Thorne's house to visit Tucker. The brown truck was gone, but Tucker was in his usual spot outside, tied to the post. After knocking on the door and getting no answer, I sat on the ground by Tucker. Wanting him to know that I had not abandoned him, I held him in my arms for a few moments, wondering how to best negotiate with Thorne. Finding Tucker a good home was proving just as hard as finding the right one for me.

Thorne's house was a mess—the paint peeled down to exposed wood, tires and car parts in the yard, and lumber strewn all about. The place looked scary to me and unsuitable for Tucker.

Armed with paper and a pencil from my book bag, I wrote a note to Thorne, opening with a little bit of salesmanship.

Mr. Thorne,
I know Tucker is a handful to care for, so if this dog is too much work for you, I'm still interested in buying him. I'm leaving for Minnesota in a few weeks, so let me know soon if you're interested.

Your neighbor,
George McCray

I stopped short of telling him that Tucker deserved a better life.

After searching for a place to leave the note, I decided to tuck it between the old, ripped screen door and the wooden front door, with its dirty glass window. As I opened the screen door, I could not help trying to look inside. As I pushed my nose against the windowpane, the front door swung open—it was unlocked. Thorne correctly surmised that there wasn't much worth stealing. Standing on the threshold, letting my eyes adjust to the dim light, I looked around.

IT WAS AS I suspected: chaos. The house appeared to be one big room with a bathroom and a bedroom at the back. There was a table covered with beer cans, newspapers, and bottles. On one wall, there were some photographs I could barely make out. One looked somehow familiar, but it seemed so out of place that it made no sense.

Before walking in to investigate further, I called out, "Mr. Thorne?" No answer. Wanting a better look at that photo, I took a chance and stepped inside. Trying to avoid piles of dirty clothes, broken car parts, and half-eaten bags of potato chips, I walked closer to the wall of photos.

I peered closely at the photo. It was a picture of my dad as a young man with his arm looped around Frank Thorne's shoulder. It looked like they were working on some old car, covered in grease, with broad smiles across their faces. Not understanding why my dad would want to be friends with Frank Thorne, I hurried out the door and pulled it shut, with my note stuck in the doorjamb.

Although it nearly killed me to do it, I turned my back on poor Tucker and walked home. I couldn't bear to say goodbye. He barked frantically and I felt awful for betraying that poor dog. I had no idea what to do or how to make things right.

During dinner, it was easy to avoid discussing what had happened with Tucker that day, as none of us seemed to want to raise the subject of the latest missing member of our household.

CHAPTER 18

The next morning I woke to the sound of the back door quietly shutting. I reached out for Tucker, but of course, he was not there. I heard my grandfather's work boots as he stepped slowly across the kitchen floor and pulled a chair away from the kitchen table. There was no "snow day" announcement, as there had been for much of the last week.

Why was my grandfather sitting alone in the kitchen with the lights off at this hour?

Huddling under the covers, knowing that something was wrong, I noticed an eerie yellow glow coming up through the floor grate. I could hear Grandma in the kitchen now, but still, they were uncharacteristically quiet. Worried and curious, I got out of bed, but when I tried to turn on the lights—nothing. We'd lost power.

After quickly dressing in the dark, I went down the stairs as best I could with no light. My grandparents were at the kitchen table, talking quietly. An old kerosene lamp with a gaudy Victorian shade rested in the center of the table.

"Good morning, George." My grandfather pushed a chair toward me. "Sit down and let me tell you what winter has blown our way." He chose his words appropriately as gusts of wind shook our house. There was a serious tone in his voice. Grandma Cora squeezed my shoulder as she rose from the table and started to make breakfast.

"George," my grandfather continued, "we have our work cut out for us today."

"Yes, sir."

"Another sixteen inches of snow fell last night and, as you've already figured out for yourself, we lost power. We still have the phone line, but that might not last much longer. We'll have to be extra careful about keeping the ice cracked on the pond and we'll have to milk by hand—just like when I was a boy. It's going to get a little uncomfortable around here. Can you help us out?"

This had to be serious or my grandfather wouldn't have taken so many words to say it. I had seen sorrow cross his face, but until that morning, I had never seen fear in his eyes or heard worry in his voice. My grandfather was comfortable barking orders, but this was different. Until that morning, I had never heard Big Bo McCray ask any man for help, and certainly not a boy like me.

There was only one answer to the question. "Of course I'll help. What can I do?"

"If you'll go down and crack the ice on the pond, I'll start the milking. Later today, I'll show you how to drive the maintainer. The only way to get through this is to take turns, working in shifts, night and day, until we dig out of this storm."

"Drive the maintainer!" I said, nearly falling out of my chair. This was a big step up from milking alone. I felt a mix of fear and excitement.

"He's only thirteen!" my grandmother warned. "Bo, I told you earlier, it's not a fair thing to ask him to do." Her voice cracked and tears began to fall.

"He's old enough, Cora, and you know I need his help."

"Then I'll take a shift driving, too," she said, wiping her eyes. Like many farmwives, Grandma could drive a truck on a dirt road and a tractor across a field, but I couldn't recall her driving the maintainer in a snowstorm.

"Cora, you're strong, but you can't handle this. And you need to stay and take the emergency calls and help George with the milking when I'm gone. You'll have your work cut out for you, too. I'll take two shifts to his one. That way I can sleep a few hours. Let's eat now and we can start to work at first light. George, you'll start by cracking that pond ice."

Certainly there was better help around somewhere in Cherokee County, but I was available, and Grandpa McCray thought I was the man for the job. Maybe my grandfather was just used to partnering with McCray men and wanted to keep it that way. It felt good to be trusted, though I still could hardly believe he was about to trust me with the job of driving the maintainer.

"Use the twelve-pound sledge and make sure the hole

is plenty big. You'd better bring a shovel so you can dig down to the ice."

These were my grandfather's last orders as I set out for the pond from the back door of our old Kansas farmhouse. It looked as if the entire sky had lost power, too; only a weak diffused light passed through the blowing snow and steel gray clouds. I wore rubber boots that were a good protector from the snow and the pond water but were poor insulators, and my toes were quickly cold. The weather turned harsh and unforgiving as it swept down from the north. No jacket could keep you warm, and the cold was only tolerable if you kept moving.

Intermittently, when the sun poked through, there were strong, defined shadows on a winter white pallet of freshly fallen powder. I suppose it might have been a nice day, if you were a caribou or a polar bear.

As I walked down to the pond, the daunting task of driving the maintainer weighed heavily on me.

CHAPTER 19

The drifting snow was up to my hips as I pushed my way to the pond, dragging the shovel and the sledgehammer. As I walked, I followed a path to the water that the cows had already trampled down. Every time I veered off the path, I stumbled into a little ditch or ravine hidden by the sea of snow.

In the winter months, because they were not foraging for grass, the cattle spent most of their time in the barnyard. We kept water for them in heated stock tanks. But with the electricity out, the tanks would freeze and they would have no other choice but to wander down to the pond for water.

In the brains department, cattle are way below horses and pigs. If they can't find a water hole, they'll wander onto the ice looking for one, and sometimes they'll break through and make their own opening to drink from—a farmer can only hope it happens near the bank, where it's shallow. Every few years some poor cow won't be so lucky. If it's cold long enough, she might wander out toward the middle of the pond toward deeper water. When the ice breaks, she can't get out. This is another reason we kept the stock tanks by the barn and why my grandfather wanted me to make sure there was a large, clear opening.

At the water's edge, I found a small hole the cattle had been using. I used the shovel first to clear the snow away from a four-foot-by-four-foot opening near shore. The ice was smooth and clear beneath the snow.

I raised the sledge and brought it down hard on the surface of the ice. The sledge seemed to only glance off the frozen surface, with sparks of ice blasting into my face. I looked down at the half-dollar-size dent and tried again, and still again, with little result to show for my efforts.

It seemed that the ice was more determined and a lot tougher than I had given it credit for. I tried again, this time closer to the small opening the cows had made on their own, and had some success. I was able to break off a piece the size of two bricks. I pulled the piece of ice out of the water and in the process soaked my gloves.

From that small beginning, I grew encouraged and chipped away, but still, it was not nearly a large enough opening.

With visions of Paul Bunyan and Babe the Blue Ox in my head, I swung down as hard as I could. The sledge glanced off the ice and twisted out of my control. The next solid object it came into contact with was my foot. Even though the ice absorbed much of the force, it still hurt, sending a jolt of pain up my leg and knocking me clean off my feet. After letting out a yelp, I fell, bottom down, into the very hole I had cut into the ice. This was not going well.

I was hoping that no one could see me in this most ridiculous of positions, seemingly resting my backside in a giant frozen toilet bowl, when I heard the first howls of laughter.

"Are you okay?" my grandfather asked between spasms. He had been standing there all along watching me, holding a sixteen-pound sledge in his hand.

"I guess. I sort of hit my foot."

"What did you do that for? You were supposed to break the ice and not your foot. And, George, if you needed to use the pot, you should have gone back up to the house."

My grandfather let out another laugh from the deepest part of his belly and offered me his hand. I stood up, sore foot and all, looked at my wet backside, and laughed right along with him.

It was nice to see my grandfather laugh. I hadn't seen him do that in months. I teased him right back. "Well, what are you standing around for? We've both got work to do."

I swung the sledge again, this time with force and control, as much as anything to prove that he had not chosen a boy for a man's job.

He bellowed, "Good shot! We'll do this together, like old-time railroad workers."

He brought his sledge down hard on the ice. It was as

if our pond had become a bass kettledrum, booming in the early-morning hours.

Soon we found a rhythm and chunks of ice gave way to our assault. My grandfather used the shovel to flick the blocks of ice out onto the pond's surface. When we had the four-foot area cleared, he knelt down in the snow to catch his breath.

His voice took a serious tone. "Do you remember when Mr. Riley lost eighteen head, all drowned?"

"Yes, I remember."

"It's an important job I'm giving you. Do you understand?"

"Sure."

"Until we get power, can you keep this hole wide open?"

I nodded my head up and down. "Yes, I can do it."

"Now that we have the hole cut, it'll be much easier just keeping it clear of ice. Why don't you go inside and change your clothes. When you're ready, we'll start the hand-milking."

As I put on dry things, I thought of the maintainer again. I knew more about hand-milking—which wasn't much—than I did about driving that big machine. But I would let Grandpa teach me in the order he saw fit. I joined him at the barn and we let the cows in, six at a time.

Once in the barn, each cow buried her wet, steaming snout into the trough filled with the feed that we stored in the grain bin for the winter. While they enjoyed their breakfast, my grandfather and I went to work on the other end, milking the old-fashioned way.

Bo McCray could milk twice as fast as any man alive and certainly faster than me. By 7:30, we had all of the milk up and into the cooler, where it would stay until we could move it to the end of the driveway. Though the cooler could not refrigerate the milk since we had no power, it was still cold enough to hold it at the right temperature.

I asked my grandfather, "Why aren't we putting it out by the road for the dairy truck?"

"Until you and I get the roads cleared, there won't be a dairy truck or a school bus or much of anything else getting through. You can go inside and stay warm. I'll start the maintainer and meet you in the driveway."

This was it. He was expecting me to actually drive the maintainer in the snow. Farm boys operate machinery, big machinery, by the time they are thirteen, and I was no exception. I'd learned to drive a tractor as soon as I was tall enough to reach the pedals. But this was more involved. This machine was enormous and even in 1962 probably cost my grandfather as much as a small house. The county paid him by the hour to operate the machine, but he owned it.

A machine this big surely needed a pilot of similar proportions. Besides, I would be expected to navigate it on roads and not through empty, flat farm fields. It was an entirely different set of operating rules. I did not even have a driver's license.

I had ridden with both my father and my grandfather in the cab of the maintainer many times before. On a couple of occasions, during the summer months when they were just grading gravel, they had let me operate the grader on my own, but they were in the cab with me, so there was little risk. It seemed like it was "just for fun." This was for real.

I was very confident that I could grade gravel on a warm day, but grading snow, alone, was a different matter. There was something else, too. As I was walking up to the house, Grandma Cora's words came to me. "It's not a fair thing to ask him to do."

My father had been killed working on a medium-size piece of farm machinery, and now my grandpa was asking me to climb on the maintainer—the biggest, most dangerous, and most difficult machine parked in the implement shed. At first I'd been flattered that Grandpa was trusting me to do this, but now I was downright scared, not sure this was a fair thing to ask of me. Maybe the time would come when I could do this, but now?

As I changed my clothes, these doubts continued to race through my mind. As cold as it was, a clammy sweat formed on my back. When I got ready to leave, my grandmother handed me a sack with cookies and two thermoses—coffee for my grandfather, hot chocolate for me. She tied a scarf around my neck. It was one that my sister had given to my dad last Christmas. She gave me a long hug. "George, *please* be careful."

"Grandma?"

"Yes?"

"I want to help, but I'm not sure I'm ready to do this. Not yet."

She grabbed my shoulders and looked me straight in the eyes and smiled. "If you don't want to do it, just don't do it. He'll ask someone else. He might not like it, but he'll understand. There will be more snow to plow in Kansas on another day."

I don't know why, maybe because I trusted her so much, but I wanted to be totally honest with her. My voice had one of those embarrassing cracks as I told her exactly how I felt. "I'm kind of scared."

She put her arm around me again and pulled me tight against her. "Of course you are. You should be."

"I don't want to disappoint Grandpa."

She looked at me very seriously. "The choices we make when we are young can define us for the rest of our lives. There is nothing wrong with being cautious."

I choked out my words. "How do we know?"

"If your mind can't tell you, then either trust your gut or follow your heart."

I had been struggling trying to figure out a lot of things in the last few weeks. For once, something difficult made sense to me. Instead of trying to figure out where to live my life, I needed to concentrate on how to live it. My grandfather's request for help was like an ancient horn sounding from a mountain-top—a call to courage. It reverberated not in my ears but in my soul.

In the future, I would have to answer the call alone. This time, the first time—the most frightening of times—I had my grandfather to stand beside me when I answered the call.

I kissed my grandmother on the cheek, pulled on my hat and gloves, and smiled the biggest, most confident smile I could muster.

"I've got work to do." I turned and walked out the door and in some ways never came back.

That morning in December, I became a maintainer. Lifting the blade, adjusting the angle, correct grading speed were all subjects introduced by Big Bo McCray before we left the driveway. But it would be many years before I realized what was really being taught. My grandfather was giving me a new book of adult rules so I could shred the childish primer that had so let me down that year. I learned to become suspicious of rules rooted in entitlement and my needs, and to instead respect rules mortared by truth and concern for others.

The memories of the days that followed, of working side by side with my grandfather, would carry me through other times in my life when I needed to heed the call not just to maintain roads but to maintain my life—times when I needed rules that would never let me down.

CHAPTER 20

My grandfather took one task at a time and tried to explain as we moved down the road toward town. "The transmission exchanges speed and power. The lower gears give you more power to move heavier loads of snow, but with less speed. You'll do most of the grading in third gear, unless the snow is deep; then, you should use second."

There was a lever on the right of the driver's seat that adjusted the blade height. "I want you to listen very carefully as I lower the blade just an inch."

I felt the maintainer's engine struggle and our speed reduce slightly. The sound of snow coming off the road was interrupted by occasional pings of gravel bouncing off the blade.

"Now look behind you at the stream of snow coming off the blade. What else do you see?"

"Pieces of gravel mixed in with the snow," I said as I glanced over my shoulder.

"That's right. In the summer months, Cherokee County spends a lot of money putting gravel down on these roads. They don't want the McCrays spending the winter months putting it in the ditch."

"Now listen again. I'm going to raise the blade a few inches above the perfect height." The maintainer seemed to surge forward and the engine was less burdened. "Now turn around and look again. What do you see?"

"The maintainer's tires are leaving a trail through the snow."

"Good boy, George; that's when you know the blade is too high. You shouldn't be leaving enough snow for the tires to form big tracks."

"Makes sense."

"George, there is something else you need to know. This is a big, strong piece of machinery. If you take it where it's not supposed to go, you will get into trouble."

I was painfully aware that he was alluding to my dad, but I asked anyway. "What do you mean, Grandpa?"

"You've got to know exactly where you are on the road at all times. Too far to the right or the left and you can drop a tire into the ditch and get stuck, or worse. If you don't watch ahead of you, you can hit a car. If you don't watch behind you, you can't tell if you're doing your work right."

"How can I watch all four directions at once?"

"You can do it. It just takes practice. Go slowly at first, until it comes naturally to you." He slowed down, turned left down a county lane, and brought the maintainer to a stop by the side of the road. He opened the maintainer door, moved off the seat, and stood tall on the running board. "Well, scoot over and give it a try."

I stood up from the small space to his left where I

had been perched and settled into the driver's seat. My grandfather nodded at me to proceed, staying on the running board. Stretching my legs out so I could reach the clutch pedal, I placed the transmission in third, opened the throttle, and slowly let out the clutch until it reached the friction point. With the door open, snow and cold air was blowing into the cab, but I ignored it and tried to chart a course down the lane. I looked at the road in the rearview mirror and could see my tracks, so I inched the blade down a little.

Before I had gone too far, my grandfather gave me some more instructions. "Practice starting and stopping a few more times and try to keep the left edge of the blade in the dead center of the road. That way you'll clean the entire road when you come back at her from the other direction."

When I looked behind me, I could see that I was not staying on a straight course but was meandering on and off the center line. "I'm having a hard time keeping it straight."

"You're doing fine. Just draw an imaginary line on the side of the road and keep your right wheel right on top of it."

By midday, after a few dozen instructions and corrections, my grandfather and I had cleared Moonlight Road, Prairie Center Road, and Four Corners Road. We were now ready to head home for lunch.

That morning it seemed my grandfather spoke more

words to me than he had in the months leading up to December, and he seemed very pleased with my grading.

Over lunch, my grandmother went over the list of emergencies phoned in by locals.

"The Rathers' daughter is pregnant and the due date is only a week off. They are worried about getting to the hospital and hope you can keep their road cleared."

"Sherry Rather," my grandfather mused. "That would be off of Waverly Road."

"Do you know Waverly Road?" he asked me. "It's south of the highway and north of Lone Elm Road."

"Sure, I know that stretch and I know right where the Rathers live."

My grandmother picked up the next note. "Mrs. Slater only has two days of insulin left. She lives just off the highway on Crossing Trails Road."

"Yeah, I know where that is, too."

My grandmother turned to the last scrap of paper. "Old Mrs. Reed called and wants to make sure you don't forget her."

My grandfather rolled his eyes. "I just cleared her driveway two days ago."

My grandmother laughed and said, "You know how those old people are, worrying all the time."

"Cora, Mrs. Reed is only four years older than me!"

My grandmother smiled but said nothing. My grandfather took out a piece of paper and drew me a map. "George, take a look at this. Does it make sense?"

I looked it over and I knew exactly what he had in mind. "Sure, Grandpa. I get it."

"Now, take your time and do a good job. I am going to sleep a few hours and when you get back, you rest up and I'll do another shift. Do you have any questions?"

"Just one."

"Yes?"

"What if I have a problem? A breakdown?"

"You're never going to be more than about eight miles from home, since we're in charge of an eight-mile radius of roads. So, if need be, you can walk home. There are extra gloves and hats in the cab. Stop at any neighbor's house, if you need to, and they can try to get you home. I've been clearing snow for twenty-five years with that old beast and she hasn't let me down yet. I wouldn't worry."

He then turned to the sink and filled his tin cup with water and handed it to me. "Drink up."

My grandmother gave me a sack of her chocolate chip cookies, refilled my thermos, and sent me out the back door to clear the roads of Cherokee County.

Forgetting all my fears and feeling as if I'd grown five inches that morning, I pulled open the door to the cab, put the maintainer in gear, eased out the clutch, and started down the driveway on my first solo job. Going a little slower than necessary, I built my confidence one step at a time, heading east.

As I passed Thorne's shack, I slowed down to get a better look. His brown truck was there, but Tucker was no place to be seen. Thankfully, Thorne had enough sense to keep Tucker inside in this snow. I wondered if he was ignoring my note or even if he'd been sober long enough to think about it.

The maintainer thrust the snow away effortlessly. Still, I had a hard time keeping the blade centered in the middle of the road, and more than a few passersby must have wondered if old Bo McCray was losing his touch.

There were few drivers out that day, but those I did see waved and seemed surprised to see me behind the wheel. The sight of Bo McCray's grandson on that giant maintainer was probably enough to discourage them from any further use of the roads.

While I graded, my grandfather did the afternoon milking. Around five o'clock that evening, approaching home, I slowed again near Thorne's place and looked for Tucker. Thorne's truck was in the driveway and Tucker was tied up outside, but this time closer to the porch, where he at least had some shelter from the snow. He must have known it was me, for he pulled on the chain, wagged his tail, and barked in a familiar way. I considered pulling in but thought it might only make things worse, so I headed up the hill and called it a day. Before going inside, I checked with Grandpa to make sure he didn't need anything. He sent me, sledge in hand, down to crack the ice on the pond.

Once a quick dinner was behind us, Grandpa headed back out to refuel the maintainer from the three-hundred-gallon diesel fuel tank we kept by the barn. With a full tank, he climbed back in the cab, pushed the throttle wide open, and didn't quit grading until early the next morning.

Lying in bed that night while he worked, I remember being a little skeptical about Grandpa's nighttime grading. I had tried to plow in the dark before. Even with headlights, it was very hard maintaining a straight line and an accurate plow depth. Grading in the dark would be even more difficult. Still, I had a lot of confidence in my grandfather and told myself that he was up to the task.

We repeated this same process the next day. It was still snowing, but not as hard, and Grandpa looked tired. While we did the milking together, he told me about the old days when he had to maintain the roads with horses, like Dick and Dock. He said it was slow going, but there were fewer roads.

The horses could not move snow this deep and the county would be left waiting for a thaw. It was different then; people were more self-reliant, and there was no electricity and no phone lines or ambulances in the county. It didn't matter much if the roads were clogged.

He kept the harness and the old horse-drawn blade stored in the implement shed along with other McCray prized possessions: an International Harvester and a Massey Ferguson tractor, plows, cultivators, seed drills, rotary and sickle-bar mowers, hay rakes and balers.

Some of the farm equipment was new, most was old, but all of it was constantly breaking.

The old road blade had not been pulled by horses for

decades, but from time to time my grandfather would ride Dick or Dock, most always in the Crossing Trails Pioneers' Parade each spring.

My guess was that he kept the horses and old blades around for a reason. If the maintainer ever broke, he was prepared to clear the roads with horses, though by 1962 they were far too old to do the job. If the horses couldn't pull the blades, he owned countless shovels and we would get at it one scoop at a time. Some people might have described him as stubborn, but that was only part of the story—Big Bo McCray was a fighter.

CHAPTER 21

The next morning, after I finished milking the cows and clearing the ice on the pond, my grandfather and I went to the barn. He asked me to remove a milk can from the cooler and help him pour it into twenty sterile glass bottles. What was left in the can he took outside the west barn door and let spill out onto the ground. "What are you doing?" I asked.

"The dairy trucks can't get through and the cooler is full. The dairy won't accept milk that's not fresh."

"Aren't we keeping the roads clear enough?"

"We're doing fine, but the other county maintainers are behind. They have not been able to get north to the dairy road and the last six inches of snow has really slowed them down. The dairy can't take the risk of coming this far out and getting stuck. If that happens, they lose an entire day of collection. It's safer for them to wait until the roads are better."

"Why don't we help? We could do the road to the dairy for them. I can do it today. Right?"

"Getting through to the dairy might be what's best for us, but there are others in this county that we have to think of, too. How would it look if I did what was good for us and ignored all the other people that have needs?"

"Not that good."

"That's right. We have a list of priority roads that have to be cleared first and the road to the dairy does not happen to be one of them."

After we sat down to a quick breakfast, he drew up another map and put two large milk crates on the table. Not only did I have roads to grade, but I also had deliveries to make.

"People can't drive on the roads and we've got milk to give away. I will put twenty quarts of milk in the back of the maintainer in the crates. There's already a box in there with eggs and other staples. I'm collecting extra food and supplies along the way from our neighbors and trying to redistribute to the families that don't have enough. With more and more phone lines down, and roads blocked, people are short on basics."

"What do you want me to do, Grandpa?"

"I want you to pull into every house you pass and clear their driveway for them. Most of the farmers have small driveway blades they pull behind their tractors, but with the maintainer you can do in two minutes what would take them all day. Next, get off and knock on the door; try to make sure everyone is getting along all right. Offer them anything they need from our supplies and try to collect back their extras in exchange, including empty milk bottles, so we can refill them." He hesitated and looked up at me. "Can you do this, George?"

I hesitated for just a moment. Tired and unaccustomed to working so hard for so long, I needed a break. My grandmother's words were still lodged in my mind. This was getting to be very hard work and still I couldn't help wondering if there wasn't someone else who could do it better than me. It seemed to me that my grandpa and I had to do all of the work for the entire county. While I wished my dad were here to help, I knew what he would tell me. It was our job to take care of the roads. It was our duty to help our neighbors. *Just climb back up on the maintainer, George, and clear the way.*

"I'll do my best."

"We need to move faster, George, before things get worse. I have a few tricks saved up for big storms. First, let's bring up the blade and leave three inches of snow on the road. Cars can push through a few inches and we can move faster the less snow we have to push. You should be able to stay in third gear that way. Next, we're going to clear one lane on all the major roads. We'll come back and clear the other lane later."

"That way the emergency trucks can at least get through?" I asked.

"That's right. But here's what you need to do. We're creating a lot of one-lane roads. The problem is when two cars meet, no one is going to want to yield the right-of-way for fear of getting stuck. There will be problems."

"So, what do we do?"

"First, I want you to ask everyone to stay off the roads for forty-eight hours and give us a chance to get both lanes cleared; essential and emergency driving only. Next, every quarter mile or so, you'll need to back up and create a wide space, like a turnaround, where two cars can squeeze by each other."

"I can do that."

"You can follow a half mile or so of what I did last night and get a better idea of what I mean. George, there are two priorities today—things you have to do."

"What?"

"First, you've got to get the road cleared into town so the fuel truck can get out here and deliver us more diesel. We've got only a two-day supply left."

"Okay. What else?"

"There's insulin in the box for Mrs. Slater that I picked up from Dr. Richardson last night. She has to get it today. She could get real sick without it, maybe even die. Do you remember where she lives?"

"Crossing Trails Road."

"That's right."

My grandmother handed me a bag lunch and a thermos. She kissed me and said, "Be careful, George."

"Don't worry, I'll be fine." I said these words as much to convince myself as to convince her.

On that cold December morning, I set out clearing the roads my grandfather had outlined on the map, stopping at each house along the way. My first stop would be the hardest of all. Frank Thorne's house.

CHAPTER 22

With the maintainer in second gear, I pulled into the driveway. From the placement of the tire tracks in the snow, it looked like his truck was stuck. As my grandfather had requested, I graded his driveway, such as it was, parked the maintainer, and mustered my strength to knock again on that old front door to make sure Thorne was not in dire need of supplies.

Tucker immediately started barking, but I could tell it was not an anxious or cautionary bark. He knew it was me and was just excited. I knocked again, but still there was no answer.

I opened the door slightly and was greeted by Tucker trying to push through to the porch. Though I wasn't an experienced dog owner, I recognized the whines of a canine that needed to get outside and do its business. After a moment he came running back to me and I opened the door again, letting him back into the house. He was jumping up and down excitedly. It seemed that he was missing me as much as I was missing him. I leaned in across the threshold. "Mr. Thorne, are you home?"

The house was dark and the morning light was not strong enough for me to see well. I pushed Tucker aside and stepped in and gave my eyes another second to adjust to the dimness. I tried again. "Mr. Thorne, are you here?"

I heard a wheezing noise. By the door, there was a small table with a lamp on it. I found the knob and tried to switch it on. Thorne had lost power, too. The only light came from the dying fire in a potbellied stove.

Even in the shadows, I could tell the room was dirtier than it had been the last time I was there. Frank Thorne had not let Tucker out and the dog had left a mess or two of his own, which added to the stench. No wonder he'd been so desperate to get outside. On the sofa in the corner, not far from a window, Thorne looked up with a half-dazed stare. "What do you want, boy?"

I felt myself quiver.

"Go ahead, boy, spit it out." He seemed impatient.

"Mr. Thorne, my grandfather asked me to stop by. I mean, I'm grading the roads. We're taking shifts because of all the snow. I graded your driveway for you. He wanted me to stop in and make sure you were all right and see if you needed anything. I've got some extra milk and eggs, if you need any."

He struggled into a sitting position. "I am too sick to eat a thing. Come over here, kid."

As I approached, I realized how icy cold the room was, its only heat source the dwindling embers in the stove. No wonder he was sick. I tried to navigate around the mess on the floor. When I got closer, I could see that Thorne was trembling.

"I got that note of yours. So you want my dog?" His tone was scornful.

Of course I wanted Tucker, but I didn't like the way he asked the question. "I think I could take real good care of him."

"That dog is the only thing I got that is worth a plugged nickel to me." He looked around and waved his arms. "This ain't no palace." He called to Tucker. "Come here, Red."

To my surprise, Tucker wagged his tail and went to Thorne's side. The sick man ran his hands through his coat and talked to him affectionately. "You're a good boy, aren't you?"

He looked up at me. "I tell you what, George; you drive that maintainer up to Wild Tom Turner's place, on Blackberry Hill, and you tell him that old Frank Thorne is in a tight spot and needs two bottles of his best . . ." He hesitated and added, "Medicine. You bring that back to me and then we'll talk about my dog."

He pulled his blanket around him and said, "How 'bout that, kid?" He coughed and collapsed back into the sofa. He was definitely sick with something, but I wasn't sure if this was the alcohol or something else.

"I'll think about it," I said quietly. I'd never heard of Wild Tom Turner or Blackberry Hill and I wondered if it was worth it.

"Don't think too long, boy. While you are thinking about it, throw a couple of logs into that stove."

I spotted some kindling and opened the stove door

and tossed it in. It was not enough to make much difference. "Do you want me to bring in more wood?"

"Ain't more, unless you're going to chop it. You just bring me my medicine and old Frank Thorne can take care of himself."

Having work to do and feeling uncomfortable, I turned to walk out. "Goodbye, Mr. Thorne." However hard it was to leave Tucker behind, I was glad to be out of there. Bending down before opening the door, I pulled Tucker close to me and whispered, "One way or another, I'll get you out of here."

When I stood up and turned back around to face Thorne, I couldn't help but sneak a glance at the picture of my dad and Thorne. It still made no sense: the man I respected the most and the man I respected the least in the same picture.

I climbed back onto the maintainer and headed east. Having so much work to do helped to reduce the number of times a day I thought of running away with that dog.

All of our neighbors were grateful to see me, and they wanted me to come in and get warm, but I told them that I did not have time. They all wanted to know what they could do to help. I explained about the food and the staying off the roads, and they handed over any extra food or supplies they could spare—matches, bacon, flour, lanterns, and more.

I pulled into the Fisher driveway next. Hank Fisher knew everyone in the county. It occurred to me that he could confirm the suspicions I'd been trying to push to the back of my mind. "Mr. Fisher, do you know a man named Tom Turner who lives someplace called Black-berry Hill?"

He was quiet and looked at me in a perplexed way. "Now, tell me this, George, why do you need to know that?"

"Frank Thorne asked me to pick up some medicine from Mr. Turner and deliver it back to him."

Hank Fisher rubbed his mustache like it itched something terrible. His eyes narrowed as if he were trying to make a decision. "George, I guess you're old enough to know this, so I'll tell you straight. Wild Tom Turner is a lot worse than Thorne. Stay away from him. Let Thorne run his own errands. The medicine that Thorne wants is alcohol."

I figured as much. I knew this was not something I should do for Thorne. On the other hand, if he was going to drink anyway, maybe it wouldn't hurt anything for me to help him out, particularly if doing so might bring Tucker back to me.

Doubting that Mr. Fisher understood my dilemma and what was at stake, I climbed back onto the maintainer and continued my work, trying as best I could to put Thorne's demands out of my head.

A boy driving a maintainer loaded with food and supplies must have been a strange sight, but each house where I stopped held friendly and grateful people who somehow knew me even though I did not know them. Invariably, they asked about their neighbors and wanted to know if there was anything they could do to help me or anyone else.

As the day progressed, I was reminded that the citizens of Cherokee County were one of a kind—generous, compassionate, and self-sacrificing. I was proud to be one of them, and I knew it would be hard to leave this community—my community—behind. I pushed Minnesota out of my head again, as I had done so many times in the last few weeks, and wondered at the number of people who wanted to lend a hand to their neighbors. Many offered to take a turn on the maintainer, but I knew that things would have to get much worse before Grandpa would accept help from anyone who wasn't a McCray.

Many folks, hardy as they were, seemed frightened by the extreme weather. For some, my grandfather and I were the only contact they had with the outside world that week. Whether friend or stranger, they all wanted news and information, but most of all they wanted Grandpa and me to know how much they appreciated what we were doing for them. Several commented that it was so quiet without television, radio, or phones and that all they had heard for days now was wind and snow blowing up against their windows—that, and the welcome sound of the giant maintainer in their driveway.

As I did my work, trying to properly grade the road, thoughts of Thorne and his proposition turned over in my mind, though Mr. Fisher's reaction gave me second thoughts. Still, what harm would it do if I got a couple of bottles for Thorne? If I didn't, he would find some-one else to get them for him. If I did, maybe I could get Tucker back.

On this, my third full day on the job, I worked straight through lunch, pulling off bits of my sandwich as I watched the road, and by 3:00 that afternoon, I was a little ahead of schedule.

If I went west six miles and two miles north to Cross-ing Trails, maybe I could get the road cleared for the dairy truck, but there was Mrs. Slater to worry about, so I decided not to risk it. She lived to the east, so I headed the maintainer in her direction, pushing snow out of the way as I went.

I had my eyes open, wondering if fate might put Tom Turner in my path. Like most people looking for trouble, I quickly learned that it is seldom hard to find.

There was no answer when I knocked on Mrs. Slater's door, and I wondered if she was staying with neighbors. After knocking again and waiting, I circled around the house and tried to look in some windows. I could see Mrs. Slater, who lived alone, lying on her sofa. Consider-ing the medicine more important than her nap, I rapped on the window. She stirred and turned her head to the noise but didn't get up, so I rapped again. She looked confused.

I went around to the back door, which was unlocked. I stepped inside.

"Mrs. Slater. It's George McCray. I have your medi-cine."

"Please come here." Her voice was weak, like she was sick.

I found Mrs. Slater perspiring despite the cold, and a little shaky.

"Do you have my insulin?"

Digging into my pocket, I gave her the small glass vials. "Yes, right here."

"Thank goodness you made it. I was all out."

After inoculating herself, she said she was feeling better. I went out to the maintainer and brought her back some milk and other groceries and promised that either my grandfather or I would look in on her again soon. She gave me a big hug and just would not stop thanking me.

As I made my way home on the maintainer, coming from the other direction, I noticed an overturned mailbox sticking out of the snow and a remnant of a driveway— more of a dirt trail and one I'd never noticed before. Then I saw the black lettering on the mailbox, U R N E R. This was it. A long lane wandered off the county road and up a hill covered in timber and brush. I was to clear all the driveways and this looked like a driveway to me. I backed up the maintainer and slowly climbed Blackberry Hill, moving snow as I went.

CHAPTER 23

At the top of a hill was a trailer, set amid a tangle of steel barrels, tires, and junky-looking car fenders protruding from beneath the deep snow in the front yard. I turned the maintainer around and sat for a second, trying to get up my nerve to either get out and go to the door or just put the maintainer in second and head back down the hill. Before I could decide, an old man came banging out the door, two scrawny black-and-tan coon dogs on his heels. Wild Tom Turner wore filthy jeans and cowboy boots, and spat brown tobacco juice into the white snow.

As he approached, I turned the engine down to idle and opened the door of the maintainer, staying put in the cab. He looked up at me, as if he were sizing me up.

"My name is George McCray. My grandfather asked me to check in and make sure you were all right. If you need food, I've got milk and groceries to tide you over."

He smiled shrewdly, flashing yellow-stained teeth, seemingly pleased to be getting something for free. "Neighborly of you, son."

"Also, wanted to ask if you could stay off the roads for the rest of today and tomorrow. We're going to try to clear one lane first for emergency traffic. We'll come back and do the other lane later."

"I'm not going anywhere in particular."

"Thanks." I paused, trying to muster the courage to ask for what Thorne wanted.

"So, you're Big Bo McCray's son?"

"Grandson," I corrected.

He nodded his head approvingly and said, "I'll take some milk if you're giving it away."

I reached back and gave him two bottles. He took them and started back to the trailer.

"Wait," I called after him. "You're Mr. Turner, right?"

He turned and spat again. "What of it?"

"My grandfather also said that if you had anything extra you could share with neighbors that I should get that, too."

"What kind of 'extras' did your grandfather have in mind?"

"Mostly food, but if you've got an extra lantern or kindling . . ." I hesitated and tried to add my next request like an afterthought. "Also, Mr. Thorne, our neighbor, he's been sick and he said if I came by this way that I should ask you for, uh, two bottles of your best medicine."

He smiled in a way that made me uncomfortable. "So, Frank drank up all his own and he can't get to the pharmacy in town for more, eh? Wait here." Turner disappeared inside his trailer and came out with two mayonnaise jars filled with a muddy brown liquid. He handed them to me, chuckled, and said, "You tell Mr. Thorne that he should take two cups every night before he goes to bed, and I'll be sending him my doctor bill."

I nestled the jars inside my extra coat so the liquid would not spill. "Thanks, Mr. Turner. I'll tell him."

"Listen, son, this business is between me and Mr. Thorne." A vicious look crept across his face. "No one else need know, you understand?"

"Yes, sir, I understand."

"Good. Now you get back to your work and I'll get back to mine." He gave a halfhearted wave as he turned around and went back to his trailer, the dogs following.

As I made my way down off of Blackberry Hill, that cold sweat was back, along with an uncomfortable knot in my stomach.

Plowing the roads toward home, I had no idea what to do. I contemplated emptying the jars, but it occurred to me that I had already done the hard part. All I had to do now was give them to Thorne and take back Tucker. Everyone would be better off. I would have what I wanted. Thorne would have what he wanted. Tucker would have a decent home.

When I returned to the farm that evening, I hid the jars in the implement shed before Grandpa and I milked again. I was quiet and my grandfather worried about me.

"You tired?"

"Yes," I answered.

He looked at me and nodded his head up and down approvingly. "That's okay." He turned and walked off, climbed onto the maintainer, and was off for the night-time shift.

While he went off to work, I went into the living room. Behind the puzzle table where my grandmother and father had spent so many hours stood a bookcase with leaded-glass doors. My dad proudly displayed his encyclopedia on the top three shelves. I took down the first volume, sat in Grandpa's recliner, and started to read about alcoholism in the dim light of the kerosene lamp that I rested on the puzzle table. More than halfway through the entry, I realized that my grandmother was standing beside the chair, at my shoulder.

"Catching up on some schoolwork?"

I slammed the book shut and tried to act casual. "No, just something I was interested in."

"Okay, but you better get to sleep. Your shift will begin soon."

I replaced the volume on the shelf, brushed my teeth, and went to bed, still uncertain of how I would handle Thorne.

CHAPTER 24

George!" Grandma yelled up the stairs. "Time to get up!" Every morning, as my fatigue built, it grew harder and harder to wake up. I could hear the maintainer idling in the driveway. It had been running nonstop for four days straight and the roads were still a mess.

After a quick breakfast, I joined my grandfather in the barn to help him finish the morning milking. My mind quickly went to the jars in the implement shed, and I felt a queasy mixture of nerves and shame brewing inside of me.

"Grandpa, Frank Thorne is sick," I blurted out. This was my guilt talking. I hadn't intended to bring up the object of my anxiety, but a part of me hungered for some direction. "I think he has the flu, or it could be tremors. His house is cold. He needs wood."

"That's kind of you to be concerned."

"Actually, I was thinking more about Tucker than Thorne." This was partly true, but I was still on a fishing expedition, hoping for some kind of sign from Grandpa Bo that would send me in one direction or another.

"We've got plenty of wood. I'll put some on the steel shelf behind the cab and you can unload it on your way out." I started out the barn door, excited to see Tucker and now feeling less guilty since Grandpa had given me a legitimate reason to stop at Thorne's. "Don't forget to crack the ice on the pond before you leave," he reminded me.

By the time I got out of our driveway and into Thorne's, even though I had been working for hours, it was still early in the morning and I did not want to wake him. Tucker watched me from the door, tail wagging, as I unloaded the wood onto the small front porch. I thought of the mayonnaise jars that I'd snuck back into the cab, but I didn't want to leave them out in plain sight with the wood. I considered slipping them through the perpetually unlocked front door, but I was afraid I'd cause a ruckus with Tucker and disturb Thorne. I would come back later to finish what I'd started. I glanced through the door at the big red dog, his eyes full of expectation.

"I'll be back for you later, Tucker," I said softly before I set out on my shift.

When I got to the far eastern edge of our clearing territory, I stopped and checked in with the Sloan family.

Mr. Sloan had a new job for me. The mailman had left all of the mail for our section of the county with the Sloans because it was impossible for him to get down most of the roads. I picked up mail for the roads that were on our route and promised to distribute it as best I could. There was another letter from Minnesota addressed to me from my mother. I stuck it in my coat pocket to read when I had time.

By 4:00 that afternoon, my shift was ending and I was

heading west. I slowed the maintainer and considered whether or not I should stop at Thorne's. My resolve to finish my "errand" was suddenly less firm, the guilt creeping back in to fill the void. Still, I wanted to check on Tucker, and unfortunately, there was no way to separate him from Thorne. All day long, the jars had been buried beneath my extra coat, and I had wanted to get rid of them. Now, as I plowed up Thorne's driveway and put the maintainer into idle, I decided to leave them in their hiding place.

There were considerable footsteps and paw prints in the snow, but Thorne's truck was still parked in the same place. A good bit of the firewood I'd left on the porch had been taken. Before I even knocked, Tucker was at the front door, pawing anxiously for me to let him out.

"Mr. Thorne, it's George," I called.

"Come in, boy."

I pushed the door open and stepped inside. Everything was so different that I was disoriented. The inside had gone through the most amazing transformation I had ever seen. The curtains were pulled back, the windows cleaned so that light cascaded into what now seemed more like a cozy cabin than a broken-down shack. The place was spotless. Though the house was still without power, a fire burned warm and full in the stove, and I could smell soup simmering and cornbread in the oven. The floors were clean, the clutter and garbage gone. Thorne was still on the sofa, but he was wearing clean clothes and was shaven.

Tucker whined. "Let the dog out, would you, son?"

"Sure." As I did so, I tried to take in the transformation. I looked at the wall of photos. Something else was different. The picture was gone. For some reason, he had taken it down.

Thorne looked so much better. I was pondering what had brought this about when he got down to the business I was dreading.

"Did you bring me the medicine?"

It wasn't medicine. It was poison. However much it might have gotten me what I wanted, I knew that even Thorne deserved better. "No, I didn't," I lied, mustering my strength. "That's not the kind of medicine you need, Mr. Thorne."

He grimaced. But what he said next surprised me.

"Good. You're a pretty smart kid, aren't you? Just like your dad."

I didn't know how to answer.

"It's not something I should have asked you to do." He smiled. "But I do have another favor to ask, and this one won't bother you. My dog is tired of being all cooped up. Why don't you take him with you while you're working on that maintainer? He loves to go for a ride. All he does is sit around here and whine to go outside. Can you do that for me?"

"Yes, sir. I could do that." I struggled to control my excitement, but inside I wanted to pop.

"Good. Now, you get on home before your grandparents start worrying about you. Frank Thorne will be fine."

I went out the door and bent down, allowing Tucker to nuzzle his cold snout into my face. "As soon as this snow lets up, you and I are going romping again! And in the meantime, you can come to work with me on snow days." I pulled him close, knowing that I'd made the right choice, for Frank Thorne and for myself. I held the dog tight to me for a few more moments before I opened the door and put him back in the house.

The maintainer climbed up McCray's Hill, grading all the while. As soon as I parked, I carefully carried what I'd hidden in the cab to the back of the barnyard, out of sight of the house. I opened the mayonnaise jars and poured Turner's homemade rotgut into the snow, hiding the empties at the bottom of the trash cans we kept behind the barn.

With the crime scene neatened up, and no discernable scent of alcohol lingering in the cold, clean air, I ran up to the house to give my grandmother the good news about Tucker. When I opened the door, a familiar aroma confused me, until I put the pieces together. On the table was fresh-baked cornbread. My grandmother stood at the stove, stirring a big kettle of her bean soup. These were the smells in Thorne's cabin.

"Grandma," I said, as I hugged her extra hard.

"What?" she asked.

"Oh, nothing."

She smiled and went back to work and I just watched her busying herself. No one else in our family would ever know how or where she spent that particular day. The idea of angels is appealing to me. Whether they exist or not, I can't say. I do know that some people are called on to do good deeds. Grandma Cora was the closest thing to an angel I ever knew. It was not lost on me how our days had differed when it came to Thorne. I had tried to take advantage of his illness to get what I wanted; she was trying to support his recovery.

My grandfather and I worked the maintainer in shifts for the next three days and nights, Tucker at my side to keep me company. At first, he was a little reluctant about jumping into the cab, but after a little coaxing he was right at home. I made a bed for him behind the seat from old blankets and coats. Having Tucker with me made the work seem more tolerable and the hours passed by quickly. From time to time, I imagined he would shout up little commands to make sure I was paying attention. "Look out there, George, you're drifting to the right."

I let him know who was boss. "You can't even walk a straight line, Tucker. So don't tell me how to plow!"

The snow let up, but the real problem was the wind, which caused drifts into the roadway so that we were having to redo what we had previously done. Still, we made progress, having cleared all of the main roads and shifting to the more isolated side roads and country lanes.

We were exhausted, but the winds were dying down and we were gaining ground. The dairy truck was coming again, and both the power and phone companies were able to start making repairs. The temperature was also climbing, and as we thawed out from the big storm, things were getting back to normal. Soon, McCray's Dairy had power and phone service, and the worst was behind us.

There were only a few days of school left before the Christmas break and I was hoping that all the canceled days would mean a free pass for me on both algebra and memorizing lines for the school play.

My grandfather gave me ten dollars and suggested that I do some Christmas shopping with my grandma— at least as soon as I cracked the ice and did the milking.

The next morning, Grandma and I decided we needed rest, so shopping would wait another day. After breakfast, I re-read the letter from my mom that I had stashed very carefully in my pocket. She said that they would be driving to Kansas and hoping to arrive no later than December 24, roads allowing. She said that I should be packed and ready to go by December 27. School started in Minnesota on January 5. I tossed the letter aside and tried not to think about it.

CHAPTER 25

On December 19, my second day off in a row, I took Tucker for a long walk. It seemed that Frank Thorne's health was continuing to improve. When I brought Tucker back, Thorne even asked me to come inside and sit down. I did not have much to say, so after a few awkward moments, I said my goodbyes and headed home.

Grandma made a huge lunch and I must have eaten too much. I felt exhausted, so I stretched out on my bed for what I thought would be a short nap before I helped with the afternoon milking. I did not wake up until 7:30 the next morning.

Stumbling out of bed, embarrassed, I wondered why no one had woken me. Downstairs, both of my grandparents were very quiet, probably a bit irritated at me for sleeping in and not helping with the chores, I thought.

It was up to me to make some conversation. "I better go check the pond and clear the ice."

My grandfather barely looked up. "Thanks, you do that."

It went quiet again, and I ate in silence until my grandfather spoke.

"George, I took the trash down to the dump and I

pulled out two empty jars that looked strange to me. You probably think that I'm too old to have noticed, but there had been alcohol in them."

As I gulped the last of my oatmeal, I'm sure my face turned as white as the snow I had been plowing.

"Do you have any idea how those jars got in the trash?"

Rising from the table and pulling on my coat, I planned to toss a quick "don't know" over my shoulder and head out.

"George, get back over here and sit down."

I sighed, knowing I'd have to tell them everything, wondering if they'd understand. "Yes, I know how they got there, but it's not what you think."

"Try me," my grandfather said.

I told them the whole story. My grandmother had her hands on her hips, her irritation with me slowly dissipating. Grandpa Bo listened with an impassive look on his face, until he cracked a bemused smile and spoke.

"Well, can we agree that'll be your first and last trip up to Blackberry Hill?"

"Yes, sir."

"I'm disappointed that you chose to run that errand for Thorne, incomplete as it was, but I'm proud of you for one thing."

"What's that, Grandpa?"

"You were able to correct your course after you made a wrong turn. That's a good skill for a maintainer. Now get on out of here and crack the ice."

Not until I had my own children did I realize how

skillful my grandparents were at parenting. It is extraordinarily difficult to simultaneously correct and support a teenager. They actually made me feel better about myself and them when I made mistakes. My misjudgments and wrong turns were opportunities to learn from and not events to be ashamed of.

Walking out the door to crack the ice, I realized I had no idea how I was going to say goodbye to two such wonderful people, whom I loved to the core. What would life be like without them?

When I got to the pond, I discovered there was no need to chop the ice. It had grown so warm, almost fifty degrees the day before, that the opening had not frozen over. The cows were ambling down to the lake for a drink and the heifers were bawling for their mothers. There was a strange smell in the air—at least for that time of year. I looked to the sky to confirm what I thought.

Snow clouds are a light gray color and just reach right down to the trees so that the spaces between the sky and the land all come together without dramatic contrasts. The sky that morning was very different. Overhead it was clear and bright and to the east the sun was giving us everything she had to give. But to the west, the sky was black as night and I could hear thunder booming on the horizon. I smelled rain. Thunderstorms were for spring and summer, not winter. This made no sense to me.

Although I might have recalled occasional lightning strikes, I could not remember ever seeing a winter thunderstorm.

I went up to the dairy barn to help my grandfather finish the milking and ask about the weather.

"Grandpa, have you seen the sky to the west?"

"I sure have and I've listened to the weather report, too."

"What's it doing?"

He grunted. "It's not good."

"What do you mean?"

"George, you've done a good job helping us dig out of two feet of snow and now you just might find out what's ten times worse than snow for a road maintainer—ice."

"Ice?"

"I'll take a foot of snow over an inch of freezing rain any day. Freezing rain coats every piece of gravel and every tree limb. The maintainer's tires can't get enough traction to do any work. On top of that, after an inch or so of freezing rain, branches, limbs, and eventually entire trees will crumble under the weight of the ice. Falling timber will block the roads and the power lines will be ripped straight off the poles. It's a maintainer's nightmare. We could be down for weeks."

"What can we do?"

"Nothing, son. Nothing at all."

My grandfather and the local weather forecasters thought we were going to pay the price for the warm air that had blessed us the last few days. A cold front had marched down from the north and was prepared to do battle with the warm air that still lingered from the south, and just like it was during the Civil War, Kansas was stuck right in the middle. Thirty miles to the north, it would be several degrees colder. They would get snow— to be pushed aside with minimal difficulties. Thirty miles to the south it would be a few degrees warmer and they would get a cold but harmless rain. Stuck right in the middle, we would get paralyzing ice.

By 2:00 P.M. on December 20, 1962, the freezing rain hit, dumping a little over an inch of hard frozen ice on the road. It was a mess, just as forecast.

However bad it might have been for the roads and the trees, it was beautiful outside. The ice coated everything and made the whole world glisten and shine. It was as if the universe were flash-frozen, leaving all life suspended.

It could be weeks before we thawed out. Anything that could get wet was also now coated in ice: trees, buildings, horses, cows, sheep, rocks, and, worst of all for us, roads.

Cherokee County, Kansas, ground to a total halt.

While I knew what a mess snow would cause, I had no idea what damage a solid inch of ice could do. I hoped that people had learned their lesson and had stocked plenty of supplies in the few days we had between storms. We were in for a very tough week leading up to Christmas and probably into the New Year.

We did not even bother starting the maintainer. My grandfather and I cracked the ice on the pond, milked the cows by hand, and dumped the milk on the ground, and we all went to bed early, not knowing what the coming days would bring.

CHAPTER 26

It was less than a week away and the prospect of a decent Christmas was fading fast. My scheme to get Tucker back was not working. We had no power and the phone lines were down. I had not talked to my mom or sisters in over a week. While hoping that the weather and the road conditions would improve, I was left wondering if they would be able to make it through the final thirty miles of the trip home, where the snow had turned to ice.

The tree I had cut for Grandma Cora had made it as far as the tree stand in the living room, but we'd been so busy with snow days that it had sat, undecorated, for all this time. Just like our milk, it seemed like the holiday was going to be thrown out. I was trying to act like I didn't care, but it was hard to give up on Christmas.

Lying in bed that night, I could hear tree limbs creak and moan under the weight of the ice. This storm was bad for us, but for some of our neighbors it had to be worse. Mrs. Slater needed her insulin, Sherry Rather had her baby to deliver, and old Mrs. Reed would be worried sick. Most everyone was frightened and here I was just lying in bed doing nothing. It left me feeling rather useless and sick to my stomach.

I wondered if we should just walk the frozen roads of Cherokee County. Maybe we couldn't maintain the roads, but we might still be able to help the people who lived along them.

The next morning I brought up my idea.

"Grandpa, maybe we should check on some of our neighbors and make sure they aren't hurt or in need of anything."

He looked at me, equally disgusted by the whole situation. "There is just not much we can do."

My grandmother reached out and patted my arm. "It's nice of you to think of them."

"But how about Mrs. Slater and old Mrs. Reed and the people who aren't so healthy?"

"They have good neighbors that live much closer than we do. In this ice, a person would be lucky to walk a mile an hour. Mrs. Slater lives eight miles from here. It might take you eight hours to just get there and another eight to walk home. What could you do if she did need help?"

"I guess you're right, but it just doesn't seem right to sit and do nothing."

My grandfather didn't say anything. My grandmother looked bothered, too, but she seemed to accept there was little we could do. "We're hoping the weather will warm again in a few days and we can melt our way out of the ice."

"Well, what if it doesn't? Christmas will be over. How will Mom and the girls make it here?"

"We'll still have Christmas, George. A lot can happen in a few days. You'll see."

After breakfast, my grandfather started up the chain saw and began clearing our yard of the branches and limbs that had cracked and fallen to the ground from the weight of the ice. I was out helping him in the yard when the back door opened and Grandma called, "George, come up to the house."

She was waiting for me at the back door with two plates full of warm food, covered in aluminum foil. "Just the man I was looking for."

I eyed her suspiciously. "What?"

"I need a delivery. Top plate to Frank Thorne and the bottom plate is for a red dog, but don't stay too long; lunch is almost ready and your grandpa promised me I could have you to myself this afternoon. We have some Christmas work to do."

I took the plates away from her. "Sure, I can take them!"

Once out of her view, I stopped and peeked under the foil. Thorne's plate had several pieces of cornbread and the remaining space was filled with fresh-out-of-the-oven Christmas cookies—cut into the shapes of trees and snowmen that were colored red and green and covered with sprinkles. Tucker's plate had a soup bone with plenty of meat carelessly left attached. I shuffled down the icy road, trying not to fall and spill the food, smiling most of the way.

As I suspected, both Thorne and Tucker were pleased by my delivery, and playing the role of Santa improved my spirits, too. The soup bone was a big hit and Tucker immediately went to work on it.

When I got ready to return, Thorne put his hand on my shoulder. "Why don't you come around tomorrow, too, when you can stay longer. Maybe, if it's a little nicer out, you can take him for a walk."

I reached down and gave Tucker a farewell hug. "I'd like that."

Tearing himself away from his treat, Tucker looked at me gratefully and seemed to say, "That'll work, but could you bring another bone, too?"

THE LUNCH MENU that afternoon was exactly what I expected: soup, cornbread, and Christmas cookies. As soon as we had the dishes cleaned and put away, my grandmother and I carried up boxes of decorations from the basement and we finally attended to the tree I had dragged from the creek.

We put lights on it and I hung what was left of the cookies that she had baked for Frank Thorne, as well as all the decorations from past McCray Christmases. As I handled the old ornaments, it was easy to let my mind drift back to happier times, when we'd all been together. Grandma Cora had grown quiet, too, and I'm sure she felt the same odd mix of melancholy and forced holiday cheer that was taking hold of me.

It was too early to start making new Christmas memories, it seemed, but I didn't want my grandmother to slip back into sadness, thinking of her lost son. There seemed to be a few extra cookies and the kid in me took over, once again. When my grandmother wasn't looking, I would pop them into my mouth and quickly chew and swallow them, another McCray tradition.

"Something seems to be getting into our cookies," Grandma announced.

"How can you tell?"

She reached out with her thumb and touched my cheeks. "He's got green crumbs all over his face, and he's got the same silly grin on his face his dad used to get."

I smiled even bigger, and I think we were both glad to have acknowledged my father, even in this small way. By doing so, it was as if we could now allow ourselves to have a little fun decorating the tree.

When we were finished, Grandma plugged in the lights and, with the power out, they did not come on. She shrugged her shoulders and said, "I guess that pretty much sums up our year, doesn't it, George." I am sure at that moment that neither of us knew whether to laugh or to cry.

CHAPTER 27

The next morning, I knocked on Thorne's door and he tossed out a friendly "Come in."

The little house was still reasonably clean and warm, and Thorne was busily tinkering with a carburetor that rested on the kitchen table. He pointed to a leash that hung by the door, knowing precisely why I was there. "Take the leash and be careful. It's pretty slick out there."

I snapped the leash on Tucker's collar and we headed out the door. "Thanks, Mr. Thorne. I'll bring him back in a few hours."

It felt good to have Tucker walking beside me. We made our way to Mack's Lake and knocked around his old cabin, but it was too cold to stay out for long, so after we took in our frozen surroundings we headed back to civilization.

We were living atop a polar ice cap that had hills and crystallized trees pushing up through the ice like statues protruding from stone ruins. With four legs, Tucker moved through the glassy terrain easier than I could, but still he had to be careful. With so little traction, I slipped around and could not get my footing.

There was the eerie sound of tree branches cracking

and snapping all around us, like distant cannon fire. Periodically, giant crashing noises came from the forest that flanked Kill Creek. Ancient tree trunks snapped under the weight of the ice and fell to the ground with thuds that echoed for miles along the riverbank. Tucker and I steered clear of the tree cover as we walked toward our farm.

My grandfather had worked all day with his chain saw, trying to clear the yard of branches and debris, and he still had a lot more to do. Tucker followed me around for an hour or so while I tried to stack the logs and branches that Grandpa had cut out of the way. There would be plenty of firewood for years to come.

After two weeks of being the first assistant to the Senior Road Maintainer, I naturally thought of my job. I walked to the end of the driveway and looked in both directions to see a tangled mess of ice and fallen debris. Eventually, I took Tucker back to Thorne's cabin. Thorne was still intently working on his project, so I said a quick goodbye to Tucker and just released him inside the door. As I headed home, I grew a little gloomy. It was hard to think of Tucker like a neighbor friend whom I could walk with from time to time but not do much else with.

All of these snow days were also making me miss my friends. I wanted my normal routine back, even if it meant going to school.

The time I had left in Cherokee County was running out with each passing day. As best I could, I tried to accept that this was the way things had to be.

When I got home, my grandfather stopped his cutting and we did the milking together. For yet another day, our cows' efforts were ultimately poured on the ground. We started inside for dinner and I wondered aloud why we could not at least make some effort to beat this weather.

"Grandpa, I want to start up the maintainer and give it a try. It doesn't feel right doing nothing."

"George, you've never tried to drive a maintainer on ice. It can handle a half inch, but a whole inch of ice is too much. You're going to have to trust me; it can't be done. You'll slip all over the place."

I dug my heels in. "I want to try."

He turned and walked away. "Suit yourself."

After I warmed the diesel engine, it turned right over, sputtering, and then it evened out. With very little light left, I put the maintainer in reverse and eased slowly out the barn door. The weight of the maintainer cracked through the ice and reached the solid frozen grass beneath me. There was enough traction to back straight out. Encouraged, I moved through the barnyard and to the entrance of our gravel driveway without slipping around too much. Slowly lowering the blade, I tried to inch forward and turn over the gravel. The second the blade hit the ice, the resistance caused the machine to lose traction, and my wheels started to spin.

Backing up, I tried again at several different speeds and blade angles. Same result. Sitting there in the cab, I could hardly stand it. My own anger and frustration started to build. Backing the machine up, I got a good running start. When I had built up enough momentum, I dropped the blade violently, hoping to crack the icy surface. The maintainer spun hard and rocked up into the yard, where I had no business being. When I tried to back out, the maintainer's tires spun.

I was stuck. Reversing didn't work, either.

Knowing my grandfather would be unhappy with me, I started to feel very foolish.

He walked out the back door, right past me, without saying a word.

Not knowing what else to do, I just sat and waited. Soon I heard the sound of the big International Harvester tractor coming toward me in the last light of the day. He parked the tractor pointing downhill from the maintainer, where he would have more traction, and then got out of the cab and connected the tractor to the grader with a long chain. The tractor's tires were twice the size of the maintainer's, so it had much better pulling power. Still, there was no guarantee he could pull me out.

My grandfather walked up to the cab door. When I opened it, he didn't appear mad. In fact, he just smiled and said, "Can't grade in the ice, George." Apparently, Big Bo McCray had passed some of his legendary stubborn streak onto his grandson.

For once, it was me who didn't say a word.

"Put the transmission in reverse. When the chain is taut, let out the clutch slowly. I'll try to pull you to level ground. Let's hope we don't both get stuck."

It took us several tries before he was able to get me

pulled back to a flatter area where the maintainer's wheels didn't just spin. Maybe it was because I didn't know better, but I didn't want to give up.

After we had both implements back in the barn, I got my nerve up to keep pushing. "Grandpa, why can't we hook up Dick and Dock, like you used to before you got the maintainer, and try to grade the old-fashioned way?"

"George, Dick and Dock are twice as old as me in horse years. They'd barely make it down the driveway before they dug in their heels and turned back to their warm stalls. And what if one of them slipped and broke a leg?"

"Well, don't we use chains on the car tires sometimes? Couldn't we put chains on the maintainer, too?"

"They don't make chains that big. Besides, with ice this thick, I doubt chains would make a difference. A car just has to push itself forward; a maintainer has a much harder job. It has to move itself forward and scrape thousands of pounds of ice off the road at the same time. That takes traction, and lots of it."

"There just has to be some way."

My grandfather looked pained. It didn't occur to me that this was bothering him just as much as or more than it was bothering me. "Why don't you go inside and let me think about it. Sometimes we just have to accept that there are things we can't fix. Things are not always the way we want them . . ."

His words trailed off and I heard something I didn't think was possible. There were no tears in the eyes of Big Bo McCray, but there was a pained break in his voice that probably surprised him as much as it did me. I walked over to my grandfather and put my arms around him. He gave me a big hug. "I'm sorry, George. None of us like to feel helpless."

He squeezed me a little tighter and for a moment it felt very much like I had a father again. He released his grip and turned and walked away. Walking back to the house, I felt a little sorry for the way I had behaved.

By the time I got back inside the kitchen, it was dark out and Grandma had lit the kerosene lamp. My grandfather did not come up to the house for dinner.

At first, Grandma did not seem that worried. She just left his plate of food covered in the oven and we ate without him. By 7:15, when there was still no sign of him, she began nervously looking out the back door.

"Do you want me check on him, Grandma?"

"No, I'm sure he's fine. It's just not like him to stay out so late."

A little past 7:30 that night, we heard the maintainer engine turn over.

"What is he up to out there?" my grandmother asked.

The maintainer eased out of the barn and turned into the driveway and stopped. The light from the headlamps reflected off branches encased in glass. The cab door swung open and my grandfather came up to the back porch. I did not realize why at the time, but he moved sure-footedly on the ice.

Grandma pushed open the back door and called out to him.

"Get inside, Bo! It's late!"

But he made no move to come into the house and just looked at her.

"What is it, Bo?"

"Maybe I'm a fool, Cora, but George is right. People are counting on us. There is something I want to try. It just might work. Don't wait up for me; I'll be back when I'm finished."

"Bo, you can't go out in this ice. You and George couldn't even get out of the driveway. This is crazy. Where are you going?"

"It'll be fine. I've got it all worked out." He turned and headed back to the maintainer, climbing into the cab and releasing the brake. I watched silently as he headed down the driveway at a snail's pace.

Grandma was furious. She paced about the kitchen for the rest of the evening, carrying on an angry monologue under her breath, and eventually she went to bed early without saying goodnight.

WITH THE EXCLUSIVE use of the kerosene lamp, I wandered into my parents' room and looked around. It seemed that I had been avoiding this room for many months now.

There were still pictures of my dad on the bedside table and on the wall along with the other family photos. This room had been his when he was a boy and the same dresser had stayed in there all of these years. I opened some of the drawers in the chest. There were four or five worn-down pencils, some firecrackers he had taken away from me, change, ticket stubs, and the yellow pocket-knife, with a bone handle, that I gave him for Christmas. A strong feeling came over me that my dad would want me to have that knife, that somehow it was rightfully mine. I slipped it into my pocket and held it close. It felt good to have something on me that connected us.

There was no reason for me to sleep upstairs where it was so cold and leave Grandma downstairs by herself, so I just climbed into the double bed. It seemed luxurious having that giant bed all to myself. It would have been even better with a big, furry, red pillow, even if it did tend to wiggle and lick my face. Reading by the dim light of the lamp, I quickly felt drowsy, so I turned it off and listened to the wind blowing against the window. The iced-over branches sounded like wind chimes knocking up against the house. While wondering what my grandfather was up to, I drifted off to sleep.

CHAPTER 28

It was light out when I woke up. It had been a long, snug, and secure sleep, but I wondered why no one had bothered to wake me. I threw off the covers and raced into the kitchen. My grandmother was standing over the sink, looking out the kitchen window. "What's wrong, Grandma?"

"Your grandfather still hasn't come back and I am worried."

"Don't worry, Grandma. He'll be all right." While I could tell my grandmother not to worry, I wasn't so good at following my own advice. I couldn't imagine where he was and was hoping he had not slipped off the road in the middle of the night, or worse. Pushing him the way I had to do something about the roads made me feel responsible.

We ate breakfast in silence. Perhaps because I just wanted to stay busy, I went straight to the chores. And since I got such a late start, I did the milking first and figured I would chop the pond ice later. After letting in the first six cattle, I milked as furiously as I could, working up a sweat despite the cold. The whole time my worry climbed and my mind raced to terrible possibilities. Why had he not told us where he was going or what he was doing? I didn't even know where to look. The milking seemed to take forever.

Finally, I got to the last six cows. When finished, I shut the barn door, closed the latch, and ran to the house, hoping that there was some good news.

My grandmother was dressed in her winter coat and was standing by the back door. "Where are you going?" I asked.

"I'm going out to find your grandfather."

"Now?"

"Yes."

"I'll go with you."

"No, you better stay here. In case he shows up, we can't all be roaming around trying to find him. I won't be gone more than an hour."

I didn't want her to go, but I knew I had no say in the matter. The door shut behind her and just like that I was left alone, more alone than you could imagine. It came to me that I had lost my father and because I lost my father, I lost my mother, albeit it to sadness, loneliness, and a move to Minnesota. She was alive but she was absent from my life. Now my grandfather was lost and that meant my grandmother would wander about in freezing weather looking for him. Losses compound and impact us like falling dominoes. It was just me—alone in the old farmhouse listening to the wind shake our house down to its foundation.

I pictured my grandparents pushing against the snow, determined to find each other. Needing to get my mind separated from my worry, I tried to read, but it was no use. I should have insisted that I go with her, but I was thirteen and generally did what I was told. We could have left a note. There was some solace in remembering how strong she was when we searched for the Christmas tree. I paced about the house and tried to formulate a plan of my own. When more than an hour had passed and still no one had returned, I reassured myself that she probably did not have a watch and when she said an hour it was only an estimate.

When she got back, I would bundle up and go in the opposite direction. We could take turns like that, one-hour shifts each. I searched around for the heaviest winter clothes I could find and arranged them around the periphery of the downstairs furnace grate. As soon as she returned, I'd dress in my pre-warmed things and go out. I thought about survival. If I got lost I would need food. I placed a few apples and some cookies in a knapsack and went to the basement and dug up an old army canteen that had belonged to Dad.

Back in the kitchen, I took a drink from my grandfather's tin cup, which so reminded me of him, and then pressed my face against the cold window. I peered outside and into the ice-land of meadows to the south of our old home, hoping for some sign of my grandparents' return. Amid all of the worrying, a sickening realization came over me. I had forgotten to clear the ice on the pond for the cows.

Quickly, I pulled on my warm winter suit and headed out the door.

CHAPTER 29

The faster I tried to go, the more I slipped and fell, which only caused me to worry more about my grandparents. It was hard going forward when the elevation increased and nearly impossible to stop sliding on the downhill sections. Fortunately, our farm sat on the top of a hill, and at least for the first several minutes, I could move across the barnyard using a skating motion.

Not wanting to take the time to skate over to the open gate, I squeezed my way between the strands of the barbed-wire fence that separates the barn pasture from the lake meadow. My extra clothing added to my girth and my jacket caught on one of the small barbs. Backing out, I reached around and pulled the fabric from the barb and tried again.

Once through the fence, I slid to the bottom of the hill and tried to make my way up the back side of the pond, where a dam held the water back. It was too steep to go over, so I followed the dam around to the east of the pond. As I made my way around the spillway, where the water overflows in strong spring showers, my heart sank.

Forty feet from the shoreline, two cows and two calves

had wandered out onto the ice and fallen through a weak spot. They were treading water as best they could. One calf was barely holding his head above water. The remainder of the herd stood precariously close, tempting their own fate. Nausea and panic came over me in waves. There was no one home to help me. My grandfather's words came back to me. "It's an important job I'm giving you. Do you understand?"

How casually I had said, "Sure."

Now I needed help, and a lot of it. I yelled as loud as I could. "Help!" My voice echoed over the hills and valleys and cruelly reverberated off the ice-covered ground. Again, I was alone.

I wanted to stop right there and just sob at my helplessness. I wanted to jump in with them. Give up. At least that way, we would all go together. The sight of the first floating carcass snapped me to my senses. The poor creature's body bobbed up and down like a grotesque black-and-white ice cube. It was one of the two calves.

None of my options seemed reasonable. The cows weighed over twelve hundred pounds. I couldn't lift them up and onto the ice. From my daily efforts at cracking the ice with the sledgehammer, I knew it would be impossible for me to clear a swath to the shore by hand.

There was only one way. I would have to pull them out one at a time with some rope and the tractor. Even though no one could hear me, I screamed again, as loud as I could. "Help!"

There was so little time. I ran across the ice back to the

barn, driven by adrenaline and fear. More times than I could count, I fell. I got back up. I ran. I fell again.

First grabbing two ropes from the barn and a huge bucket of feed, I dashed to the implement shed and tried to remember how to start the largest tractor we owned, the IH. I had driven it many times, but I was so panicked that the simplest task seemed impossible. I had to try three times before the engine turned over and started. There was no time to let it warm up. I released the clutch with my numb feet and backed out of the barn. I swung the tractor forward and the massive wheels spun on the ice. Backing the throttle off, I tried again.

Eventually, I gained enough traction to move forward. Not wanting to waste an instant, I crashed through the gate, without bothering to open it, and made my way to the pond. The tractor would have to be pointing downhill when I tried to pull the cows out or it would not work. As I approached the pond, I picked the perfect spot, stopped the tractor, put it in reverse, and tried to get enough steam going to make it up a gentle hill that approached the west side of the pond. I had over fifty yards of lariat and I prayed it would reach.

Parking the tractor as close to the pond bank as possible, I quickly secured one end of the rope to the steel clevis on the back of the tractor. Pouring the sorghum on the shore worked exactly as I thought it would. The remainder of the herd that was not already in the water ambled over to the edge to eat, unaware that death was only twenty yards away.

With the bulk of the herd out of the way, I raced across the surface of the pond, holding on to the other end of the rope.

There was no time to think about it. Perhaps I should have known better than to risk my life for a few cows. But to me, they were living creatures with beating hearts that I had cared for my whole life, and that stood for our family's livelihood. I couldn't let them die without trying to rescue them. I knew full well it was more than cows I was trying to salvage.

I jumped. The cold water sucked the breath straight out of me. With the rope in my hand, I dove beneath the first cow. With hands frozen stiff, I managed to tie a knot around her. I tried to lift myself out of the ice but fell back in. My boots had filled with water and they were so heavy that they were pulling me down and making it hard to tread water. I kicked them off, but still I could not find a way out of the ice. A desperate cow's hoof slammed into me and I screamed out in pain. Now I was stuck, too.

I remembered the rope, somehow managed to grab it, and pulled myself out to safety.

Running and slipping across the surface of the pond in my stocking feet, my body a shivering, freezing mass of ice, I struggled up onto the tractor and pushed it into first gear. The right tractor wheel was spinning and the tractor could not gain traction. I backed up a little bit and tried again. Still, the right wheel spun. The tractor was set up with a right and a left brake pedal, so I tried to lock down the right wheel to transfer more of the pull to the left wheel. It worked. The tractor moved slowly forward, oblivious to its load. The rope went taut and pulled the cow up onto the ice. She plopped out onto the surface of the pond and let out a frightened bawl as I dragged her to the edge.

She came to her feet but was too frightened to let me get close enough to untie the knot. To make matters worse, the harder she pulled, the tighter it made the knot.

I didn't have time to wait for her to settle down. I remembered my father's pocketknife, pulled it out, and just cut the rope.

The rope was losing its flexibility in the cold. I backed the tractor to the edge of the pond. My feet were frozen. I jumped off the tractor and yanked the rope back to the edge of the water. Holding on to the rope, I jumped in again. The water, being warmer than the outside air temperature and my frozen clothing, was not as bad this time, but still I felt like my blood was freezing. The other calf was the first animal I got to. He was struggling to get up onto the ice to follow the cow I had just retrieved, his mother. He seemed so small and helpless that I thought maybe I could pull him out by myself. Taking one end of the rope, I looped it around his backside, just under his tail, and then pulled myself up and out of the water. I was exhausted and frozen, and I questioned whether I had enough strength to pull out much more than a minnow from the frozen waters.

I'd lost my socks in the pond, too. The skin on the bottoms of my feet was wet and stuck to the surface of the ice. As much as it hurt, it also gave me traction. I yanked and pulled and cursed and screamed. The calf probably weighed close to two hundred pounds, but he was buoyant in the water. With him kicking and me pulling, he was able to work his front legs out of the water and onto the solid ice. With one final heave of everything I had left, the bawling calf slid out onto the surface of the ice. We lay there together on the ice for a moment, both of us panting, exhausted. Some skin had ripped from the bottom of my right foot and it began to bleed.

I was tired, so tired. I wanted to just lay there, but I forced myself to my feet and untied the knot from the calf. There was one left. I stared at the water, ready to jump in. Perhaps I stood up too quickly, or perhaps it was fatigue, but the pond and ice started to swirl as if a giant tornado had uprooted me. I spun, turned, and fell to the ice with a thud. I could feel my eyelids flutter and I did not know what was wrong with me. I tried to fight my way back to consciousness, but everything was slipping away, getting darker and darker.

I don't know how much time passed, but something warm was licking my face. I tried to push it away and opened my eyes. Tucker was barking wildly. I tried to lift my hands to pull him close to me, but nothing would move. It went dark. Sleep. I had to sleep.

Then someone gripped me by the jacket and yanked me to my feet and began to drag me away from the ice. I remembered where I was and what I was doing and struggled to get loose. I yelled, "The cow!"

"Leave the damn cow," my rescuer swore, tossing me over his shoulder.

I shuddered convulsively in the clothing that was frozen to my body, my feet aching. I tried to resist. "We can't let her drown. . . ."

"Yes, we can."

With me resting on his shoulder like a sack of potatoes, Frank Thorne climbed onto the big IH, slid the transmission into gear, and headed back to the house.

He pushed open the back door and carried me into the bathroom. He dropped me into the tub and immediately turned on the spigot, allowing life-giving warm water to pour over my frozen body.

Moments later my grandmother pushed open the back door and followed the trail of ice, snow, and mud into the bathroom. She took one look into the bathtub and screamed. Frank Thorne left before I could open my mouth to thank him.

CHAPTER 30

It was afternoon by the time I stirred under a pile of blankets. Grandpa Bo and Grandma Cora were sitting by my bed. I felt something that I had not known if I would ever feel again. Sweat. I reached up and brushed it from my brow. I felt another source of warmth pressing against me. Tucker was stretched out beside me, his tail thumping against the mattress the moment I woke up.

My grandmother sprung from her chair and scooped me up in her arms. "Oh, George, are you all right?"

I felt fine and knew I was going to recover. I could feel bandages on my right foot, but as warm as the rest of my body felt, my toes still seemed frozen. It would be days before they felt normal—and a miracle that I didn't lose any of them to frostbite. "I'm going to be fine. I've swum in that old pond a hundred times before, just not in the middle of winter. That's all."

"Why is Tucker here?" I said, now holding him close.

My grandma answered. "Thorne asked if you would mind taking care of him again. He said he's got some personal business to attend to, and he thought you might enjoy Tucker's company while you were recovering."

"Where's he going and for how long?"

"He was vague about that. You know by now how private a person he is. But at least a few days, he said."

"Frank Thorne saved my life, you know," I said quietly, stroking Tucker's silky ears.

"Yes, George. We know," Grandpa said, speaking his first words to me. "And Tucker did, too."

Thorne had told them Tucker was the first to hear me hollering for help and was throwing a fit. When he walked outside to find out why the dog was barking and carrying on, Thorne, too, heard my yells and found me at the pond.

Tucker's warm fur was the best medicine I could have hoped for. I held him tight, and I'm not sure which of us was more pleased to be with the other. Tucker let out a mournful little groan that seemed to suggest that some missing part of his soul was put back in place. With each other, we both felt restored, whole.

After a while, I got up and tried to walk. The bottom of my right foot hurt like crazy, so I put on some extra socks to add cushioning. Tucker followed me while I limped around, and I knew that I owed him a great debt for his loyalty. The dog may have very well saved my life. I had no idea how to repay him, or how I would ever thank Frank Thorne.

We ate warm soup at the kitchen table. I was exhausted, but at the same time it felt good just to be alive, safe and warm. More important, it felt good to have Tucker back.

My grandmother insisted that I stay on the sofa for the

remainder of the day. I slept away the rest of the evening and most of the following day. Each time I woke from my slumber, Tucker was right there.

By the afternoon of the second day, our county was still shrouded in ice, but at least I was able to convince my grandmother that I was fully recovered.

CHAPTER 31

Around four o'clock on December 21, I grew restless, wondering if my mother was going to make it. Without phone service, we could only assume that she was headed our way. How she would get through the last thirty miles on these roads was another question.

There was no more putting it off: I needed to start packing. It was hard. I tried to make two piles: things that should go to Minnesota and items that should stay in Kansas. Trouble was, I still couldn't figure out exactly which pile to put myself in. Tucker, standing there in my room wagging his tail, made that choice even harder.

While I was regaining my strength and caring for Tucker, my grandfather had been strangely absent, working on what seemed to be a secret project off-site. When I asked him where he'd gone off to in the maintainer the night before my little mishap at the pond, he'd been vague. Now he was gone again for hours when he wasn't doing the milking or other chores. He wasn't grading roads on this ice, and whatever he was doing seemed to involve daily walks to and from the farm. He did let on that he'd been at Hank Fisher's house, but what was he up to there? Maybe, I thought, he was working on some secret Christmas present for Grandma Cora and using Hank's tools, though Grandpa did not seem to have enough holiday spirit to be playing elf these days.

My grandmother, though grateful that I was okay, was not too happy about my cattle-rescuing effort, and her mood was as bad as I had ever seen it. Grandpa's project was also irritating her. She said she still had no idea where he'd gone that night, though he'd returned home right after Thorne brought me back to the house.

He had developed a nasty cold that seemed to be turning into a full-blown case of the flu, which he considered nothing more than a nuisance. She was very worried about him and, as I stood there in the kitchen, her voice rose to a point of irritation that was uncommon for her.

"Your grandfather got an extra dose of stubborn and only half a dose of common sense. He'll likely die from pneumonia before spring planting."

"Is he that sick?"

"I've never seen him sicker."

"Well, maybe I should help him?"

"What are you talking about?"

"I feel fine, Grandma. I'm ready to get at it again." For the last few days, I had been exempt from milking duties, but now I was actually eager to help out again. I felt useless sitting around the house, and I certainly did not want to pack.

She turned away in a huff. "Did you think you were a polar bear jumping into that freezing water? You swimming in the pond in the middle of winter and him hiking around on the ice all day—what is wrong with you two?"

"Nothing. I feel fine."

"That's not what I meant, George."

My feet were still tender but much better, and I could walk with almost no pain. I put on my coat and hat, and got Tucker's leash out. He grew excited the minute he saw it, as eager as I was to get outside.

"Where are you two going?" Grandma asked suspiciously, probably worried that I'd disappear with Grandpa.

"Afternoon milking, that's all."

She let out an exasperated sigh. "You are a McCray."

The wind was whistling, but the temperature did not seem unbearable. There was no sign of my grandfather anywhere in the barnyard or the implement shed. The maintainer was gone, but I hadn't heard Grandpa start it up or drive it off the property. Keeping Tucker well heeled on the leash, I pushed open the big sliding door into the milking barn. To my surprise, milking away, like nothing had happened, was Grandpa.

My grandmother was right. He looked tired and whatever he had been working on seemed to have taxed him to exhaustion. I put my hand on his shoulder; otherwise, I'm not sure he would have even noticed us standing there, watching him milk.

He looked up with his blue eyes that were mired in dark black circles. "Well, hello, George. Looks like you are feeling a lot better. I wish I could say the same." He reached over and patted Tucker, too. "Hello, old boy. You're quite the rescue dog, aren't you?"

Skipping all pleasantries, I just asked, "Are you ever going to tell us what you've been working on? I haven't seen much of you for the last couple of days, and Grandma is going crazy wondering."

"I can tell you this much, George. You are going to like it." He coughed several times and offered nothing further by way of an explanation.

Hoping to get a real answer this time, I continued, "Did the maintainer get stuck on the road that night? I didn't see it in the shed."

"Nope. Hank Fisher and I have been working on some alterations. Should be ready—real soon."

"Hank?"

"Hank has an electric generator. With no power, I needed it for the arc welder."

I still didn't understand what he was doing or why he seemed so evasive.

He coughed again and wiped sweat from his brow with the back of his shirtsleeve. "Don't worry, George, you'll see. You know, it was your idea; you said that we had to do something."

It was a two-mile walk to Hank's place and I couldn't imagine walking that distance in this weather, but somehow Grandpa had been making the trip on foot. "Isn't it hard walking that far on the ice?"

He leaned off the milking stool and lifted up one of his legs with a grin. He pulled his pants up above his ankles and showed off the bottoms of his boots. "With these little rascals, it was a nice morning for a walk." He had taken roofing nails and hammered them into the soles.

"It worked?"

"Like a dream. That's where I got the idea, the night before you took your swim."

"What do you mean?" He obviously wanted to surprise me, but I was growing impatient.

He sniffled but did not answer, so I asked, "Do you feel all right?"

"Lousy. I need to get some sleep."

Just then I heard the heavy rumbling of a big engine growing closer; the maintainer had pulled into the driveway. I hurried outside and my grandfather came along behind. Hank Fisher was behind the wheel and he had a giant smile on his face. He got down out of the cab and my grandfather shook his hand.

"Howdy, neighbor."

Hank pointed to the maintainer with pride. "Well, what do you think?"

My grandfather walked around the machine, inspecting. "You did a great job." He stopped at the wheels. It seemed that they had made a few modifications based on my suggestion.

Now I knew what they had been up to. I put my hand on one of the giant rear tires. "Wow!"

Hank stood back, proud of his work. "It was quite a job," he said. "First, I had to find every logging chain I could get my hands on and cut each one to the right length. Welding the logging chains and the clasps together was the easy part. These babies are what took me all night." He ran his hands over hundreds of small steel studs that had been welded onto the chain.

"How did you do it?" I asked.

"I had to cut steel rods into small studs. Then I laid the chain out flat so I could weld the studs onto the chain. I'm hoping the welds will hold. We won't know for sure until we drop the blade."

My grandfather coughed out his thoughts. "We'll need to adjust the grading angle so that we turn the gravel over without pushing it off the road." He pulled a locking pin up, which allowed him to swing the blade so that it was perpendicular to the maintainer. He locked it in place by dropping the pin back down in the hole.

Hank nodded. "We can try to bring the drier gravel up from the bottom of the roadbed and bury the icier gravel."

"The studs alone won't be enough, but I got another idea that will hopefully make the difference. It's an old trick I learned years ago with deep snow," Grandpa said.

I could feel his excitement growing and I urged him on. "What?"

"When the snow is deep, the maintainer will do just fine on level ground and will do even better on the downhill stretches. It's pushing snow uphill where you need more traction and power than the maintainer can deliver. George, remember that night after you got stuck in the yard? I said I needed to try something. . . ."

"Yes."

"Well, that was it. I tried grading only on the downhill sections and flat sections. In the barnyard, you were trying to push on a slight uphill grade. When I turned down our hill, going west, it was much better. It was almost there. If we only grade going downhill, with the chains and the studs, I think we can make it."

Something was missing. "I don't understand. How can you only grade downhill? What about the uphill sections of the road?"

"Easy. Lift the blade, and drive up the hill without grading, then we'll turn around and go back down the same hill with the blade dropped."

I knew he was right. It would work.

I was pushing my luck, but something inside of me wanted to do this. "Can I take the first go with it?"

My grandfather smiled at my enthusiasm, but he would have none of it.

"George, this is going to be tricky; you need to let me check it out. Maybe you can give it a try later. Driving on ice is different. You should never slam on the brakes; you've got to tap them rapidly. Otherwise, you might skid and rip the studs off the chains."

Realizing that my last foray onto the ice had not turned out well, I only nodded my head and meekly offered, "I can do that."

"I've never done this myself, so I can't really tell you how to do it. My best guess is that we should not grade any deeper than necessary. Hopefully, one to three inches will pull up enough dry material to clear the gravel roads."

"How about the asphalt roads?" Hank asked.

"We'll take it down to the roadbed, if we can."

My old Santa Claus of a grandfather looked like he was about to throw up. He bent over, anticipating nausea, before regaining his composure. "Let's all get a good night's sleep and then start up tomorrow morning. Hank, would you like a ride home? It would give me a chance to test it out."

"You look miserable, Bo. I'll walk back." He lifted his legs to show off the same modification to his shoes. "You've done it a half-dozen times in the last few days—it's my turn."

My grandfather did not argue, and as we headed back into the house, it occurred to me that there was a chance, just a chance, that Cherokee County might still have a Christmas. "Do you think we can grade all the roads in two days?"

My grandfather clapped me on the back. "We've still got problems, George."

I knew what he meant. In those days, there were no salt trucks to help melt the ice or sand trucks to help gain friction. Most vehicles were rear-wheel drive; there were no radial tires and very few people even had snow tires. Without the maintainer pushing the ice off the road, most of our neighbors would be lucky to even get out of their driveways. If they could get out of the driveway, they would not get far.

My grandfather further defined the problem. "There are trees down everywhere, blocking the roads. We'll need chain saws and men to run them and tractors to pull limbs off the road. We would have to have an army of men to get this done before Christmas. We can only do what we can do. We may not get far, but we can get some of the main roads cleared."

If it had been up to me, we would have started a night shift on the spot, with me taking the first turn, but so far my efforts at taking charge had not gone so well.

As I looked at my grandfather that evening, all tired and worn-out, I realized that it just was not going to happen. It wasn't until many years later, when I had my own family, that I realized what he was going through. As children, we feel like the adults in our lives are always pushing us to do more than we want or feel like we should have to do. I didn't understand then that for every inch he pushed me, I had been pushing him the length of an old-fashioned yardstick. He had had enough.

CHAPTER 32

Twice during the night, I had to get up and tuck my sheets back under the mattress. Laying at the foot of my bed, Tucker had been fidgeting and shifting himself around nervously, and no matter how hard I tried, the blankets did not seem suited for him. With his canine version of tossing and turning going on most of the night, it seemed like the alarm would never go off. Finally, I could stand it no more and rolled out of bed just shy of 4:20 in the morning, armed with a plan. Frankly, Tucker hadn't been the only thing keeping me up. I'd been mulling over an idea and I was ready to put it into action.

The milking I could do on my own—that would give my grandfather a head start. For once, he could sleep in while I got the chores completed and the old diesel engine on the maintainer warmed up for a day of hard work.

After bundling up against the chill in my dark bedroom, I took the leash and a flashlight from the tool drawer in the kitchen, and Tucker and I made our way down to the barn, with only a narrow beam of yellow light to guide us through the ice-covered barnyard.

Without power, we were still milking by hand. My

grandfather was right: the Babson Bros. automatic milking machine was an unparalleled invention, and I couldn't wait to get it back. The milk we were pouring out every day was making a frozen mound behind the barn large enough to feed an army of cats. There were raccoon tracks all around the milk mountain, where those resourceful creatures were determined to break off icy chunks for food.

By 7:30 the sun was up, the chores were done, and the ice was cracked, and I started the maintainer to warm it up. I had been expecting my grandfather to join me all morning long but was not too worried when he didn't show. When I got to the house, with a load of firewood in my arms, my grandmother had breakfast waiting for me. "Where's Grandpa?" I asked.

"He spent most of the night in the bathroom. He is exhausted, sick, and won't be out of bed for a week—if he's lucky. Just like I told him."

My heart sank. Of course, I felt sorry for him, but what about the roads? What about Christmas? He had worked so hard and now it was all for nothing? Although I was getting used to the rule book being ignored, surely this was not fair. I'd gotten up extra early just to help Grandpa get out the door and onto the maintainer so that we could get our shifts rolling, but now my plans were wrecked. And so was Christmas for Cherokee County.

Around 8:00, Grandpa stumbled into the kitchen. My disappointment was so deep, I could hardly look up at him.

He interrupted the silence. "Picked an awful time to get sick, didn't I?"

He looked worse and I knew he had no business being out of bed. I mumbled, "People get sick. I did the chores."

"Crack the ice?"

It was embarrassing that he had to ask, but I knew it was a fair question. "Yes, that, too."

"Is that the maintainer I hear running?"

"Yes. I didn't know you were sick."

"Well, you might as well shut it down. Maybe tomorrow."

My grandmother moved into his space like a pouncing cat. "Tomorrow! I don't think so."

Big Bo McCray knew he had met his match, and he quickly turned tail and headed back to the bedroom, mumbling over his shoulder, "We'll see."

I sat at the kitchen table, feeling defeated once more. But while I was running my hand through Tucker's fur, a rough outline of a new and improved plan began forming in my mind.

A week before, I had guided the maintainer up Blackberry Hill to visit Wild Tom Turner. There was a strange feeling in my stomach, an ache just below my solar plexus, as I headed up that driveway that led to Turner's trailer. Many years later, I would come to recognize that dull aching feeling in my stomach as the way my conscience tries to tell me to think again. Now, for the second time in a week, I experienced that feeling, knowing that I was about to do something I should not do, but willing to do it anyway. If they got really mad at me, what would they do—banish me to Minnesota?

After I shoved my arms through the sleeves of my coat and pulled on my hat and gloves, Tucker and I headed back outside. Once inside the implement barn, I sat on the seat of that maintainer, and instead of shutting it down, I did what I had no business doing. After all, I am a McCray.

"Tucker, get up here with me!" I moved over and he situated himself in the bed I had made for him.

With the maintainer in reverse, I backed out of the barn. Tucker and I were headed out to clear the roads of Cherokee County. We didn't bother looking back.

CHAPTER 33

With my feet parked by the steel heater that blasted warm air from the bottom of the maintainer, and my coat buttoned to the top, I shifted the transmission into first gear and eased out of the barnyard. As a renegade road maintainer, there was no stopping at the house for food or drink. I was sure Grandma Cora could hear the big machine go by, and that she'd see me from the kitchen and tell my grandfather, but no one was about to chase me down on this ice.

At the end of the driveway, I turned east and headed down the hill. The maintainer was sure-footed with the chains and homemade studs that Hank Fisher had spent the night welding, but the real test was dropping the blade.

I wanted to wait for a flat spot, with shallow ditches on each side, to test out the modifications, but I would be on a downhill slope for a while. Taking a deep breath, I grabbed the adjusting lever and let the blade down easy, an inch at a time.

The maintainer jerked to the right, causing me to lose control just as I had in the driveway a few days before. I panicked for fear that I would flip the maintainer, and

I did the worst thing possible and applied the brakes too hard. The maintainer started to skid out of control. Determined not to fail before I even got to the bottom of McCray's Hill, I remembered what Grandpa had told me. While it seemed counterintuitive, I tried releasing and tapping the brakes. The maintainer started to straighten and the skidding stopped. Pushing the blade farther down to the road surface gave me even more stability. I could hear the sweet sound of ice coming up and off the road. I turned around and looked behind me.

The maintainer was the world's largest ice cube maker, spewing chunks of ice off each end of the blade! Grandpa was right—the momentum of going down the hill was just what we needed.

I was ready to spring my plan into action.

First stop was our nearest neighbor to the east, Frank Thorne. After I bladed the ice right off his driveway, I jumped down and ran to his door.

I was out of breath, but when Thorne came to the door, I blurted out, "I wanted to thank you."

"It was nothing, kid." He seemed to be avoiding my gaze. "How are you doing? You were in pretty bad shape last time I saw you."

"I'm all better now. It was nice to have this guy around to keep me company," I said, nodding at Tucker.

"I had some things I needed to do and I couldn't let him tag along—thanks for watching him again."

He reached down and patted Tucker on the head.

"It was no problem."

"Hang on to him a little longer. I can see he's enjoying riding around with you on that big machine. What do you want, George?"

Excited, I struggled to get my words out. "I was wondering . . . could I get . . . your help on something?"

He looked at me suspiciously. "A McCray asking a Thorne for help?"

There was a lot of hurt in his words, but I pointed out to him an undeniable truth. "Mr. Thorne, you already helped a McCray the other day. You saved my life."

From the gleam in his eyes, I could tell that he was a little proud of himself—deservedly. "What do you have on your mind?"

Once I had explained the problem, he looked at me in a curious way and said, "Stay here." He shut the door and I waited in the cold morning air for him to return. When he did, he was dressed warmly, a chain saw in one hand and the keys to his old brown truck in the other.

CHAPTER 34

When my grandfather awoke from a nap later that afternoon, my grandmother insisted that he get up and out of bed and eat in the kitchen. He told me later how her mood had changed. One minute she'd exiled him to the bedroom, and now she wanted him up and about. Perhaps to make sure he stayed in bed, she had not shared with him that I had headed out of the driveway on the maintainer earlier that morning.

Her hands on her hips, she hovered over the bed and said, "Bo, you're a no-good lazy man. Get up out of that bed this minute and come into the kitchen for some food. Besides, there's something I want you to see."

The look on his face when he came to the kitchen window and peered out into the barnyard must have been pure astonishment. He was looking out at the "army" he and Hank said we would need to clear the roads of Cherokee County: thirteen crews of men in trucks with chain saws and fourteen tractors with driveway blades or tow chains to haul off logs. Earlier that morning, Frank Thorne had helped me and Tucker spread the word from farm to farm, and now everyone was saying the same thing: *Let's get the roads cleared for Christmas.* The

McCray farm was headquarters for this effort. It was like a contest to see who could help the most. Each driveway that Thorne and I had cleared that morning netted us another volunteer road maintainer. Although it was still well below freezing, working conditions were decent. No more snow or ice was coming down, so it wasn't getting any worse.

The word eventually spread all the way to town and the phone and power company crews got into the spirit, too.

My plan was to make the first priority clearing the roads of downed trees and branches so the utility trucks could make their repairs and the maintainer could pass through. Once the maintainer cut its initial eight-foot swath straight down the middle of the road, the much smaller farm tractors could find enough traction to take another foot or two with their driveway blades. In this fashion, the maintainer, in tandem with four or five tractors, could clear the roads in one pass. Without the maintainer leading the way, none of this would have worked.

Tucker and I kept the maintainer going all day on December 22 and December 23. Thorne changed his mind and decided to take some night shifts on the maintainer.

The road crews worked through the nights, as well. Along the sides of the roads of Cherokee County were stacks of wood and a foot-high pile of ice. On the third day, Christmas Eve, we were blessed with warmer weather that aided our efforts, and more houses, including our own, had their phone and power service restored. Things were just about getting back to normal.

Frank Thorne seemed to naturally take over the job as manager of the auxiliary road crew. I was glad to hand over the reins. It appeared he had a better ability to manage others than he did to manage his own life. My grandfather said that during the war, by all accounts Thorne had been a good soldier. Perhaps he got a little of his pride and confidence back by stepping up and taking responsibility for the crew.

Grandma Cora and other local women kept our kitchen busy with pots of coffee and massive amounts of food for the hungry workers. As I worked the maintainer, Tucker remained with me up in the cab, and I couldn't imagine working a shift without him. It was fantastic having him back with me again—even if he wasn't really my dog.

In the early afternoon of December 24, I returned home from my last shift and more fell than got off the maintainer. Everyone had gone home. The parking areas where our road crew had assembled were empty. Instead of climbing back onto the maintainer to take over, my grandfather just put his arms around my shoulders and said, "We're done. It's good enough."

I started to protest that there were still roads to be cleared, so he repeated himself. "It's good enough. I think you can take a lot of the credit for giving Christmas back to Cherokee County, son. Come inside. There's someone who would like to see you."

There were no cars other than ours parked in the driveway, so I was surprised that I had a visitor. Tucker and I made our way up to the house. After kicking off my muddy boots, I opened the back door and walked into the kitchen, with my grandfather following right behind.

Standing by the sink were my mother and my two sisters. They had decided to take the bus from Minneapolis to Crossing Trails. Thanks to all of our work the last two days, Hank and his wife were able to bring them the rest of the way in their car. My grandparents knew they were on their way, but they wanted it to be a surprise. It was the best Christmas present I could get.

Tears streamed down my mom's face. Not waiting for me to come to her, she quickly closed the space between us and held me in her arms, shifting her weight back and forth in a rocking motion. She held me so tightly I wasn't sure I could breathe. She just kept saying over and over, "Oh, honey, oh, honey . . ."

Her wet tears felt warm on my cold face. "George, you're freezing." She cupped my chin in her soft hands as if to warm me up, the way she'd done since I was a small child. "I just can't believe what you've done! I'm proud of you. Your sisters and I missed you so much."

Her warmth flowed through my veins and invigorated my spirit, but the strong emotions I felt left me tongue-tied. "Thanks, Mom" was all I could manage. I reached down and hugged Tucker. "This is our dog!" It may not have been the truth, but that was how I felt. Tucker had become a McCray.

Before I knew it, my two sisters, Trisha and Hannah,

had their arms around me, too; I realized just how much I had missed the rest of my family. They kept looking at me and saying, "George, you look different."

My grandmother stood back and gave us the space we needed to reconnect. "Sit down and rest! Eat." She herded everyone to the dining-room table, which was covered with food.

For the first time since June 14, 1962, my whole family was sitting down together, laughing and feeling joy. The absence of my father still hung in the air, but it was not weighing us down.

We sat at the table for a good long while, chatting and eating way more than we needed, as if we were making up for months of missed family dinners. Periodically, my grandmother would go into the kitchen, where she would make and receive telephone calls to and from friends and neighbors. We couldn't hear much of her conversation from the dining room, but apparently there was a lot of catching up to do. She spent most of the afternoon chatting on the phone with our neighbors—though she acted so secretive that I started to think it was her turn to be up to something.

We enjoyed recounting the day-to-day, seemingly insignificant details that had made up our lives over the last few months—the unreliable gas stove in the new house; the day a kid at school flooded the boys' bathroom; the traffic outside of Minneapolis; how I milked the cows without the help of the Babson Brothers, and much more. Of course, Mom wanted to hear every last detail of

my fall into the frozen pond, and all about Tucker's heroics. I made sure to also give Frank Thorne credit. As we
talked, Tucker made his way around the room and took
his time getting to know my mother and my sisters, with
the help of the table scraps they slipped to him.

As the afternoon came to an end and we finally began
clearing the table and cleaning up the dishes, something
wholly unexpected occurred. It started with a knock on
the back door. It being a country home, no one ever came
to the front door.

When I opened the door, there stood Hank Fisher and
his wife. "Well, if it isn't the youngest maintainer!" Hank
boomed, shaking my hand.

Before I even had a chance to ask him in, our neighbors to the west, William Foster and his family, appeared
at the door. Both the Fishers and the Fosters said they
wanted to thank the McCrays for keeping their roads
cleared. As they stepped into the kitchen, there were
more knocks on the door and more cars arriving. One
after another, nearly all our neighbors and many members of the volunteer road crew showed up.

After six or seven cars arrived and no one left, it became clear to me that these were not random instances
of neighborly gratitude, with the Fishers and Fosters
and others just happening to show up at the same time.
Grandma Cora's phone calls! She was behind all this.

Tucker wound his way through our now-crowded
house, with overflow in the kitchen, the dining room,
and the living room, where the Christmas tree that had

seemed so bare only a few days before was suddenly now wrapped in bright lights, surrounded by packages decked out in Christmas colors of green and red. Mrs. Slater, most of the Rather family (Sherry was home with a healthy baby boy), and even a quiet but smiling Frank Thorne became part of the crowd. Most of the gifts that had materialized beneath the tree were presents from grateful residents of Cherokee County.

Many of our neighbors recognized Tucker from the hours he spent beside me on the maintainer. Hank Fisher gave him an affectionate pat and then looked up at me.

"George, if firemen need Dalmatians, I guess maintainers need Irish setters!" Frank Thorne, who'd been standing within earshot of Hank, caught my eye at that moment and nodded. I nodded back, though I felt a wave of sadness as I knew my time with Tucker was running out—as was my time with all the good people who surrounded me now.

If Grandpa Bo was still feeling a little tired after his go-round with the flu and his night shifts on the maintainer, his energy was now revitalized by the crowd of well-wishers. While he may not have uttered twenty words to many of his neighbors before, tonight Grandpa spoke freely of how I had single-handedly saved his herd of cattle from certain death and how proud he was of me for organizing the emergency road-clearing efforts. He told everyone he could get to listen that it was my persistence that had cleared the roads of ice.

My family allowed my grandfather his proud boasts, though I was a bit embarrassed at all the attention, as any thirteen-year-old boy would have been. Still, I like to think that my mother and I both realized that night that she had not left me "behind" in Kansas. Over the last four months, and particularly in the last few days, I had moved "ahead"—far, far ahead.

Once the last guest had parted with his or her wish for a Merry Christmas, the evening milking was finished, and every dish was cleaned and put away, Grandma put on her coat and told us to bundle up. "We're going into town." It seemed there was one more surprise she'd cooked up.

I couldn't bear to leave my friend behind. "Can I bring Tucker?"

"Sure, but he'll have to wait in the car for part of the time."

When we did not move fast enough, she ordered, "Load up, now!"

Driving into town in Grandma's Impala, all crunched together, family and dog, we had no idea what she was up to. Apparently, my grandfather did not know, either. She issued directions as we went. "Left at the light. Now keep going. Go straight to the school."

The Crossing Trails Central School parking lot was full. When we got out of the car, my grandmother clutched a grocery sack so close to her that one wondered if the contents came from a bank vault. Before she got out of the car, my mother cracked open her window. We left Tucker resting on the backseat, burrowed beneath a warm wool blanket. He was glad to be included in our trip to town and seemed to understand that not all errands were dog errands.

Within moments, it was clear what Grandma Cora had been up to that night. With a little organizing from the women in our community, the town of Crossing Trails patched together a spontaneous pageant to celebrate the holiday that almost was not. We collected at the Crossing Trails Central School auditorium.

As the audience found their seats, some grade-schoolers on stage stumbled, rather than led us, through Christmas carols. Still, like most of the adults in the crowd, my mom and grandparents broke into wide grins at the sound of children singing. When we got ready to sit down, my grandmother, still holding firm to that grocery sack, grabbed my hand.

"Not you, George. You are coming with me."

It was clear that she was on some kind of mission as she led me to the door of the boys' bathroom and thrust the sack at me. "Put this on and go find your teacher—she's waiting for you backstage. And hurry. We don't have much time," she said before she disappeared back down the hallway. I peeked in the sack and discovered that Grandma Cora had hurriedly sewn together a Santa Claus costume. I pulled it on, including a hat with a white beard attached, and then turned to the mirror. I looked absolutely ridiculous.

"Hey, George—can you give me a hand?" I thought I was alone in the bathroom until I heard the voice of my classmate Eddie Sampson, who was trying to struggle into an elf suit. Suddenly, I felt less ridiculous.

It turned out that the centerpiece of that night's show was the production of a Christmas play by the sixth- and seventh-graders. Performing the lines that I had never bothered to memorize, while wearing my Santa ensemble, would take far more courage than driving a maintainer in a blizzard or rescuing a few cows from a frozen pond. Then Mrs. Weeks put me at ease as she handed me the script.

"We're only doing the last act, and you can read your lines." She walked out onto the stage and the cast of *Santa and the Lost Elves* followed behind. Well, I thought as I shuffled out onto the stage with my heart pounding, if a tough guy like Eddie could wear red tights in public, then I could wear Grandma's Saint Nick costume and read, a skill I had down pat.

Mrs. Weeks stepped up to the microphone, summarized the first two acts for the audience, and then concluded, "With the school closing, our actors have not had time to memorize their lines, so their dramatic interpretation of Act Three will be read. Santa Claus is played by George McCray."

My sister Trisha embarrassed me terribly by whooping and hollering at the mention of my name. That actually was the worst part. In fact, with the summary of the first two acts inserted, and with all of us practically speed-reading our lines as kids tend to do, the play was bearable and mercifully short.

As I offered my final "Ho, ho, ho and have a Merry Christmas," we exited the stage to enthusiastic applause. My friend Mary Ann was dressed as an angel; her hair was pulled back behind her plastic halo, and when I looked at her, I thought she played the part well.

She grabbed my arm playfully. "Good job, George! You didn't fall asleep once."

"That's only because you didn't have any lines," I shot back.

With no warning, she leaned toward me and kissed me on the cheek and whispered, "I am going to miss you."

Thankfully, she darted off and did not see me playing the part of George, the red-faced Santa Claus.

After I changed out of my costume and said some hurried but wistful goodbyes to a few friends—all of whom swore they'd be my Kansas pen pals forever—I found my family by the main door and we made our way out to Grandma's car. I ran ahead to let Tucker out and then we circled back to the join the group. Suddenly, there was a shout from across the parking lot. I assumed it was just another neighborly well-wisher.

"Hey, George!"

It was Frank Thorne. He walked toward us, holding a package.

My grandmother gave Thorne a big hug, which surprised me, until I remembered the role she'd played in helping Thorne shake off his old ways and take some steps forward—some very large steps, indeed.

"Our George was in the Christmas play. He was the star."

Thorne looked at me approvingly. "I saw. A damn, I mean darn, good Santa Claus."

He reached out and shook my hand. "I want to thank you, George. What you and your family have done for me means more than you can imagine. I want you to have this." He handed me the package he had been carrying.

I took the package but did not know what to say or do.

"Go ahead, open it."

The paper came off easily enough, but in the dim light of the parking lot, it took me a moment to understand what it was that I held. It was the picture of Thorne and my father that had hung on his wall. I swallowed hard and held out my hand to shake his. "Thank you, Mr. Thorne. I'm pleased to have a picture of you and my dad."

His words were soft and gentle this time, without the old edge I'd first encountered. "You can call me Frank. Your dad was a fine man. Best friend I ever had."

Thorne had taken many a wrong turn and made more than one bad decision, but in a few short weeks I learned how good a man he truly was. I had Thorne wrong, all wrong. He taught me an important life lesson that December—that rushing to judgment rarely worked in anyone's favor.

While I was grateful for the picture and the kind words, what he said next meant more.

Thorne stared down at his boots for a few seconds and then looked up at me. There was a glint in the eyes that I could only describe as profound determination. Tucker pulled on his leash and whined. I let go and he made his way over to Thorne, who bent down to pet the dog, then buried his face in his fur. When he stood up, there were small tears in his eyes.

"George, I've got a job. First job I've had in years. It's at the plant, putting together Fords in Kansas City. That's why I asked you to hang on to the dog a few extra days, because I had to make some arrangements. Red here needs to be on the farm. I wonder if you and your grandparents would mind taking him for me?" Before I could answer, he continued, "For good, this time."

I was leaving for Minnesota in a few days, but I was counting on my mom letting me take the dog with me, if not on this trip then at least on the next one. I looked to my grandfather with every ounce of *want* I could muster, but it didn't take much convincing.

Before I could say a word, my grandfather nodded his head approvingly. "Frank, we'll do it. We could use a good dog."

Thorne nodded too, as if to reassure me. "Go ahead, George. You'd be doing me a favor."

I knelt down to scratch Tucker. He cocked his head at Thorne, then looked back at me. It seemed that Tucker understood. He looked at Thorne one more time and barked.

"Stay," Frank said to him, with a little smile. "It's all going to be okay—Tucker."

As I felt Tucker's cold wet nose and warm fur on my face, I did not understand what rule allowed us to have this dog, but I felt a gratitude that seeped into the very marrow of my bones. As excited as I was to get Tucker one step closer to being mine, it was going to be very disappointing if I couldn't take him with me.

"Mr. Thorne—Frank . . . ," I stammered, looking up to thank him, but he was already walking away, heading back to his truck. The old engine turned over and with a final wave he drove off, leaving me stunned. I held Tucker like I would never let him go. As I got to my feet, I tried to think of a thousand ways to thank Frank Thorne, but I didn't get the chance. The next morning, his worldly possessions were loaded into his truck. He got in it and drove off without saying goodbye, never to be seen again.

CHAPTER 35

When we got home, Mom kept hugging me and asking for more details about everything I had been doing the last few weeks. Sitting on the living room floor, I answered her questions as best I could.

"Weren't you scared of driving that big old maintainer?"

"At the beginning. But I got used to it after the first few days."

"Tell me again about the ice."

Tucker chose that moment to offer a friendly bark at Mom. She ran her hands through his fur. "I know just how you felt, Tucker. Some days I was so worried about George, too."

My sisters and grandparents joined us in the living room to open a few presents, as we'd always done on Christmas Eve. It was quite late, but this was a McCray family tradition. I didn't feel the urge to unwrap anything, though, since to me Tucker was the best package under the tree.

It was hard to believe that he was mine. Every few minutes I hugged my beautiful red dog and let him know how pleased I was to have him back on the farm for good.

My mother sat in the chair closest to the fireplace and stared at all of the packages. Even though there was a smile on her face, her eyes still looked sad. I think we all had the same hollow feeling in our stomachs. With all the commotion surrounding our impromptu open house, followed by the excitement of the Christmas pageant and then Thorne's "gift" to me, I'd managed to avoid confronting the reality we all now faced together: the first Christmas we would share without my father.

She caught me looking at her and said, "You have a lot of thank-you notes to write, young man."

Around midnight, with yawns and droopy eyes, we opened the packages from our neighbors and friends, saving the more personal family gifts for Christmas Day. My sisters played the roles of Santa's helpers and read each gift tag aloud, all of us chuckling at how many packages were for Tucker. "Here's another one—For the Big Red Dog!" There were many presents for me, as well.

Of course, I can't remember all of the gifts that showed up that night, but there were a few that stood out, including a thank-you note from Mrs. Slater with a picture of Tucker she had drawn and a little red plastic dog Christmas ornament that I still hang on the tree.

With the fire burning warm and the gift opening behind us, I felt very content with Tucker and the rest of my family all in one room. As I became even more relaxed, I remembered how comforting it was to just experience family conversation, without listening to individual words. What they said didn't matter. It was like a symphony—the sounds of the particular instruments were lost to the larger pattern and movements of sound. Although it had been a very long time since I had heard it, and one important instrument was missing, it was still an old familiar concerto that played through our home once again that night.

I drifted off listening to my sisters and my mother sitting around the table struggling to find the shapes that would fit into a still unknown pattern. The last words I remembered were "Grandma hasn't touched last year's puzzle."

CHAPTER 36

On Christmas Day, while Grandma and my mother made breakfast, Trisha and Hannah gave the Mc-Cray men their first present for Christmas day—helping with the chores. Even with electricity, it still took us over two hours to do the milking. Watching Trisha and Hannah try to strap the Babson Bros. automatic milking machine onto a cow not only made me feel like an old pro but kept me laughing for most of the morning. Grandpa and I could knock our routine out in an hour and a half, but I doubted with as much cheer.

Breakfast was served in the dining room. Special occasions, like Christmas morning, usually brought forth the same menu of warm buttermilk biscuits, smoked bacon, and scrambled eggs piled high on an antique dish. Our appetites were intact and before long we pushed away from the table content.

We were all trying very hard to be thankful for what we had and not dwell on what we had lost. But try as we did, the excitement from yesterday wore off and we were all faced with the difficult realization that John McCray, our father, son, or spouse, was gone. It was one of many firsts that we had to get through.

With a wet dish towel in my hand and the breakfast dishes almost behind me, my mom took me aside. She handed me a sack and whispered into my ear, "Merry Christmas." I opened the bag to find that it was full of my favorite oatmeal cookies.

"Thanks, Mom."

She gave me a big hug and said, "George, you've turned into such a nice young man, but I still think I am going to miss my boy."

Of course, I beamed when she called me a man.

"Your dad and I are both so proud of you." She held me tightly a minute longer before she took my hand and said, "I've missed you. It's going to be good having you home with me again."

I didn't know what to say. There was no use telling her that I was torn in two about leaving. It would have broken her heart. Still, she could tell that something was bothering me.

"Come on, George, we've got family presents to open. It's Christmas!" She wiped her eyes quickly and headed for the living room.

We were about to gather around the tree, but we could not find my grandfather. Grandma Cora yelled for him several times, but he did not appear. She went to the bedroom to look for him. When she returned, her energy seemed drained and she asked us to be patient; Grandpa Bo would need just a few more minutes. When he finally came into the living room, he looked so worn-out that I thought he must have journeyed a hundred miles from that back bedroom. In some ways, I suppose he had.

Before he sat down, he placed under the tree a package wrapped in brown paper, cut from a grocery sack.

Typically, we unwrapped presents in a frenzy, but this year we took our time, offering polite thank-yous along the way. Hannah handed the gifts out one at a time. Eventually, the presents dwindled down to that little brown package.

Hannah cried out, "We forgot this one!" She held the last little brown paper package in her hand. "It says, 'To Tucker, from the McCray family.'"

She passed it over to me. "Here, George, you open it for Tucker."

We were all excited to have something to offer our newest family member. His brushed red coat was perfect for Christmas and his fine figure adorned the living room floor with as much flare as any ornament on the tree. I pulled the simple wrapping off the package. I gasped.

My grandfather had carefully sculpted the most beautiful dog collar I had ever seen. It was made of soft brown leather and he had burned in the words TUCKER MCCRAY. There were brass rivets to hold the buckle in place. I put the collar around Tucker and it stayed there for many years to come.

As everyone dispersed about the house, Grandma called me into the kitchen. She and Grandpa were standing by the sink. Grandma spoke first.

"Your grandfather has another gift for you. It's a going-away present."

"George, I want you to know how much I appreciate all of the help you've given us these last few weeks. You're going to be a tough hand to replace." He then handed me a box wrapped in red paper. There was a handwritten note that went with it, scrawled with words in my grandfather's old-fashioned handwriting:

To: The best maintainer this family ever had!
From: Grandma and Grandpa McCray

I unwrapped the box and lifted the lid. It was my grandfather's tin cup that had sat by that kitchen sink for so many years. It would have gone to my father, but instead it came to me.

I stared at the gift for a long time, strangely touched by the simple tin cup that had been handed down from father to son for four generations. My grandfather must have been holding two very different thoughts in his head at the same time. He was glad to pass this piece of family history to me, but how sad he must have felt to skip a generation.

Trying to break the solemn mood, I put the ancient tin cup to my lips, drank the imaginary contents dry, and let out a long "Ahh."

The moment touched Grandpa. The cup was not valuable to anyone else, but it signified something important to him. I drew nearer to give him a hug. "Thank you,

Grandpa." He held me tight in his still strong arms. Of course, I was thanking him for much more than a cup.

Many years later, my mother told me something that had never crossed my mind. Losing my father had broken Bo's heart, but on that Christmas day, the thought of me packing up and leaving just about finished him off.

My grandmother spoke up. "Now that you're an official road maintainer, you'll need a good cup to drink from. That cup has sat by our sink for sixty years; now it can sit by your sink in Minnesota."

CHAPTER 37

Even on Christmas day, there were chores to do. We trusted Tucker around the cows now, but I still kept him tethered with his new collar and long leash in the barn while I milked. I insisted on taking both shifts that day, but I had a new partner that afternoon.

"You didn't think I knew how to do this, did you?" My mom swung the Babson Bros. milker into place.

"You're good, Mom, but I think you need a little more practice."

She looked up from the milker. "I've got two more days to learn, before we leave."

I tried to smile. "That's right."

She seemed to be testing the waters with her next comment. "I am looking forward to being your mother again."

"You don't need to worry, Mom. Grandma has been taking good care of me." It didn't occur to me how it might hurt her to hear this.

"I'm glad for that . . ." Her words trailed off and she worked quietly until we were finished and walked back to the house.

The day's activities and a dinner of turkey and dressing made us all tired. That evening, I just read and once more enjoyed the presence of my family and my dog. My sisters gestured to the puzzle table. "Grandma, why don't you help us?"

Grandma Cora stood in the dining room with a pained look on her face. I don't think she knew how to go back to that table, where she had passed so many hours with my father, without feeling his absence. It was safer to avoid it. When she didn't answer, it was clear to me that the idea of puzzling was causing her discomfort.

"I don't think she wants to do the puzzle," I blurted out.

Apparently my observation did not help matters. She turned and walked away. My sisters realized what they had done and raced after her into the kitchen, with my mother close behind.

There were tearful sobs and apologies. It was quiet for a very long time, and I began to wonder what they were doing and why it was taking so long. My grandfather set down his newspaper and was shifting his weight nervously.

Suddenly, my grandmother's clear-as-a-bell voice echoed through the house. "Come on, girls."

Seconds later the McCray women emerged from the kitchen, composed and determined. They stopped for a moment, and with a measure of strength and beauty that I would never forget, my grandmother spoke just two simple words. "It's time."

They sat down at the puzzle table, grasped hands, and

closed their eyes. They were silent for a few moments and I felt a knot form in my throat. When my grandmother opened her eyes, they were clear and alive. An unclaimed joyful presence seemed to flow in the room like a refreshing spring breeze.

She tucked a stray white hair behind one ear, smiled, and said, "We have work to do."

With eight hands they made fast progress.

Around 11:00 that night, with the last embers of the fire pulsing with a warm dry heat, Hannah calmly observed, "Finished."

I was half asleep on the sofa, but I smiled from my daze.

Grandma Cora motioned to me. "Come see, George."

Rolling off the sofa, I went over to the puzzle table. What I saw took me by surprise. It was an aerial photograph of our farm cut into a puzzle.

Grandma grabbed my hand and said, "You know, George, your father liked to give me puzzles that were darn near impossible to put together. This time he almost did it."

It was late, so I just leaned over and kissed each of the four women I loved most in the world on the cheek and went to bed. Within a few minutes, my sisters and Tucker followed behind. It seemed that he, too, needed a good night's rest. Tomorrow I would have to finish packing. Again, it seemed that some rule was strangely off-kilter. Young men should not have to leave the homes they love—nor should they be separated from their parents.

I couldn't sleep. Around midnight, I heard voices coming up through the floor grate. Like me, they were all wondering what would come next.

My mother's voice was agitated. "He is just playing at packing. He hasn't asked about his new room, our house, or his new school. Don't you think if he wanted to go, he would say something?"

My grandmother tried to reassure her. "Sarah, this is the only home he has ever known. He can be both sad to leave and happy to be back with you at the same time."

My mother seemed to know exactly how I felt. "I don't think that's it; it's clear to me that he doesn't want to go."

"Of course he wants to be with you and his sisters."

"Has he ever said anything about not wanting to go?"

My grandmother was silent for a few moments before she did something I never thought possible. She lied. "No, honey, George would never say that."

Finally, my grandfather asked in his to-the-point way, "Is he old enough to decide on his own?"

My mother's voice cracked. "I won't do that to him. It puts him in an awful place: choosing between people he loves. This isn't about me and my needs. It's about what's best for him."

I heard the old kitchen chairs being pushed away from the table. Tired, weary, and familiar-sounding steps creaked on the staircase. I closed my eyes, the way kids do when they pretend to be sleeping and a parent comes into the room, just as my mother pushed open the door.

I felt her weight on the bed as she came and sat beside

me. She ran her hands through my hair for a few moments. Tucker got up from his resting spot on my bed and walked over me to get to her for a pat, which gave me the perfect excuse to "wake up."

I sat up and my mom took me in her arms like she was just giving me a big goodnight hug. She held on to me for a very long time. It was a hug she knew would have to last for many years to come.

"George, I want to talk to you. Are you awake enough to listen?"

CHAPTER 38

My mother's winter visits back to the farm in the years to come were some of the best times of my young life. Even after my sisters were married and had families of their own, Mom faithfully returned every December for the holidays. I spent Thanksgiving and six weeks of the summer in Minnesota. In between, we exchanged endless letters, spoke regularly by phone, and made extra trips when we could. There may have been some distance between us, but there was no lack of connection.

It's been a long time now since she made her last Christmas visit to our farm in Kansas. A very long time. That's what makes today so special.

She should be arriving any minute now. I have Tucker's collar, my grandfather's tin cup, and the last puzzle my father gave Grandma Cora, all sitting here beside me. Mom's memory is fading. The doctor encouraged us to show her objects when we recount the past to her. It was up to me to be the curator for this exhibit, to put together just the right pieces from our family museum.

When the time is right, I want her to sit by the fire, hear our stories, and be comforted by our history—to know how important her place is. There are things I want to tell her, things I want her to understand. I don't know what she remembers, what is lost, and how much more time I have to let her know how I feel. I practice the story one last time. . . .

Grandpa was the road maintainer for Cherokee County. His name was Bo McCray and my grandmother's name was Cora. After Dad died, I stayed here on the farm, with my dog, Tucker, to live with my grandparents. They helped bring me up. Of all the courageous people from that period in my life, my mom was one of the bravest. She let me stay here because she knew it would have hurt me too much to leave.

Having children of my own, I know how hard it must have been for her. Sometimes the strongest people in the world are the ones who let go so the rest of us can hang on.

In the winter of 1962, I learned how to be a maintainer. Some might think that it wasn't an important job, but I'm convinced that most of the important tasks in our lives all amount to the same thing: clearing away the burdens that block our way.

Tucker and I had five more warm summers and cold winters together before he became an old man of a dog. Many of those winters had snow days, but nothing like the snow we experienced that year. How it piled up.

Within a few years, I was driving Grandpa's old Ford truck to school and dating a young woman. Mary Ann had been my best friend on the bus for years. She was an angel in that Christmas pageant. When the pageant was over, I looked at her in a different way. I am still looking at her like that forty years later.

Grandma Cora told me that Tucker could hear me approaching in that Ford truck from miles away. He would begin pacing the back of the porch, his tail wagging furiously and letting out little happy greeting barks when I pulled into the driveway. He was a beautiful dog—the dog of a lifetime.

When I graduated from high school, I went to Vietnam. Tucker and Cherokee County were left behind on a Friday and I would not return for two very long years.

Tucker hardly left the back porch for months. He assumed I would return home after school, just like I did most every other day of his life with us. He thought there was a rule. I knew how he felt—day after day, hoping that someone you love is going to come, as always, right through that back kitchen door.

On an April morning, Tucker became restless. Grandma Cora watched as he got up and looked south to Kill Creek. He whined and ran off for Mack's Ground. Maybe he was looking for me. Maybe he just knew his end was near and wanted to spend his last days in full flower.

People saw him all over the county that week and they would say, "Isn't that George McCray's big red dog?" They would call and let Grandma know that he had been roaming far afield, but no one could ever catch up to him.

After a week, he returned home exhausted but content. He collapsed on the back porch and never got up again. He died there, having led a full and happy life. A truer and better friend I have never known. He was a gift. I will always miss old Tucker.

Grandma Cora and Grandpa Bo found it hard to say goodbye to him, too. They carried him to Mack's Ground and buried him by the lake, the place where he was the happiest. He still rests there. Grandpa made a simple wooden bench and placed it beside the lake. To this day, my family and I can walk to Mack's Ground, sit by the lake, skip stones, and, when the weather permits, dangle our feet in the cool water. Sometimes I tell them about Tucker. His collar has hung in the barn all these years.

I've got it here beside me now.

Grandpa and Grandma are long gone, too. I miss them more than words can tell. When I come in from a day of running McCray's Dairy, from working in the barns and meadows and fields that still surround our farm, I take a long drink from this old tin cup that I still keep by the sink. When it's empty and I've quenched my thirst, I say "Ahh," long and slow.

There is one last thing I will share with my mother. I will tell her that I've had a good life on the farm pictured in Grandma Cora's puzzle by trusting in my father's simple rule: no matter how much falls on us, we keep plowing ahead.

That's the only way to keep the roads clear.

ABOUT THE AUTHOR

GREG KINCAID is a practicing lawyer who helped to start the Changing Lives Through Literature Program in Kansas. He is also involved in pet advocacy and the mentoring of young people. The father of five children, he lives in Johnson County, Kansas, with his wife and two dogs.

AN EXCERPT FROM *NOELLE*

FEATURING THE McCRAY FAMILY

CONVERGENT BOOKS

ON SALE EVERYWHERE BOOKS ARE SOLD

Prologue

This was Lulu's fourteenth litter. Because her puppy count was down, it was also likely her last. She had given so much but was now worn out. She'd been Lester's mint: a golden retriever who had produced twenty thousand dollars' worth of puppies over nine long years. It was hard for Lester to make it on traditional farm income alone; the puppy business helped him bridge the gap. Lulu's large, uniform litters meant eager buyers and good profits for the reliable holiday puppy market. A smallish litter of four, like this brood, was hardly worth the effort. Next year Lulu would have to be replaced with a younger dog.

While the market for soybeans, corn, oats, milo, cattle, and hogs goes up and down, Lester Donaldson counted on puppies for a stable income that came at an opportune time—the long winter months when nothing else grew on his 160-acre farm in north-central Kansas. It was still early November, but in five weeks Lulu's new litter would be ready to sell.

Lester owned seven dogs: four goldens, two Labs, and one standard poodle. The regulations imposed on commercial dog breeders were applicable only to those with more than four females on their premises. To dodge any scrutiny, Lester kept three of the animals on his own property and then rented space from neighbors, where he set up makeshift pens for the other mothers and pups. He sought out silent partners, like his cash-strapped neighbor Ralph Williams, who knew not to ask too many questions and who were satisfied simply to look the other way, leave the dogs be, and take Lester's rent money.

Lester was getting a little ambitious—building more pens, finding more neighbors—so that next season he could expand his inventory even further. The market for the giant breeds—mastiffs, great Danes, and Irish wolfhounds—was excellent, and he wanted to take advantage of it.

The commercial breeders, who owned well over a hundred dogs, were like factories. Lester enjoyed the money, but he was small-time and wanted to keep it that way, flying under the radar. He didn't need people from the government telling him how to keep cages clean or when to call the vet. He could do just fine without any supervision. He sold his inventory over the Internet and in classified ads. He could never keep up with demand. He had a web page that he'd built by dropping in stock pictures of dogs running carefree through flowers in open spring meadows, with cuddly puppies tagging along behind. For one hundred dollars paid online with a credit card, you could reserve your puppy months before the holiday rush. He called his business Dream Dogs, LLC. After he uploaded puppy pictures, he added descriptions that he stole from other web pages and animal shelters. "We call this little guy *Zorro*. When puppy play gets out of hand, he loves to come to the rescue of his baby sister. Great with kids! Hurry, this little dude will go fast!"

Lester felt as if dog breeding was honorable enough work. Puppies make people happy and provide the finishing touch on the perfect family fantasy. He also knew that their living conditions might raise the hackles of some, but puppies, like hamburger and milk, are sold as commodities. Santa was coming, and in that run-up to Christmas no one much cared about how his puppies were raised or how clean their cages were kept—that was all in the past. What mattered now was price, appearance, and availability. Some mom or dad would meet him at an agreed-upon halfway spot, excitedly pick up the chosen puppy, hold it in the air, say something predictable, like, "He sure is cute," turn to Lester, and ask, "Would you take four hundred and fifty dollars?"

Lester would scratch his chin and say, "He's worth every bit of six hundred." He would pause for effect and then ask, "Cash?" and when the buyer nodded his or her head, he'd say, "It's more important to me that little Zorro have a good home than I get every dollar for him that he's worth. How about five hundred?" They'd shake hands, and the deal was done. No expense spared for a happy holiday. Lester would drive home with a fat stack of crisp twenties in his wallet, freshly minted from the neighborhood ATM.

Lester entered the numbers for the still-tiny puppies from Lulu's most recent litter in the register he kept on his iPad as #4118 through #4120, with one anomaly, #4121. He weighed each puppy on a small portable scale and kept the data in the column to the right of each dog's number. The anomaly was three ounces too light. It happened sometimes. Nature does not always offer the uniformity that the dog market craves. It was simple. Golden retrievers have a certain look. Same with Ford Mustangs and BMW 325i's. Without that look . . . well, the dream just didn't come true.

He explained this to his neighbor (and sort-of land-lord, as far as the dogs were concerned), Ralph Williams, and his twelve-year-old daughter, Samantha, that morning as they peered through the wire mesh at the new litter. "If they lack that golden look, you just can't sell 'em." In this particular case, Lester thought that the anomaly had problems that went beyond confirmation or size. The puppy did not even look like a golden—her color was not too far off the mark, but seeing her tiny, too-short legs, he could already tell the proportions were all wrong.

Lester had suspected something that would explain the dog's appearance. Now, as he noted how quiet

Ralph's usually talkative daughter was, he was virtually certain. Samantha had taken Lulu out of the pen—something Lester asked her not to do—and had left Lulu unattended. It was his own fault. He should have put a padlock on the door. This little misfit looked very different from her siblings, and even at this stage Lester could tell she'd grow up to lack the elegant proportions of her mother, though maybe she resembled her father. Like other breeders, Lester had seen it before—different dads, same litter. Some mongrel had wandered onto the Williams property while Lulu was still in heat. Samantha had let Lulu out of the pen, or at least failed to properly shut the gate. That was the only explanation.

He held the strange-looking puppy up for inspection and quizzed Samantha. "You didn't let Lulu out, did you?"

Samantha's father frowned at his daughter. He liked the extra income from housing Lester's pups, but he didn't like his daughter being exposed to the underbelly of the industry. He'd asked her to stay away from the pens. Truth was, he felt bad for the dogs, too, and kept his own distance. This was Lester's project and not his—certainly not Samantha's.

For the life of her, Samantha could not figure out how Lester knew her secret. She thought she'd been very careful. She denied it. She shook her head back and forth. "No, sir. Maybe she got out on her own."

Lester knew she was lying, but it made no difference. What was done was done.

Thinking about the tractor that needed to be fixed before springtime, the hit his crop yield had taken from the latest drought, and the usual bills piling up, Williams brushed off a twinge of guilt he felt over what he was about to say to his daughter. He had to show Lester he was still committed to their partnership. "Samantha, you need to leave the dogs alone. They're Mr. Donaldson's business, not ours."

The look on Samantha's face suggested guilt. "Yes, Dad."

Lester smiled, knowing he'd made his point. "We won't worry about it. We'll see how she matures. You never know, I might be able to find a buyer at a discount." He slapped Ralph on the shoulder as he turned to walk away. "Kids!"

Samantha did her best to ignore the puppies as she was told, but as the weeks passed and their eyes opened and they became more mobile, it was harder. Samantha would bend down near the bottom of the cage, and the puppies would bolt toward her, yapping excitedly and licking and biting at the fingers she poked through the mesh. This, she could have resisted. What pushed her over the edge was the cold weather and their less-than-clean living conditions. The poor puppies huddled near old Lulu. With limited windbreaks on the open cage, the winter poured over their bodies. Samantha thought it was wrong, but she knew better than to say anything.

Or do anything. Her father had made it quite clear: the puppies were not their business.

Finally, in early December, when the temperatures dropped even further, she acted. One of the puppies, the misfit, appeared to be sick. The last few days, listless, she had barely moved from her mother. Lulu moved very little as well, lying on her side as the puppies tried to stay warm and nurse. Lester fudged a little when he advertised that the puppies had been completely weaned.

It was Saturday morning, and Samantha's father had gone to town to run errands and drink coffee with neighbors. Alone, she opened the door to the pen and stepped inside. Because Lester was so busy delivering puppies from the other litters to his buyers, his day-to-day attention to the pens had waned. She had to step carefully. Conditions were worse than normal. The earthen floor was a mess, and the puppies were covered in their own waste. Lester's policy seemed to be to protect and keep his investment clean only when he had a buyer. Surely no one would complain if she cared for the dogs. What could be wrong with that? She was helping Lester and her dad in a way, and she wasn't asking to be paid. Or even thanked.

First she picked up the little runt and tried to warm her body. The puppy squirmed and wiggled, and Samantha felt reassured that she was at least alive. Nonetheless, there was something wrong with the pup's right eye, which was swollen almost shut. Samantha set the puppy down by her mother and got to work. She used an old shovel that Lester kept leaning against the pen just for this purpose and tried to remove the waste. She redistributed what was left of the unspoiled straw, creating a layer of fresh bedding.

Lulu seemed oblivious to Samantha and didn't do what mother dogs ordinarily will do when someone approaches them and their litter: growl, snarl, and bark. Instead she stayed still and as Samantha continued to clean up, even allowed the girl to pick up her puppies. The animals were so soiled that Samantha was reluctant to handle them, so she ran back inside and drew a bucket of warm water and returned to clean each one, then Lulu. She carefully dried their damp coats with an old towel. When they were clean, she sat down on the cold December ground and allowed the puppies to crawl all over her, vying for attention, while Lulu watched, as if she were content to have a teenage babysitter on hand. The exhausted dog lay prone, resting.

Samantha liked the way the runt snuggled up into her neck and whimpered lovingly. She wiped the crusty yellow substance from the puppy's face and asked her, "Are you feeling okay today, little runty?"

Before an hour passed, Samantha's fingers ached with the cold, so she said good-bye to the puppies and Lulu and closed the door to the pen. She hoped no one would notice that the pen and its furry contents had all been cleaned.

If Lester noticed her handiwork, he didn't say anything about it, but he did offer the misfit to Ralph—"Your daughter might enjoy a puppy of her own"—but

Ralph thought that could start a dangerous trend, so he declined. That next week Lester delivered three more of Lulu's puppies to buyers across the state, leaving only Lulu and the misfit. Lester told Ralph that he would be closing the pens for the winter. "Lulu's been a fine dog, but she's practically barren." Samantha had grown up on a farm, and she knew what that meant. She also knew what it meant for the runt.

"Samantha, hon," her father said, not unkindly, "we need to say our *good-byes*."

Samantha wanted to cry, but instead she just turned and walked away. *They think I'm stupid*, she thought, *that I don't understand what's happening.*

Her sadness gave way to anger, and she felt helpless and small as she headed for the farmhouse.

Lester dropped his voice. "I'll come by tomorrow night, after she's gone to bed."

"That might be better," Ralph confirmed.

While Samantha buried her head in the pillow of her twin bed and cried, the men talked about their future with rottweilers, wolfhounds, and mastiffs for a few more minutes before Lester left to make another delivery from his own farm—the last of the Labs. It was a two-hour drive to Abilene.

Lester spent most of the next day closing the breeding operation for the winter. By evening there was only one task left. It was an unpleasant one, but he couldn't put it off any longer. He had a cousin, Hayley Donaldson, who used to run a no-kill animal shelter in Crossing Trails, an hour or two away, but it had closed for lack of funding. There simply was no place for him to take an unwanted dog and her unsellable puppy. It wasn't a part of his job that he liked, but he was a businessman, not a charity.

Around ten that evening, he pulled in to the Williamses' driveway, got out of his truck, and walked toward the pen carrying a muzzle and a leash. Poor old Lulu was so broken down that he'd probably have to lift her into the bed of his truck. One way or the other, he'd get them back to his place, where he would do what had to be done.

It was dark, so he left his headlights on and carried a flashlight. The wind blew hard, unwelcome, so he drew his coat taut, trying to stay warm. He hadn't seen any point in coming out here to feed or water Lulu that day, as he knew it didn't matter at this stage. Lester made his way around the barn and flashed the light toward the pen. He stopped and stared for a moment. The door was wide open. Lulu and the runt were both gone. The girl? Probably. He shrugged and went back to his truck. There was nothing he could do.

In this weather Mother Nature could do the job her way or he could do it his way. The outcome would be the same. It was the end of another profitable season.

Dr. Welch, the burly chief veterinary surgeon at Kansas State University, was still at home the next morning when the phone rang shortly after 7:00 A.M.—good thing he was an early riser, he thought as he picked up the receiver.

"This is Dr. Welch," he said.

The man on the other end of the call sounded upset. "Dr. Welch," he began, "it's her eye, and her breathing seems . . ." The man paused to find the right words. "Her breathing is shallow. Dr. Welch, what should I do?"

Dr. Welch tried to calm the man down. "Okay, first thing. Who am I talking to?"

"It's me. Todd. Todd McCray."

The surgeon knew Todd, but his voice sounded so upset that at first Dr. Welch hadn't recognized him. Todd was a bit of a legend at Kansas State, a caring kid and now a grown man well into his twenties. Todd had been calling Dr. Welch and the other vets at the university for over ten years. As a boy, Todd had been a homing beacon for injured animals—a broken wing on a hawk, a litter of abandoned coyote puppies, or a raccoon that had strayed onto a busy road. He had a way with them all, but above all Todd McCray knew dogs.

Dr. Welch found the adult Todd to be a painstakingly, almost irritatingly, thorough dog trainer, working at one of the nation's most impressive training facilities—the Heartland School for Dogs, in Washington, Kansas. Nowadays Todd called monthly with questions on dog behaviors. He was a hard worker and had risen almost overnight to head trainer. Dr. Welch had heard all the stories about Todd's success rate in training dogs and of his gift for matching the right dog with the right human. Todd expected a lot from a service dog, but when it didn't happen, he put it on himself and not the animal.

"Todd, slow down. It's early, and I haven't had my coffee."

Dr. Welch listened carefully to Todd's rescue narrative. A farmer whom Todd knew found a lifeless golden retriever by the road, either hit by a car or dead from exposure. It was hard to see in the dark of the early morning, so he got out of his truck with a flashlight to check for tags, and that's when he'd heard a faint whimper from a nearby culvert. Before the farmer had crawled more than a few feet into the large aluminum tube that passed beneath the road, a small puppy stumbled toward him, bloodied and with a badly damaged eye. The farmer tried to warm the little pup but knew she needed more care than he could give her. With his own dog close beside him on the bench seat of his pickup truck, he drove straight to Washington, hoping to find Todd.

Todd greeted the farmer at the door of Heartland well before the rest of the staff had arrived. "I'll take her. Don't worry." Todd quickly inspected the puppy and, without wasting a moment, punched in Dr. Welch's phone number.

"I'll meet you at my surgery in two hours. Bring her in, but don't speed."

Todd pulled on his coat, started his old truck, and drove the two hours to Kansas State University with the small dog carefully cradled beneath his shirt and resting against his abdomen.

Hastily parking the truck and leaving the driver's-side door wide open in his rush, Todd ran full speed through the front door of the surgery. "Dr. Welch!"

The puppy's breathing was labored, as if it would stop for good at any moment. Todd knew that men weren't supposed to cry or act frightened, but, glancing at the little bundle as he raced toward Dr. Welch, he couldn't help it.